MAY 6 2010

P9-CMS-961

ONE MAN'S PARADISE

ONE MAN'S PARADISE

DOUGLAS CORLEONE

MINOTAUR BOOKS ✠ NEW YORK

This is a work of fiction. All of the characters, organizations, and events portrayed in this novel are either products of the author's imagination or are used fictitiously.

www.minotaurbooks.com

ISBN 978-0-312-61158-3

First Edition: May 2010

10 9 8 7 6 5 4 3 2 1

To Joel Price

ACKNOWLEDGMENTS

After *aloha*, the second word I learned upon arriving in the Hawaiian Islands was *mahalo*, which means *thank you*. A damn good thing, since many *mahalos* are due in connection with the publication of *One Man's Paradise*.

Firstly, great thanks to everyone at Minotaur Books and Mystery Writers of America for helping me shed the suits and ties I wore as a litigator in New York City in favor of the Tommy Bahama shorts and sandals I now wear as a writer in the Hawaiian Islands.

Special thanks to Kelley Ragland, Andy Martin, Hector De-Jean, Matt Martz, and to everyone else at St. Martin's Press, not only for helping to bring this book to publication, but for making me feel so welcome during my initial return to New York.

Thanks to my agent Ann Rittenberg for stellar advice and guidance. I couldn't ask for a better partner in my writing career.

Thanks to Alison Hart for discovering *Paradise* amongst the piles and for judging it kindly. And to the competition's inaugural winner, Stefanie Pintoff, for holding my virtual hand from contract through publication and promotion.

Thanks to Maura Kye-Casella for her invaluable editorial advice and for being among the first in the publishing industry to see potential in my manuscript, in Kevin Corvelli as a character, and in me as a writer.

For their unyielding support and for offering to read earlier drafts of my novel, special thanks go to Vincent and Ashley Antoniello, Ariadne Bonano, Joyce Calderone, Denis Dooley, Joe and Andrea Gaydos, and Martin Marlow.

Finally, *mahalo* to my beautiful wife Jill, who rode The Bus and spent countless days and evenings on her feet at Hawaii nursing homes and Wahiawa General Hospital so that I could lie on Waikiki Beach, sip rum punch, and pen my debut novel. From today until the day I type *The End* on my final manuscript, I will never once forget that it was you who made this all possible.

The law is a sort of hocus-pocus science.

—Charles Macklin,
Love à la Mode [1759]

PART I

THE MALIHINI

PROLOGUE

They pawed at each other against the black backdrop of night, the restless Pacific waters purring at their feet. The moon, a sliver of its former self, hung low and lopsided as if by a thread, as the pair dropped in tandem, imprinting their shapes in the wet sand like children forming angels in freshly fallen snow.

She atop him, then he atop her, they rolled around like newlyweds in a private luxury suite, the nearest sounds emanating from the line of bars a few blocks away. It was nearly 3:00 a.m., the witching hour, when he carefully unwrapped her sarong and tossed it overhand to higher land, safely out of reach of the ocean's tide.

There was a pause in their movements, a break in their sounds, then off she pulled his palm-tree-patterned shorts, and her head hovered deftly above his middle, bobbing gently like a buoy in a harbor. He grasped her by the hair and pulled her upward toward him, locking her in another mouth-to-mouth embrace, as he worked at her thong. The underwear moved quickly

from her thighs, over her knees, down around her ankles, until fi-
nally she flipped them from her toes into the ocean.

He stood on his knees, over her, and worked himself inside,
her soft moans carried off by the trade winds into the night.
Then suddenly, a noise, a clank, like metal on metal, yards
away from the pile of flesh on the sand, and the couple fell still,
the sounds of lovemaking replaced by silence.

When no one emerged, he continued inside her, unconcerned
with the possibility of an audience. She was more daunted, im-
mediately pushing against his chest, her voice rising above the
tide, her body squirming to free itself from his. "Stop!" she hissed.
"C'mon!" he countered, aspiring to reach his crest. Her right hand
clawed at his face as he pinned her left down into the sand. Strug-
gling beneath him, she raised her leg as swiftly as she could, con-
necting with his groin. They rolled over passionately, this time
fueled by anger rather than lust, her body thrashing beneath his
like an animal caught in a trap. As she started to scream, he struck
her with a closed fist, a solid right jab to the face.

He rose from the sand and gathered his shorts, moving quickly,
his eyes locked on her, as she lay still, a fixture in the sand. He
scanned the blackness, then set his sights on a destination in
the distance. From the slow, deliberate steps he took away from
the Pacific, it seemed as though the beach itself were melting
around his feet, trying to grasp his ankles and slow his progress
as he trudged uphill, away from her and what he had done.

CHAPTER 1

I am trying not to yawn.

A hell of a way to start a new life, yeah, I know. But that's what I'm doing. I'm trying not to yawn. And trying not to yawn is counterproductive, definitely making things worse. It's a psychological thing, I think. Something I'll have to look up on the Internet when I get back to my apartment. *If* I get back to my apartment. If this son of a bitch ever stops talking.

I scan the surface of the desk between us. Nothing interesting. It's too tidy. Way too tidy for a lawyer. My desk back in New York was a fucking mess. It was a lawyer's desk, covered in closed client files, calendars, bar journals, half-used legal pads, unpaid bills. A messy desk is a sign of genius. Someone told me that. Someone with a really messy desk.

From the looks of his desk, Jake Harper isn't too bright.

His walls are pretty bare, too. I wonder if that means any-thing. There's a calendar marked sporadically with court appearances and a single birthday, that with a note that reads *send card*. There are no photographs or framed pic-tures. The furniture is utilitarian: an old, solid-oak desk; a battered, rusty filing cabinet; a couple of client chairs with worn upholstery, one of which I'm sitting in, digging into the torn arms with what's left of my chewed fingernails.

The furniture doesn't mesh with the freshly painted ivory-colored walls and new beige carpet. The furniture is more like Jake. Jake, who's giving me a goddamn history lesson on his life. Jake, the Irish Texan, who five years ago packed his bags and fled the Lone Star State for sunny California only to fail the bar exam three times. Jake, my soon-to-be office landlord here in downtown Honolulu.

I study his face, shocked that his lips are still moving. Jake's face is weathered, worn especially around the eyes. His nose is peppered with tiny gin blossoms, miniature-size merit badges earned through the decades of hard drinking he's just told me about. He says he's sixty-six but he looks at least a dozen years older. His hair is thin, a shocking white with streaks of gray, his face as wrinkled as the aloha shirt on his back. He looks as though he might drop dead before he stops talking. It might be the only way.

Jake, whose ad for office space I discovered this morn-ing on Craigslist, speaks slowly, as if to a child, as though calculating every word in his head before allowing it to escape his sun-chapped lips. He does convey trust, I'll give him that. Trust is undoubtedly what keeps him in clients here on the island. Certainly not competence, he conveys no such thing as that. Only trust. Right now I trust that he'll never close his trap.

We're thirty-three stories up and I contemplate throwing myself out the large bay window behind him. But the view of the azure Pacific in the distance reminds me why I'm here. To calm the fuck down. My shrink warned me that I couldn't escape myself but I'm determined to prove him wrong. So I take a deep breath, sit back in the ratty old client chair, and try to relax, letting Jake take me through the wilds of his seemingly endless career.

For more than thirty years, Jake was a lawyer in private practice in Houston, appointed by the courts to represent indigent defendants in capital murder cases.

"When people talk about the death penalty," Jake says, "they talk about Texas. Well, Harris County is the capital of capital punishment, son. It is the single most productive death row pipeline in the western world."

I nod politely. I've done so much nodding during the past forty-five minutes I feel like one of those bobblehead dolls they used to sell in the eighties. Maybe they still sell them, I don't know. Something else to check out on the Internet.

"The prosecutors are mean," he says, "and the judges are all former prosecutors, all of them mean as hell. They stand around the courthouse hallways joking about capital defendants, about the next inductees into what they call the Silver Needle Society. And what's more amazing is their follow-through. Punishment handed down is punishment carried out. It's a very efficient system, son. Execution dates are set by the courts. Appeals are streamlined. And the U.S. Court of Appeals for the Fifth Circuit is the most conservative in the country. The Fifth Circuit is so loath to reverse convictions that it even reinstated the death sentence of a fella whose attorney slept through half the trial. As a criminal lawyer in Houston you spend a good deal of time holding clients' hands on the way to the death chamber."

I suppose his passion against capital punishment and his empathy for his clients should sound refreshing to my cynical New York ears. And maybe it would have sounded so years ago. But now it's all static. White noise. He may as well be speaking Japanese. Actually, I may have an easier time with Japanese. At least there's a *Complete Idiot's Guide* to understanding it. In fact, I picked up a copy when I moved here to the island of Oahu two months ago.

I don't practice law for the clients or for any special cause. I practice law because I went to law school and because I borrowed $200,000 to pay for law school. Now I have to pay it back and the only way I know how is by taking money from desperate clients in return for helping them avoid their just deserts.

I don't like my clients and I don't care if they like me. We're each means to the other's ends. I lie to them when it suits me and they lie to me because it's all they know how to do. I don't make friends with them and I don't invite them to dinner. I don't even shake their hands when I can avoid it.

Like my old boss Milt Cashman always said, clients ruin the practice of law.

"But it's the front line, son. You fight against something worth fighting against, like the machine in Texas, it makes your life worthwhile. You feel fulfilled at the end of the day, even when you lose."

I'm tired of the Texas twang, but I'm curious, and my curiosity often leads me to regrettable actions, such as when I ask Jake what brought him to the Hawaiian Islands.

"In a word, beauty. That and the bar exam here isn't state specific, so if you know the basics of the law, you have a fair chance of passing, unlike California. I'm not dumb and I'm not lazy. Just stubborn, I guess. I refuse to study for an exam I passed four decades ago."

A look of disgust is on Jake's face, as if the California bar exam were a living, breathing entity that set out to spoil his plans.

"Now that I'm here, I'm grateful things didn't work out in California. I mean that. From the moment I stepped out of Honolulu Airport and felt that sun on my face in the middle of February, I knew this was my home. Once you've been here awhile, son, your priorities change. Part of it's the warm, soothing weather and the serene atmosphere. But mostly, it's the people. They have a gentle spirit unfettered by all that mainland get-ahead bullshit. It's pleasant here, relaxing." He adds, "I didn't always talk this slow, you know."

With his cowboy boots resting on the desk between us, Jake leans so far back in his old leather swivel chair that I fear he'll tip over. He's as tranquil as a corpse on Valium, so completely free from agitation that it worries me, sends me into near panic. Hawaii seemed so appealing on the Internet, what with the palm trees and hammocks, the fruity cocktails with tiny umbrellas. And the pineapples. The pineapples really sold me. But now I feel as if I entered some bizarre *Twilight Zone* episode, where Honolulu is the mirror opposite of Manhattan, and Jake the mirror opposite of Milt. Nothing feels right here. Anxiety, the fuel on which my body runs, is in short supply here and I fear myself shutting down. I realize I may have made a terrible mistake. I don't even *like* pineapples.

Questioning is as instinctive for lawyers as lighting cigarettes is for smokers. And it's just as nasty a habit. I don't want to think like a lawyer, especially now. What I want is to get back to my apartment and beat myself up for giving away my New York law practice and moving here. But I can't help it. And although I know I'll get an answer that can be made into a seven-part HBO miniseries, I ask Jake why he left Houston.

"I was tired, son. Tired of fighting mean prosecutors with endless resources. Tired of compromising my independence to please judges so that I could continue getting appointments. But most of all, I was tired of hearing court-appointed lawyers being bashed. It made me sick. We worked our asses off fighting this death machine commissioned by the state and all we received in return was criticism. Criticism from the media, even from other defense lawyers who didn't have the balls to take the cases themselves. It turned our clients against us. You know as well as I do, you have a client who doesn't trust you, the state's gonna get a conviction. I'd had enough. So five years ago, after a surprising acquittal that epitomized the Texas system, I packed up my office and left. I've been practicing here just under three years."

There I have it. Jake Harper in a nutshell. A bleeding heart who spent his life fighting a losing battle against the Texas criminal justice system. Crusader. Defender. Landlord. It must be nice to have a passion but I know one thing's for certain. Passion doesn't pay the piper. And it doesn't pay off student loans.

Now that I'm here in Hawaii I have to make a fresh start. And this law suite seems as good a place as any to do just that. With Jake the only occupant, the suite is quiet compared to the hustle and bustle of the thirty-eight-lawyer space I shared in downtown Manhattan near the South Street Seaport. As I tear off the last of my thumbnail with my teeth, I think I feel a little calmer already.

"Jake, I'm impressed with the suite and I'm impressed with you. If it's all right with you, I'd like to rent the large office right across the hall from yours."

"It's yours, son. But we can talk business later. Tell me a little more about yourself."

Let's see. First off, I can't stand small talk. The only thing I hate worse than talking about myself is listening to someone else tell me about their life, as you, Jake, just did for well over an hour. But I don't say that. Because I'm so nice.

"Well, Jake, I practiced criminal law in Manhattan for six years. While I was in law school, I worked for Milt Cashman—"

"Wait a minute," Jake interrupts. " 'Not Guilty Milty'? The high-profile lawyer that represented all those rappers? What were their names? Shaved Dog and Melted Ice?"

"Rabid Dawg," I say, "a solo artist who was falsely accused of rape, and Shave Ice from the hip-hop duo Death on the Rocks, who keeps getting framed for cocaine possession. Yeah, that's him, the one and only Not Guilty Milty. He was the reason I was able to open my own practice downtown the moment I was sworn in."

Jake removes from his desk drawer a silver flask and unscrews the top. "Hope you don't mind, son. It's time for my medicine." He winks, gives me a large Texas smile, and takes a pull. He offers me a sip and I pass. "Continue, son. But speak slower. We're in no rush."

Sitting back in the chair, feigning serenity, I tell Jake how Milt launched my career. While I was still a law student, Milt introduced me to attorneys all over the city. As soon as I hung out my shingle, those attorneys began sending me their overflow business, mostly misdemeanors they were too busy to handle. Thanks to Milt, I already knew my way around the courtroom and had established a good rapport with the assistant district attorneys and judges, and it paid off in handsome plea deals and light sentences for my clients. This impressed my clients, especially those fa-

miliar with the system. Clients began referring their friends
and family members, and as luck would have it, their friends
and family members were committing felonies. I started
taking cases to trial and winning. I began raking it in and
making a name for myself. Kevin Corvelli, "the Acquittal
Kid."

After two years, I was sending my overflow business to
other attorneys and collecting the referral fees. Then, about
a year and a half ago, it came. My first press case.

Before my name hit the headlines I was like a little kid,
admiring and envious of his big brothers. I wanted what they
had. Not a later curfew, not a cigarette or a bottle of beer. I
wanted a taste of fame. I wanted photographers and camera
crews to wait for me outside the courthouse. I wanted to
give interviews and sound bites. I wanted ex-girlfriends and
old classmates to see my picture in the paper and call my office so that my secretary could tell them I was unavailable.

Sometimes that little kid wants it all too soon. And sometimes he gets it. Sometimes it's not all it's cracked up to be.
And sometimes it just turns out dead wrong.

CHAPTER 2

Brandon Glenn was a premed student at Pace University's Manhattan campus when he was charged with murdering his biology professor. The professor, Samuel Moss, was openly gay, and witnesses attested that he'd made overt sexual advances on Brandon in the months preceding his death. Witnesses further stated that the advances infuriated Brandon, who was a homophobic marine reserve born and raised in the Bible Belt. The professor was found dead on Valentine's Day in his East Village apartment with a screwdriver embedded in his throat.

Milt Cashman was conflicted out of the case, having represented the victim on previous marijuana charges. Of course, his past representation of the victim wouldn't have adversely affected his representation of Brandon Glenn, but no assistant DA in Manhattan wanted to lock horns with Not Guilty Milty, so the office zealously moved the court to have Milt removed from the case. The DA's office succeeded and the result was my first stint defending a high-profile accused killer.

Brandon had been in the professor's home, there was no doubt of that. His fingerprints were found on a light switch, on a doorknob, and on a glass coffee table in the living room. Carpet fibers from the professor's apartment were on Brandon's clothes when he was arrested, and likewise, fibers from Brandon's clothes were found in the professor's humble abode.

Science isn't sexy, doesn't get the adrenaline pumping, and isn't something I realized I was signing on for when I first decided to defend criminals for a living. During the trial I found myself feeling like a fraud, wishing I had paid at least some attention to my professor when I took a forensic-science class in college.

Brandon didn't take the stand. He didn't tell the jury what he told me: that he went to the professor's apartment to threaten him with an administrative complaint if the sexual advances didn't immediately cease. I knew it was a lie, but that isn't why I refused to put Brandon on the stand. I refused to allow him to testify because it was a lie that the jury wouldn't believe.

I dismissed Brandon's protests of innocence and attacked the case on the assumption that he was as guilty as hell, just like the rest of my clients. The assistant DA presented a strong case, hitting us steadily with a fierce series of punches, a left jab of motive here, a right hook of opportunity there. I tried to put their case down with a single punch. And I missed.

The professor's ex-boyfriend, Carson Reese, had both motive and opportunity and thus was dubbed around the office as our Reasonable Doubt Fairy. I had interviewed Reese and I was convinced he wasn't the killer. Yet his being dateless on Valentine's Day gave my client a chance at freedom, and me a chance at a dramatic victory that would adorn the covers of every major newspaper in New York.

I was playing for the press. With the media decorating the front row I posed for the courtroom sketches and concerned myself more with making the defense dramatic than with making it effective. After I put on what the *Daily News* called a "brilliant defense," the assistant DA called a rebuttal witness, a priest of all things, who testified that he was with Carson Reese on the night of the murder and he had the used condoms to prove it. Father Thomas White hadn't come forward earlier for obvious reasons, and of course because no one had asked him to. The priest put the final nail in my client's coffin when he testified that my client was romantically involved with the victim, that he had seen them kissing in Central Park. Yes, his testimony buried my client. And I had handed him the shovel.

It took the jury less than an hour to return the guilty verdict. Father White had been on the prosecution's lengthy witness list, I assumed as a smoke screen, and I'd never bothered to interview him. I was too busy deciding which tie would look best in a black-and-white photograph.

Thirty minutes after the verdict was read, Brandon Glenn confessed to me. He *was* having an affair with Professor Moss. He was at the professor's apartment often, but

Brandon insisted he was not at the professor's apartment on the day he was murdered. He would rather let the world think him a killer, he said, than know he was as queer as an $8 bill.

The day after the verdict I got just what I wished for. My face was plastered on the front page of the *Post*, along with the headline HE BLOWS IT! and an inset photograph of Father White positioned conveniently by my crotch.

Five days after the sentencing, I received a telephone call from Rikers Island. Brandon Glenn had been raped and murdered while in general population awaiting transfer to an upstate facility.

I didn't leave the office for the following three days. I decorated the conference room with the Brandon Glenn file as if I were preparing for trial and pored through every piece of evidence I had to assure myself of his guilt. Alone in my office I prosecuted him again posthumously to unburden myself of the overwhelming guilt I felt over his death.

After those three days I received a telephone call that convinced me I needn't continue. It was the assistant district attorney who had prosecuted Brandon Glenn's case. A Bronx man charged with multiple murders on the Lower East Side had confessed to the killing of Professor Samuel Moss.

The media circus reopened and pitched its big-top tent right in front of my office. Milt was none too pleased anymore at being labeled my mentor and put some distance between us. New clients stopped calling, and the clients

I did have watched me with a wary eye, as though I were the criminal. All I thought about was Brandon and how I'd failed him. I didn't force the truth, not even from Brandon himself. I looked innocence in the eye and blinked. I didn't recognize it, and an innocent man was dead for my short-comings. Had I believed in his innocence, I might have looked a bit harder. I might have been able to convince the jury, if only I were able to convince myself. But I was a liar, a fraud, and I'd just figured everyone else was, too.

A firm believer in running away from my problems, I sold my practice for practically nothing, tucked my tail between my legs, and headed as far west as I could without sacrificing my ability to practice law, which translates into my ability to pay my student loans.

"That's some story, son," Jake says, removing his feet from the desk. "Are you gonna continue practicing criminal law?"

"Yeah. But I'm sticking to misdemeanors. No more rapes, no more murders. The stakes are much too high and I don't want that kind of responsibility anymore. Any client whose case might pique the media's interest is walking right back out my door and finding another attorney. I intend to refer all felony cases elsewhere."

"Well, son, we'll see about that." Jake lifts himself off the chair and places the flask back home in its drawer. "C'mon. Let me show you around your new office."

Jake leads me to the large empty space across the hall and I feel a twinge of excitement, that short-lived high that comes with something new. A new car, a new home, a new girl. He points toward the colossal window centered on the back wall.

"You have a *mauka* view," he says. "Means your office looks out on the mountains. It's a stunning view, even when the clouds gather over them. You'll see more rainbows than you can count."

"The only rainbows I ever saw in New York were in puddles, right before a taxi would plow through and splash my suit pants on the way to court."

"You're in a different world now, son," he says, resting a hand on my shoulder. "My office has a *makai* view. I considered turning my desk around to take advantage of the view of the Pacific."

"Too awkward for you to have your back to the door?"

"Nah, I just figured I'd daydream all day while my clients sat in jail exchanging cigarettes for blow jobs. By the way, did you bring a girlfriend with you here to the islands?"

I give him a slight shake of the head and a look that lets him know I'm uncomfortable with the subject. I have commitment issues, deep-seated difficulties in sustaining relationships for longer than a couple of weeks. Once that new-girl smell is gone, so are they. I move on. I'm not proud of it, and my shrink and I were working on it when I left New York. I have found, however, that the mechanisms of psychotherapy can turn as slowly as the wheels of justice.

"How about you, Jake? Are you married?"

"Nah. There are very few women, especially in Houston, who fancy a man who comes home from work late every night, mad and frustrated as hell because he can't keep his clients alive. A man that spends his life fighting losing battles for shit pay, all the while getting criticized by yellow journalists who wouldn't know a lethal injection from a blood test even if they had a front-row seat."

Outside my new office window is a picture-postcard view. Rolling green mountains kissing soft, white clouds. I press my nose up against the glass and know that I'll never again stand in awe of the New York City skyline, or anything else man-made for that matter.

"C'mon," says Jake, peeling me away from the glass. "Let me introduce you to Hoshi, our beautiful, young, brilliant, bilingual receptionist."

After introductions are made, Hoshi leaves us in the conference room, an immense space lined with five-foot-high windows, the length of two walls. Jake points out a few landmark buildings but my eyes focus on the natural beauty behind them all.

Jake sits down and motions for me to do the same. I look at my watch, but a different body language is spoken here, so I sit.

"These islands," Jake says, "are populated with thousands of people who came here to escape something on the mainland. Some came to escape their stressful jobs, some their overbearing families, some their abusive spouses. Some created worlds for themselves on the mainland that they could just no longer bear to live in. Some made mistakes larger than those mountains that cast shadows so far, the only land they felt they could stand tall on was here on the most remote archipelago in the world. Many of my clients escaped from their home states on the continental U.S. figuring the law would never catch up to them here. And most of them were right. The problem was that they repeated their mistakes and ended up in jail having to pay my fees.

"So the first thing I tell people who just moved here is to make it a point not to repeat the mistakes that led them here to begin with, and to avoid at all costs placing themselves in that same kind of situation they escaped from on the mainland. For me, that was easy, since Hawaii is enlightened enough not to have the death penalty.

"The second thing I tell them is to make sure whatever they escaped from doesn't follow them to the islands. For example, the DEA or that abusive spouse, or that fucking mother-in-law they left in Scottsdale.

"The third and most important thing I tell them is to constantly remind themselves that we are *malihini*, newcomers to these islands. Don't be misled. We use U.S. currency and have American laws. English is the primary language. Still, we live in a world very foreign to mainlanders. Be conscious and considerate of where you are. We're not in Houston. We're not in Manhattan. We live in a tropical paradise, but don't allow that to lull you into a false sense of invincibility. Sometimes bad things happen on these islands, which is lucky for us or we'd be out of work.

"Now, I have to make one quick phone call, son. Then what do you say we grab Hoshi and the three of us head over to the Sand Bar for some mai tais?"

CHAPTER 3

I wake the next morning with my first island hangover, a sickly sour stomach and a headful of hurt. I consider returning to sleep but the tropical sun is already peeking through my blinds, tapping me on the shoulder like a mother pestering her child to get up and get ready for school. I fall out of bed, hoping a hot shower will wash the sick away, but this kind of sick is as clingy as a one-night stand that doesn't realize she's worn out her welcome.

I drank last night on an empty stomach, unwittingly extending my hunger strike until the restaurants here scrap what they pass off as food in favor of something acceptable to my discerning New York palate. I'm finicky, I know, fussy as a prep school girl. I've lost twelve pounds since my arrival and I didn't have twelve extra pounds to lose. It's just that every night I go out, I have my heart set on a thick, juicy, ten-ounce filet mignon, cooked medium rare with a warm, pink center, topped with mushrooms, and a side of steak fries. Instead I get an overcooked hamburger without the bun, dripping with a watery brown sauce that looks like . . .

Shit. A wave of nausea that would easily dwarf the twenty-foot waves up North Shore hits me like a ton of bricks. Stubbing my big right toe along the way, I barely make it to the bathroom on time. The rum isn't nearly as sweet coming up as it was going down. On my knees, sweat pouring from my forehead, staring at last night's liquid dinner, I've reached a new low point in my life. I deserve this. As the acrid taste of bile lingers in my mouth and the stench hits me in the face, I vomit again. Welcome to the island of Oahu.

Okay, I'm now at least another pound lighter and I had to brush my teeth three times.

I step barefoot onto the lanai and let the gentle trade winds wash over me, cooling the surface of my skin. I live in Waikiki, on the twenty-ninth floor of an older but well-renovated high-rise two blocks from the beach. It's 7:00 a.m. and the balmy Pacific sea is already littered with tourists and their playthings. It's the same scene every day, rain or shine, they are out in droves: kids hopping around wildly in the surf, surfers riding six-foot waves, the less ambitious sunning on the beach or lounging in the water on inflatable neon rafts.

The sun crawls over me like a newborn kitten, painting my skin with yet another coat of bronze. I close my eyes and tune out the sounds of nearby construction, wish away the tourists, merchants, and hotels.

I moved to Waikiki to ease the transition to island life, certain I'd be soothed by the familiar lines of cars stuck in traffic, the masses of people pushing their way to nowhere in particular, and the musical sound of police and ambulance sirens. Waikiki is a veritable mecca for families and honeymooners, all of whom parade up and down Kalakaua Avenue in their aloha shirts and muumuus with the price tags still hanging out, searching for the next Kodak moment. Mimes and musicians, hucksters and prostitutes, line the streets at night, providing a little New York flavor without the New York steak.

I don't pretend to know a man until I've drunk with him, and last night I got to know Jake Harper really well. He doesn't have the charisma or business sense of Milt Cashman but he does have something Milt sorely lacks. Selflessness. Sure, Milt does the occasional good deed. He even takes on some pro bono clients whenever the New York Bar threatens to suspend his license. He hands out favors the way Planned Parenthood hands out condoms, only the favors are handed out in typical *Godfather* fashion. *Someday, and this day may never come, I will call upon you to do me a service.*

Jake has offered to show me around the courts, introduce me to some of the local players in the Oahu justice system, though he doesn't claim to have the least bit of clout here himself. Still, it's a selfless act that gives me some hope that my tenancy on South King Street will work out well. So long as Jake doesn't camp out in my office expecting lengthy fireside chats.

The freight train blazing around in my head speeds up with the goddamn drilling going on halfway up the block. I pop two more aspirin and chase them with some Pepto, sit at the kitchen table with yesterday's *Honolulu Advertiser* spread out before me. I peruse the articles on a copter crash on Kauai, rising home prices on Maui, and an editorial on the state Supreme Court decision that recently decided the fate of Hawaii Superferry.

A headline on the front page of the local section catches my eye. NEW JERSEY MAN ARRESTED IN WAIKIKI SLAYING. With homicides averaging only twenty per year on the entire island of Oahu, this one is a real treat. I study the booking photograph of the accused, one Joseph Gianforte Jr., a twenty-four-year-old Hoboken man charged with murdering his former girlfriend.

The photo sends a shiver down my spine because Gianforte reminds me of someone I've had a love-hate relationship with for the past thirty-one years. Myself. The look in his eyes is familiar, not much unlike the look in the eyes of Brandon Glenn, the look displayed in the booking photo now tattooed on my mind. It's the look of a man suddenly faced with the specter of a forever confinement.

Not all men charged with murder have that look. Many have eyes that are vacant. Their look says only one thing: I knew this was coming. Some know it from their early teens, from the mere fact of where they live, who their family and friends are, by fact of the wares they peddle. Others, those like Gianforte and Brandon Glenn, never see it coming. They have jobs or go to school. They live in high-rises or costly houses in wealthy suburban neighborhoods. They call their mothers and volunteer in local elections. Some are innocent, others are prone to fits of rage, a single propensity that can end two promising lives in one fell swoop.

According to police, Gianforte boarded a flight early Sunday from Newark to Honolulu to follow Shannon Douglas after the couple had broken up. Police speculate that Gianforte discovered his ex-girlfriend with a local man, who had been seen leaving a bar with the victim earlier that night. The local man, twenty-eight-year-old Palani Kanno, a former suspect in the case, told police he left the victim alive in a secluded area on Waikiki Beach just hours before her body was discovered. Shannon Douglas was found dead by a band of surfers shortly after sunrise Monday morning, apparently killed by being struck with a blunt object to the head.

A police affidavit states that Gianforte has a history of domestic violence against the victim with one misdemeanor conviction in New York, where Shannon Douglas was studying law. Gianforte was arrested without incident late Monday night at his Waikiki hotel and is being held in lieu of $3 million bail.

I fold the paper and my mind shifts back to Brandon Glenn. My fingernail tastes like newsprint, so I pull it from my teeth. An airplane descends in the distance and I wonder if it's coming from New York. I wonder if it carries anyone I know or anyone I will someday know. I wonder if it carries anyone who could tell me how to clear my conscience of Brandon's death.

———

My hangover finally subsiding, I find myself outside my new office building for my first day of work. With no clients, I have little to do but prepare for the day I *will* have clients. My furniture and computer should arrive by week's end, along with a small treasure of office supplies. My marketing strategy includes an elaborate Web site and several cost-effective advertisements in the local publications. Without Milt and his army of referring attorneys, I fear my finicky eating habits will soon not be the only reason I'm going hungry.

I'm decked out today in an aloha shirt and khakis, my beloved suits sitting idly at home in their closet. Jake assured me that this is the lawyer's uniform when the lawyer's not in court. I'm distraught over this, although I'm taking at least some comfort in that my sandals were made by Kenneth Cole.

When I reach the thirty-third floor, I'm hit with my first surprise. My name is already emblazoned on the gold plate next to our door. I take a deep breath, ready to savor the newness of the experience, somewhat relaxed because my calendar is empty for at least the next few weeks. I can use that time to learn the Hawaiian justice system, to find the courthouses, and buy some new linen suits. I also need to check out a few things on the Internet, such as yawning, for instance, and those bobblehead dolls from the eighties.

"Aloha, Hoshi."

"Aloha, Kevin! Jake's been waiting for you. He wants to see you about something. I'll let him know you're here."

As Hoshi buzzes Jake on the intercom, I worry my check to him may have bounced. Those goddamn debit cards. I constantly forget to record my purchases when I'm out. And my nine different student loans are all automatically debited at different times of the month, and the amounts constantly change to reflect ever-fluctuating interest rates.

"Kevin's here," she tells him.

Son of a bitch. It's too late to run out the door. I haven't bounced a check in six years. I should never have taken that trip to Cabo San Lucas before I moved here, knowing I wouldn't have income for a couple of months. It's too late. He's telling her to send me right on back to the conference room.

"Jake's in the conference room, Kevin. Go right on back."

"*Mahalo,* Hoshi." That's Hawaiian for "thank you." Because I don't yet know how to say "I'm fucked."

As I open the door to the conference room, I'm hit with the glare of the sun and Jake's broad smile, complete with yellowed teeth. "Come in, come in," he says. "I'd like you to meet some very good folks."

Two figures are seated with their backs to the conference-room door, both shielding their eyes from the glare of the sun. Jake lowers a shaded film over each window so that the glare is gone but the breathtaking view remains. It's as if the conference room is wearing sunglasses.

The male is heavyset, with a bald spot the size of a silver dollar on the back of his head. The woman is thin, with tight curly locks, golden all the way through except at the roots. I step around the table, putting on my bullshit smile, assuming they are clients of Jake's.

Wrapping his arm around my shoulders, Jake says, "This young man is Kevin Corvelli. He is an excellent trial lawyer from New York. He's tough, he's aggressive, and he specializes in violent felonies."

One lesson I learned from Milt is to wear my poker face at all times, no matter what the situation. Another lesson I learned is to always act as though I know exactly what is happening, especially when another lawyer might be making a play, even when I don't have the slightest fucking clue.

"Kevin, allow me to introduce you to two fellow mainlanders," says Jake, his hand still resting on my shoulder as if he's afraid I might run away. "This lovely woman is Gina."

Gina stands and holds out her right hand. Her eyes are wet. She's been crying. Her mascara is smeared around her eyes, making her look like a pretty blond raccoon. I take her hand in mine and manage an "I'm pleased to meet you." Her hand is wet and black from wiping at the tears and mascara. This is why I don't shake hands.

The man stands, all 250 of him. His look makes you

think he's never cried in his entire life. He takes my hand, gripping it like a vise. Another reason I don't shake.

"And this, Kevin," Jake says, "is Gina's adoring husband. Joseph Gianforte Sr."

CHAPTER 4

"What the hell do you think you're doing?"

We are in my empty office, Jake and I, while the Gianfortes sit, twiddling their thumbs in the conference room.

"You have a new client, son," he says. "Their boy was charged with killing a young girl on Waikiki Beach."

"I *know*," I spit out. "I read about it."

"Good. So you're pretty much up to speed."

"You ambushed me, Jake. I made it abundantly clear to you just yesterday that I'm not handling felonies anymore, especially not *murder* cases."

"And I told you, 'We'll see about that.'" He grins widely, an I'm-so-fucking-proud-of-myself, shit-eating grin.

I'm fuming. I want to throw something, but there's nothing yet in the office to throw. I consider punching the wall, but my last bout with a wall resulted in my wearing a cast for six weeks. And I don't like drinking with my left hand.

"It's a press case, Jake. It's exactly what I escaped from."

"No, son. You escaped from what you perceived as a terrible mistake that you made that happened to get eaten up by the press. Do you really think you'll be content handling vandalism and shoplifting cases the rest of your life?"

No. "Yes."

"You're lying, son. Either to me, or to yourself."

"Why don't *you* take the case, Jake?"

He chuckles. "I'd rather drink turpentine and piss on a brush fire. I'm too old for this shit."

"So you want to sit on the sidelines and root, is that it, Jake? You want to get a taste, but you don't want to pay for the meal. You want someone else to carry the load. Well, I don't work for you, Jake. You're my landlord, that's all."

"Look, son. I'm trying to help you, is all. It's what people do here on the islands. We help each other. I took your checks for first month's rent and the security deposit down to the Bank of Hawaii this morning, and when I jokingly asked the teller if they would clear, she said, 'Barely.' Now, I don't give a rat's ass if you can pay the rent at the office on time every month or not. We can work that out. But you're a young guy living in paradise, and from the way you were dressed yesterday, I don't figure you have cheap tastes.

"That paper sitting there on the conference-room table between the Gianfortes is a retainer agreement on letterhead Hoshi printed up for you on the fly. Under that paper sits a check already made out to you in the amount of fifty grand."

"How much?" Yeah, I heard him, but I want to hear it again.

"Fifty. And that's just the initial retainer. I've explained to them that if there's a trial, it's likely gonna cost them six figures. They didn't flinch. I took the liberty of setting your hourly fee at four seventy-five, both in court and out. I hope that's okay with you."

"Fifty," I say aloud, because I like the sound.

"I've already made the sale, son. All you have to do is go back in there and close the deal."

Jake and I step back into the conference room, apologize for the interruption, and take our seats across from the Gianfortes. I study them, pick them apart like an inspector at the end of an assembly line. Gina is an emotional volcano, ready to erupt at any second. She has on a mask of calm. Still, the lava is there, creeping beneath the surface, I know. Tears well up in her eyes, but she now refuses to let them fall, creating within herself a wall, a dam I suspect only the most ardent cry could penetrate. She's strong, I can tell that by her face, her look, but mostly because she'd have to be, given the size and scowl of the man sitting beside her.

He's a volcano, too, only ready to spew much different emotions than his wife. His eyes are cold, steel bolts fastened into a hard, solid frame. All I read is anger. Anger, I suspect, directed at his son for getting himself into this predicament, at the victim for living and dying, at the police for attempting their jobs, and at me for sitting across from him waiting for my $50,000 check.

When selecting a jury, I attempt to discern which potential jurors entered the courtroom with their minds already made up. Some people wear it on their faces the way football fans wear face paint to distinguish without question which team has their loyalty. Both of these people sitting across from me have prejudged, in striking contrast, the guilt of their son. If given the opportunity, I doubt I'd put this boy's own father on his jury.

"Now," Jake says, slapping his hands together, "some unfortunate business brings the Gianfortes to the island." He makes it sound as though their stock portfolio is underachieving. "It seems their son, Joey, has been arrested for a homicide that occurred late Sunday night in Waikiki." This is all for their benefit, to dismiss the idea that the little meeting we held in my office was called to talk about them behind their backs.

I play along. "Yes, I've been following the matter in the papers."

"Good, so you're up to speed," Jake says slowly, measuring every word with the precision of a surgeon. "Now, the Gianfortes need an aggressive trial attorney like yourself to represent Joey and give him the very best shot at an acquittal."

"You look a little young," Senior says to me. "How long you been doing this?"

It's an irritating question, but one I'm used to, even now at thirty-one, after six years of practicing law. The query is always satisfied by the end of the interview, after I've lectured the skeptic for an hour or so on criminal law and procedure and shown that I know my shit. For now, I offer only my standard answer: "Too long."

I don't like Senior and Senior doesn't like me, and that's just the way I like it. I start with some preliminaries to calm the storm I sense brewing in Gina's head. I can hear her silent cry for guidance. I ask her, her and not him, to give me some background on their son: his childhood, education, relationships, work history, criminal history, credit history. Tomorrow, when I meet with Joey, I'll use this knowledge to gain his trust.

Gina tells me what most mothers tell me, that her son was a good boy, an angel really, growing up in northern New Jersey. He attended St. James Catholic Grammar School, Bayley-Ellard Catholic High. He played football in the fall, basketball in the winter, baseball in the spring. In the summers he worked the usual eclectic group of student summer jobs: retail clerk at Blockbuster video, waiter at Friendly's restaurant, security guard at Rockaway Mall.

They spoiled him so, she admits, but only because he was their only son. His father bought him a brand-new red Chevy Camaro on his seventeenth birthday. Two months later, he crashed it. And his father bought him another, the second one in black.

Joey maintained a B-plus average at Seton Hall University in South Orange, where he majored in political science and minored in criminal justice. He was accepted into several law schools across the country but insisted on enrolling in one in New York.

"Law school?" I ask.

Gina rolls her damp eyes and nods. "That's where he

met her," she says, the *her* dripping off the tongue like sour milk.

The law school is where Joey met Shannon Douglas and where his life altered dramatically. He fell in love with her at orientation, Gina tells me, and his world shrank in ways worlds do when one first falls in love.

Telling me about Joey's relationship with Shannon is troubling her, so I stop her midsentence, saving her from living it over today. I tell her I'd prefer to gather my first impression of Shannon from Joey himself, and this eases her, at least somewhat.

Jake briefly explains to them the procedural process of the Hawaiian justice system, and it is all I can do to keep myself from taking notes. He already promised me he would walk me through local procedure, yet the tinge of fear of the unknown still lingers within.

Finally, we come to my favorite part. The reason I went to law school. The reason I shadowed Milt for three years. The reason I opened my own law practice. The reason I'm sitting here agreeing to represent an accused killer when I swore to myself I never again would. Finally, we come to the retainer.

"Seems a little steep, fifty K," Senior says.

Of course, there's no course in law school titled Legal Fees 101, nor are there any courses devoted to reeling in clients or getting them to pay. That would be too practical. But I can tell you all about the Dormant Commerce Clause of the U.S. Constitution, which forbids states from favoring local economic interests or unduly burdening interstate commerce. Not interested? Neither was I, which explains my D in constitutional law. No, lawyers learn all about legal fees and finding paying clients on their own, usually the hard way. I was lucky. I learned from the best. I learned from Milt Cashman.

"Mr. Gianforte," I say, "I'm going to be blunt. Simply put, your son is charged with first-degree murder."

Hearing it aloud elicits a gasp from Gina, her hand fluttering to her heart. *Check*.

"This is a very serious charge," I say, "with very serious consequences if convicted. A term of life imprisonment without the possibility of parole."

Senior looks away from me, his eyes dropping down to the table. He's hunched like a boy just got caught pissing in the confessional. *Check*.

"My goal is to have your son acquitted," I say. "As Mr. Harper here will confirm, that will require a lot of hard work over a long period of time. In addition to my time and Mr. Harper's time, we'll need to hire investigators and experts to assist us in picking apart the prosecution's case."

Gina is nodding, nodding like a bobblehead doll. If they still sell them, I'll buy one and put it on my desk. She's nodding. Yes, to the acquittal. Yes, to the hard work. Yes, to the amount of time. Yes, yes, to the investigators and experts. Yes, to picking apart the prosecution's case. *Check*.

"Your son's financial situation," I say, "may be such that the court will happily appoint him an attorney free of charge. That attorney may not be able to devote as much time and personal attention to your son's case as a private attorney such as myself, but I'm sure his representation will be adequate. If not, the issue can be raised on appeal after conviction. A court-appointed lawyer will probably at some point suggest a plea bargain, and he may even get your son a decent plea offer, so that Joey will be out of prison in twenty or so years, in which case one or both of you may even live to see your son walk out of prison a free man."

Gina is shaking her head. That's it, Gina, shake it. No, to the court-appointed lawyer. No, to the conviction. No, to the appeal. No, to the plea bargain. No, no, to the twenty or so years. *Check.*

"The choice," I say, "is yours. If you'd like more time . . ."

"Joseph," Gina says, "hand him the fucking check."

CHAPTER 5

I'm pacing like a caged animal, walking in the echoes of my own footfalls, trapped in the concrete shoe box they pass off as an attorney-client conference room here at the county jail. I'm suffering physical manifestations from my claustrophobia. If that's possible. Maybe the pounding headache, the profuse sweating, and the tightness in my chest are purely psychological. I don't know. Something I'll have to look up on the Internet when I get back to my apartment. *If* I get back to my apartment. If these sons of bitches ever produce my client.

I look at my watch, the fifty-second time in the past forty-eight minutes. I don't even see the time anymore, it's just nervous habit. I've already complained a half dozen times, and each time I'm told that the jail runs on aloha time. Each time the guard serves me a broad smile and flashes me the *shaka,* the Hawaiian hand gesture for "hang loose." Should he *shaka* me one more time, he's going to get a dose of his own medicine, a common hand gesture from *my* culture. The Big Apple's one-finger salute.

I'm clawing at my forearm with my half-eaten nails, trying to get the guard from under my skin, when I finally hear a rap at the door. I open the heavy door and I'm met with a face barely resembling that of the man whose picture I saw in the *Honolulu Advertiser* just yesterday. The man in the photograph looked more human, more alive. The glint in the photograph is missing from his eyes, left behind in his eight-by-ten cell.

I thank the guard with a quiet *mahalo,* forgetting myself and the wait I was just put through. My client is unfettered by handcuffs yet shackled to a smell. He reeks like a vagrant, of body odor mixed with futility, the nauseating stench of utter despair. I wait for a scream of horror, something coinciding with the contorted look of terror on his face. Instead he quietly apologizes for his scent.

"Don't concern yourself," I say. "I knew you were from Jersey when I agreed to take the case."

My words elicit a smile, even a light laugh. The ice is smashed into a million little pieces.

Joey is dressed in the standard prison-issued jumpsuit, which is as befitting for him as a garter belt for a nun. He's good-looking, or at least was at some time, his face angular and strong, framed by closely cropped brown hair. His eyes are red and puffy, his cheeks sunken and pale. The first seventy-two hours inside are the worst. Then it's all peaches and cream.

"So you're my new lawyer?"

"What's it to you?"

"My mother tells me you're the best."

"Only in the western hemisphere." I hope Hawaii is in the western hemisphere, or else I just made a bad joke. I'll have to check that out on the Internet. When I think about it, I'm amazed at how little I actually know for certain.

I begin as I usually do, asking him questions I already know the answers to, to determine whether I can expect from him the truth, or if he'll serve me up steaming plates of horseshit at every turn, as criminal clients tend to do.

My preamble about the attorney-client privilege isn't necessary, he says. He made it that far in law school. So I get right to the meat of the matter. To the Sunday, bloody Sunday, the day he may never live down.

"What time did you arrive at Honolulu Airport?"

"A couple hours after Shannon. I guess it was around four p.m."

"Where did you go after leaving the airport?"

"I took a cab to my hotel in Waikiki, the Hawaiian Sands."

Made up of two forty-floor towers with over twelve hundred rooms, the Hawaiian Sands is one of Waikiki's bigger resorts. The towers, built around the time I was born, bracket a huge open atrium complete with a three-story, man-made waterfall. The Hawaiian Sands abuts Waikiki Beach approximately a mile from where Shannon's body was discovered.

"What did you do when you got to the hotel?"

"I checked in, showered, grabbed some dinner down-stairs, had a few drinks. Then I went out for the night."

"Where did you go?"

Joey gives me the names and descriptions of the bars, a chronology of his solo pub crawl, as best he can. He was drinking T&Ts, Tanqueray and tonics. He won't hazard a guess at how many, he leaves it at "a lot." He asked some of the bartenders to hold the tonic. My kind of drinks. He puts himself at the last bar at approximately 3:00 a.m., which is around the same time the victim was last seen alive.

Fortunately, Joey was sensible enough to say nothing to the police, other than the magic words *I want a lawyer*. If the police have Joey's timetable for that night, it's from pounding the pavement. That's right, Joey. Make them work for it. Let them earn their keep. Most clients serve up their damning facts on a silver platter, along with generous helpings of damning untruths.

"How did you know Shannon was coming to Waikiki?"

He hesitates, eyes darting up and to the left. I did pay attention in forensic-science class on that day. He's looking for a lie.

"A mutual friend," he says.

"Does this mutual friend have a name?"

"I'd rather not say."

"Is it a male or female?"

"Female."

"What's her cup size?"

"What?"

"What's her first name?"

"I'd rather not say."

"Just the first name."

"Cindy."

"What's her last name?"

"I'd rather not say."

"Would you rather smell like this the rest of your life?"

"DuFrain. Her name is Cindy DuFrain."

"Good. Now, that wasn't so hard, was it? Wasn't that fun? Don't dick me around," I bark at him. "Last time a client dicked me around, it turned out bad for him. Real bad. Now, did anyone else know that you were coming to Hawaii?"

"Just my father."

"Did your father speak to the police before your arrest?"

"No."

"And how did the police know you were here, that you were in any way connected to Shannon Douglas to begin with?"

I let him connect the dots and move on.

"What brought you here, Joey?"

He takes a deep breath, his eyes lifting to the ceiling as his mind travels back in time, to a period he wishes his body could join.

"Shannon and I were together a couple years. We'd been inseparable since law school orientation. We took the same courses. We studied together. We ate every meal together. The only time we were apart was when she was at work."

"Where did she work?"

"Newark, New Jersey. The law firm of Carter, Backman and Knight. Personal injury lawyers."

I've handled my fair share of personal injury cases, most of them against the New York City Police Department for kicking the shit out of my clients during arrest. It's a fun practice. If I weren't defending criminals, I'd throw on a pair Nikes and chase ambulances with the best of them.

"We had some rough spots," he says, "some tough times, but we worked through them. Then out of the clear fucking blue last weekend, she tells me it's over. My heart was ripped to shreds, and all I could think about was getting her back. I was so sure that if I could just talk to her, she'd realize her mistake and take me back. I hadn't done anything wrong."

Sorry, Joey. It's when you haven't done anything wrong that you know she just doesn't want you, and it's as over as over gets. If you cheated, it's understandable her leaving, so you deny it and move on. If you don't spend enough time with her, you simply promise to spend more. If you're not good in the bedroom, you order Viagra online or take out some instructional books from your local library. But when she has no rhyme or reason, when she tells you, "It's not you, it's me," then it's you, you, you, and you're done, done, and on to the next one.

"When I got to her apartment in Murray Hill, she was gone. I had a talk with her roommate, Cindy, who tried to convince me to forget about her and move on, that it was completely over. And I pretended to listen and understand. Finally, she told me that Shannon left for Hawaii. She never dreamed I'd go, but I went back to my place in Hoboken, packed a bag, and flew here hoping to find her, to talk to her, to fix whatever was wrong between us."

Without realizing it, Joey is sitting before me plotting the prosecutor's opening statement, carving up a delicious slice of motive, serving it with a heaping side of opportunity.

At this point, my file on *State versus Joseph Gianforte Jr.* consists of little more than a retainer agreement and a photocopy of the $50,000 check. Still, that Joey was charged with first-degree murder says a lot about the state's theory of the crime. The term *crime of passion* and charge of first-degree murder mix like Klan members and Black Panthers at a bar mitzvah. A homicide committed in the heat of passion typically warrants a charge of second-degree murder, a crime of malice without forethought. The state in this case either theorizes that Joey flew to Hawaii with the intent to kill Shannon Douglas, or, more likely, that Joey observed the tryst between his ex-girlfriend and the local man on the beach, which fueled a homicidal rage, which he exhibited control over while lying in wait until Shannon's lover left the scene, and perhaps then some, before acting on his violent impulse, thus establishing premeditation, the requisite ingredient for a first-degree stew.

Joey's being shitfaced on T&Ts—what is legally termed *voluntary intoxication*—is a meritorious defense to the specific-intent crime of first-degree murder. But it's a double-edged sword. While the drunkenness negates specific intent, it also makes it more likely that he committed the crime, thus at a minimum helping to establish the lesser included offense of second-degree murder. It's a pitfall we must somehow navigate around.

"What time did you get back to the Hawaiian Sands hotel that night?"

"I don't know," he says, clearly frustrated and maybe even embarrassed at his blacking out.

I can sympathize with this. I drank my way through college and law school, and there were many nights I had to be told about the next morning. Still, I ask him to hazard a guess.

"Late. Maybe four or five a.m."

I would bet the retainer that the police already have a copy of the video from the Hawaiian Sands' surveillance cameras that shows precisely what time Joey strolled in, and I would also bet that the timing is not at all helpful to our defense.

"Joey," I say, "did you see Shannon at all that night?"

"No, I didn't."

"Are you certain?"

"Yes, I'm certain."

I study his eyes and I don't know whether I am staring in the face of guilt or innocence. Before Brandon Glenn, it didn't matter, not one single bit. Guilty or innocent, my job was the same: to manufacture reasonable doubt. But now things have changed, haven't they? Brandon was innocent and Brandon's dead, dead as dead ever gets. Joey will get from me what Brandon never did: the benefit of the doubt.

Still, one issue is particularly troubling me, one item that will make a prosecutor dance down the aisles like a ballerina on speed. There's no room to dance here in the concrete cubicle, so I come right out with it.

"Joey, tell me the circumstances surrounding your conviction on the domestic violence charge in New York."

He sinks low onto his metal folding chair like a child who hasn't done his homework. He squirms, uncomfortable on the metal, uncomfortable in his skin.

"You're not gonna believe me if I do."

"Why's that, Joey?"

"Because I lived through it, yet I hardly believe what happened myself."

CHAPTER 6

Late last year around Christmastime, Joey entered Shannon's apartment with the key she'd given him on the fifth of December, their one-year anniversary. He found her drunk, completely smashed, he says, crying hysterically on the living room rug. He asked her what was wrong, what was troubling her, but she shooed him away, covering her face as if he were some sort of stranger. He kept asking, kept touching, kept trying to comfort to no avail. The more he spoke, the angrier she grew. The more he touched, the more she pushed away. The more he tried to comfort her, the more hysterical she became.

Finally she faced him, but with a face he had never before seen. She spat in his eyes, her rage raining down on him like a level-three tropical storm. She screeched at him, you bastard, son of a bitch, no-good low-life whore. He didn't know what it meant and doesn't to this day. He was neither a son of a bitch nor a bastard and has never, he assures me, whored.

Her rant, he says, turned quickly to violence, a fearsome attack on him for which he was ill prepared. She came at him with glasses, bottles, and plates. He ducked a few, batted a few more. They hit windows and walls and furniture, smashing all around him, before crashing to the floor.

Amid the bedlam and wreckage, he grabbed his leather coat and headed for the exit. She charged at him with a vase, a large, clear piece of crystal he had brought for her that night. He dodged her out of fear and watched her trip on the edge of the Oriental rug she so loved. She fell like a tree, smashing her head on the shelf of the cherry Pottery Barn bookcase they had selected together a month before.

She was bleeding, but not enough to stop her screaming. She cursed him, threatened him, threw things at him from her spot on the floor. She was alive and kicking, literally kicking, so he ran like the dickens out the door.

A nosy neighbor dialed 911 and brought the cops to Shannon's apartment. Joey was long gone by the time police arrived, and his side of the story had left with him, leaving hers, only hers, and nothing more. Still drunker than drunk, Shannon told police Joey had attacked her, beat her, left her bloodied on the floor.

A detective called Joey's home and invited him down to the station the next morning. Joey obliged, but sung nothing except the magic lyrics: *I want a lawyer.* He was booked on a domestic violence charge and spent a grueling night in the Tombs. He was released on $500 bail the following day.

Joey didn't see Shannon while the case was pending. An order of protection was issued by the court, such that Joey couldn't even go to school. Had he come within one hundred yards of Shannon, he would have been rearrested and charged with contempt for violating the court's order of protection.

Joey had no choice but to take a leave from law school. He called it a leave, though he knew even then he would never go back. He became depressed and started drinking, but sometimes drinking just isn't enough. So he experimented with drugs like a mad scientist. He snorted coke for a couple weeks until his nose bled and he could snort no more. He smoked pot for a month, but his lungs weren't built for smoke, so he put the pipe aside and tried pills. Pills were just the thing. Narcotic painkillers by day, tranquilizers by night. He didn't know, he says, until then that Shannon came in pill form.

Still, when the real thing finally telephoned, he took the call. Shannon told him that she tried, oh so desperately she tried, to rescind her story from that night. But the assistant district attorney assigned to the case was a hard-ass who threatened her with a charge for filing a false report. The assistant DA assured her that if she didn't cooperate in the domestic violence case, Shannon and Joey would end up with criminal records, both of them. The DA's office already had enough to prosecute Joey, what with the original police report and Shannon's hospital records, which revealed that she needed nine stitches to close the wound on her pretty little head.

Joey told Shannon not to risk it. She wanted to work someday for the FBI, so she needed a spotless record. He cared about nothing but her, so for him it was no choice at all. He took a plea to a misdemeanor with a promise of probation and community service. But most important for Joey, the order of protection was lifted, and Shannon had agreed to see him once again.

Joey misreads the look on my face; he thinks it's of disbelief, when it's really of disgust and disdain. I believe every word Joey just told me. But only because I've represented clients charged with domestic violence in New York before. I know the zeal of the district attorney's office in prosecuting such cases, the fervor with which convictions are pursued. I have known them to intimidate complaining witnesses who refuse to cooperate, threatening them with charges of perjury and filing a false report. I call their bluff and my clients walk. But Legal Aid lawyers, always looking to lighten their load, often advise their clients to plea, to throw up their hands in surrender to the state. Yes, I believe every word Joey just told me. But I know, too, that a jury here in Honolulu would not.

The interview is taking its toll on Joey. Hell, it's taking its toll on me, too. I'll want to see Joey regularly while he adjusts to life behind bars, so I tell him I have no more questions for today. I ask him if he has any of his own.

"Will you be able to get my bail reduced, so I can get out of jail until trial?"

Joey is a Grade A flight risk if ever I saw one. Charged with a crime that could keep him behind bars for the rest of his life, seven thousand miles from home. Without some changed circumstances since the time bail was initially set—some new evidence that weakens the state's case or makes Joey a much lower flight risk—bail reduction is a practical impossibility. I tell him this and he takes it less than well.

I don't carry a hankie, though right now I wish I did. Joey is breaking down before my eyes, streams of tears flowing down his cheeks, snot dripping steadily from his nose.

I'm losing my breath, suddenly dizzy, shaking like a leaf in fall. The shoe box we share is growing smaller, tightening around us like a vise. It's suddenly hotter in here, his smell more pungent, like a public toilet that's overflowed. My cheeks feel flush and my stomach wants to put my breakfast back on the table.

I focus on Joey, trying to soothe myself by soothing him. "Joey, look at me. You're a long way from home, confined to a terrible place. But you are not alone. I'm here to help you. I'm here to learn everything I can about what happened that night. Regardless of what happened, my job is the same. To slice and dice the state's case and see you walk. I'll overturn every stone. I'll try to tear apart every witness they put on the stand. I'll give the prosecutor a fight like he's never fought before. But in order for me to be effective, I'm telling you now, I need from you the truth no matter what that truth is. I need to know everything you know right down to the type of toothpaste Shannon used. If you don't trust me enough to tell me everything, then tell me now. Because later will be too late."

"Mr. Corvelli—"

"Kevin. Call me Kevin."

"Kevin, I didn't kill Shannon."

"Then, Joey, I have to find out who did, or at the very least, who could have."

Tears, tears, more tears. God, I hate to see a grown man cry.

"What do I do in the meantime, Kevin? What am I supposed to do?"

"You keep your mouth shut while you're inside. You don't discuss *anything* about your case or your relationship with Shannon with *anyone*. Not the guards, not your cellmates, not even your parents. The only person you speak to is me."

I stand from my metal folding chair. My ass hurts. It hurts real bad.

"Mr. Cor— I mean, Kevin, I have one last question."

"Make it quick, Joey. My ass hurts. It hurts real bad."

"Do you think we'll win the preliminary hearing? Do you think maybe the judge will just toss the case, and I'll be sent home?"

A preliminary hearing was scheduled at Joey's initial arraignment. In theory, preliminary hearings are meant to determine whether there was probable cause for arrest, so that the defendant doesn't sit needlessly in jail for an extended period while the prosecution tries to build its case. Prosecuting attorneys have the option of taking felony cases to the grand jury or to a preliminary hearing before a judge. They take most cases to the grand jury, where defendants lack the right to confront state witnesses. The right to confrontation is guaranteed in preliminary hearings. Thus, if the prosecutor drags his ass and a preliminary hearing must be held, the accused has a better shot at avoiding trial. Evidently, however, the Honolulu prosecutor's office doesn't run on aloha time.

"There's not going to be a preliminary hearing, Joey. The Oahu grand jury handed down an indictment this morning."

Another downpour of tears from his side of the table.

Poor son of a bitch. The accused is always the last to know.

CHAPTER 7

This morning Jake and I sit in the conference room with the contents of our growing file on the case of *State versus Joseph Gianforte Jr.* spread across the table. The Hawaiian sun peeking over our shoulders is no doubt wondering, like us, how the hell we're going to knock down the house of cards the prosecution is quickly building. After meeting with Joey yesterday, I strolled over to the Office of the Prosecuting Attorney with a written request for preliminary discovery. I fully anticipated being met with dirty looks and leaving with empty hands. Instead I received a warm reception and was immediately directed to the Screening and Intake Division, or SID.

SID is responsible for screening felony cases brought to the department by the Honolulu Police Department and other state investigative agencies. Consisting of one division chief, thirteen screening deputies, seven support staff, and two paralegal assistants, SID reviews search warrants and felony cases, deciding which ones to accept, which ones to reject, and which ones require follow-up work. SID also handles preliminary hearings in district court and presents cases to the grand jury.

I was greeted by the division chief, a pretty, middle-aged woman wearing glasses. I was prepared for a fight. I was prepared to sit and wait, to be shuffled from division to division while people talked about me behind closed doors. I was prepared to raise hell, to threaten and complain my way to getting the discovery on Joey's case. I was prepared to throw things, really I was.

"Aloha, Mr. Corvelli, my name is Barbara Davenport. How can I help you today?"

"I represent Joseph Gianforte. I have a written request for discovery."

She took the paper from me and smiled. "Very good. We are about to transfer this case to the Trials Division, but I'll have my assistant photocopy everything for you right away. It shouldn't take much longer than five minutes. Do you mind waiting?"

"Of course not."

She was so pleasant, it angered me. So helpful, I half-expected to get hit from behind and kidnapped. This had to, just had to, be some sort of ploy. Prosecutors aren't this nice. They are evil robots with badges. Or maybe I *was* in some sort of *Twilight Zone* episode. Or maybe I was on *Candid Camera*.

She returned four minutes fifty-three seconds later with a manila envelope in her hand. "Here you go, Mr. Corvelli," she said, handing me the envelope. "I'm sorry about the wait."

"Not at all."

"I understand you're new to the islands. Let me be the first from our office to say, 'E komo mai.' Welcome. If you need anything else or have any questions, please feel free to call me at any time. And best of luck with your new practice."

"Mahalo," I managed, still befuddled over my first-ever positive experience in a prosecutor's office.

This morning I brought the envelope to the office and found Jake already in the conference room, sipping from a steaming cup of store-bought coffee, the aroma suggesting he added ingredients of his own.

I pored through the contents of the envelope as soon as I got back to my apartment late yesterday afternoon. It consisted primarily of witness statements, photographs, an autopsy report, pleadings, and police affidavits. It also contained three DVDs.

"Let's start with the victim's timeline on the night of the murder," I say. "It seems the victim started the evening at around eight p.m. with some dinner at Margaritaville on Kuhio Avenue."

"So we find the lost shaker of salt and the case is closed," Jake says between slurps.

"I went there last night," I say, leafing through my yellow legal pad scribbled with notes. "The bartender puts Shannon there from eight to eleven, during which time she had a cheeseburger and four Tiki Gods."

"Tiki Gods?"

"It's the bar's variation on the mai tai. They're strong, full of Bacardi 151. I had a couple while I was there."

"You're a very thorough investigator, son."

"That I am, Jake. That I am."

"Where did she go after that?"

"After Margaritaville, she went directly to the Bleu Sharq, across from the beach. Two of the bartenders who worked that night don't remember her. The third had last night off. She's off tonight, too, but she works tomorrow night. I'll go see her then."

"Any credit card receipts?"

"No, she paid cash. Either that or someone else bought her drinks."

Jake picks up a witness statement and squints so tightly his eyes disappear. "Perhaps this fella here, Palani Kanno."

Palani is a local, a doorman at the Waikiki Winds, a moderate-size hotel not far from the Bleu Sharq. On Monday, when the body was first found, Palani quickly became the primary suspect in the case. He was seen leaving with the victim twenty minutes after last call. The police brought him in for questioning, at which time he admitted to having sex with Shannon Douglas on an isolated stretch of Waikiki Beach, a couple blocks from the Bleu Sharq. He also admitted that there had been a physical altercation, but only after Detective John Tatupu informed Palani that his skin had been found under the victim's fingernails.

That skin had been found under the victim's nails was true. Whether it was Palani's or not, the detective did not know. Although the visible claw marks across the left side of Palani's face probably gave him some clue. DNA tests would take time, so the detective lied to get from Palani what he wanted. That's what detectives do, they lie. And it works. Palani folded like a piece of paper. He even admitted that in defending himself, he may have struck Shannon Douglas in the face.

Judging from the witness statements and police affidavits, Detective Tatupu must have thought he was seconds away from a full confession when a pair of honeymooners arrived at the station. The newlyweds—a Mr. and Mrs. Timothy Knowsley—had spent their first night on the island walking the deserted beach in the dark, drinks in hand, not wanting the magic to end. The next morning, they saw the commotion on the beach and feared they might know something about what happened. After being shown a grim photograph of the victim, they confirmed that, yes, indeed, they had seen the girl alive on Waikiki Beach at approximately threesomething a.m. Although it was pitch-black outside, it was apparent to them she had been crying, and more important, that her face had been badly bruised.

Palani had told Tatupu that he left Shannon Douglas there on the beach, alive and well, and walked straight to the Waikiki Winds to "pick something up." After a few tough questions from Tatupu, that "something" turned into *pakalolo*, the Hawaiian word for marijuana. Luckily for Palani, the friend who sold him the weed—one J. J. Fitzpatrick—was so high himself that he begged Palani to take over his shift. Palani grudgingly accepted it and remained at the hotel the entire night, unwittingly creating for himself an alibi that would keep him from being formally charged in the death of Shannon Douglas.

After the honeymooners provided sworn witness statements, Tatupu quickly confirmed Palani's story with the doorman's supervisor at the Waikiki Winds. Tatupu also secured the hotel surveillance videos, which evidently convinced him to clear Palani as a suspect.

I had intended to view the videos when I returned to my apartment last night. But after a couple Tiki Gods at Margaritaville and a few margaritas at the Bleu Sharq, that just wasn't happening.

"This guy's useless to us," Jake says, flinging Palani's witness statement across the table to me.

"I'm going to talk to him tomorrow morning. Maybe Shannon said something to him that'll help us."

"Son, I don't think she could've done much talking with his dick in her mouth."

"Still," I say, "maybe he told the detective something that was conveniently left out of the statement."

"Okay, son, let's move on to this Cindy DuFrain, who ratted out our client for taking this impromptu holiday."

"According to the police affidavit, she didn't volunteer the information. Far from it."

It seems that once Tatupu cleared Palani as a suspect, he started digging and digging fast. Tatupu contacted his colleagues in New York and asked them to find and interview anyone and everyone connected to Shannon Douglas.

They started at Shannon's apartment, where they found her roommate, Cindy DuFrain. After a good amount of prodding DuFrain admitted to police that she had told Joey of Shannon's trip, and that after hearing it, Joey left the apartment in a hurry.

Jake picks up his coffee and moves to the window. "Aside from one hell of a fucking motive, what else do they have on our boy?"

I leaf through my notes, a summary of the police affidavits and witness statements. "A surveillance camera at the Kapiolani Surf Hotel puts Joey not far from the crime scene at two thirty-five a.m. Then, a surveillance camera at the Hawaiian Sands shows him stumbling back to his room at four forty-five a.m. At least that's what Detective Tatupu attests to. I haven't watched the videos yet myself."

"Do we have the medical examiner's report, son?"

I find the ME's report and gloss over what I already know. "The cause of death is listed as blunt-force trauma to the head. Her skull was fractured. Massive blood loss. The death blow was likely delivered by a right-hander, taller than Shannon's five feet ten inches, with fairly significant strength."

"Sounds like our boy," Jake says.

"Sounds like a lot of boys," I counter.

"How about the murder weapon, son?"

"We have a photo of it and an initial lab analysis."

I find the photograph of the alleged murder weapon. The ivory-colored reef rock is larger than a baseball, smaller than a softball, peppered with crevices and grooves, lightly smeared with a gruesome rust.

"Dried blood matches the victim's," I say. "No prints. It was found in the surf. Must've been on the shore long enough for the blood to dry. Then, the surf came up and rinsed off the prints, if it would've held any to begin with."

I'm guessing. I'm pretty sure we never studied dried blood and latent prints found on reef rocks in that semester of forensic science I took back in college. We sure as shit didn't study forensic science in law school. Again, that would have been too practical. But we did have vested remainders subject to complete defeasance shoved down our throats. Whatever the hell they are. The science doesn't matter this early in the game anyway. Besides, that's what experts are for.

"That doesn't sound like a law student, leaving the murder weapon there in the sand near the body," Jake says. "The ocean's right there. Why not throw it in, as far as you can? It would've never been found."

"The prosecutor will argue that all legal training and logic fly out the window when there's a body at your feet."

"Or perhaps," Jake says, holding one finger in the air as if he's just solved a Scooby-Doo mystery, "the killer didn't know it was a body at his feet. Perhaps the killer struck her once and thought she was gonna wake up in the morning with nothing more than a really bad headache."

I get up from my chair and hand him a set of photographs, these of the victim as she appeared within an hour of being found. Jake sees his theory take an arrow through the heart.

Jake squints at the photos with his aging eyes. Upon seeing the close-up shot depicting where Shannon's head had caved in, he lets out an eerie gasp. This from a seasoned Texas death-penalty attorney. I shudder to think what sounds of horror will escape from the mouths of jurors who live and breathe on Oahu, a remote island in the Pacific that sees less than twenty homicides a year. He shakes his head slowly. "Jury sees these, it's all over."

"There's no way to keep them all out," I say. "We'll have to put them in context, convince the jurors that it wasn't Joey who caused this carnage."

"Then, who was it, son?"

"That other guy."

"Oh, yeah. Him. That's not gonna be easy. The victim is a girl thousands of miles away from home with no acquaintances on the island. That eliminates all the usual suspects. Those with motive have no opportunity. Those with opportunity have no motive. She wasn't raped. She wasn't robbed. It boils down to a crime of passion. We may be facing a plea situation here, son."

I concede that the situation is grim, but I tell him Joey is unlikely to take a plea.

"What's your take on him?" he asks.

Joey is a frightened little boy, locked in a closet, fearing he will never be let out. His parents are helpless to save him, capable of nothing but listening to his screams through the door. I'm the only one both inside and out. I'm the only one capable of finding the key to set him free. I'm the one he'll blame should that closet become his permanent home.

What's my take on him? It doesn't matter, does it? I promised I would help him. That didn't mean much before Brandon Glenn. But it sure as shit means something now.

"Let's just say I'm withholding judgment, Jake. I don't know if he did it or not, but I can't risk thinking him guilty and finding out later I was wrong, after it's too late."

"It's dangerous ground you're treading on, son. The law itself, she's a jealous mistress. Add to that the need to save the world one case at a time, and you wind up growing old too fast. It's easy to forget it's his ass on the line, not yours. Hell, the state of Texas executed me more times than I can remember. I'd like to think I've done some good over the years, but I can't argue I've done much good for myself. If I had it to do all over again, I'm not so sure I would."

Just then, the conference-room door swings open, and Hoshi steps in.

"Sorry for the interruption," she says. "But I was just over at the Sand Bar picking up my lunch, and the television was on. There's something I think you guys should see."

CHAPTER 8

The Sand Bar looks like an Irish tavern that got lost, found itself in downtown Honolulu, and tried too hard to fit in. Look to your left and find a leprechaun on a surfboard. To your right, a statue of a beautiful hula girl wears a T-shirt that reads KISS ME, I'M IRISH. Behind you on the shelves are Polynesian tiki gods covered in four-leaf clovers. And in front of you, behind the bar taking drink orders, stands a man named Seamus adorned in a lei and grass skirt.

"Aloha, gents," says Seamus in his thick Irish brogue. "Top o' the mornin' to ya. What can I get for you today?"

I ask Seamus to turn up the volume on the television, and Jake orders us two Jameson Irish whiskeys on the rocks.

"Isn't it a little early, Jake?" I ask.

"Hell, you're from New York. It's six hours later over there. You've got to take into account the time difference, son."

Seamus turns up the volume on one of a half dozen television sets over the bar. Gretchen Hurst fills the screen, touting what is still to come on her national cable news show, *All Ears*. She began her career on radio, but was later given her own cable news show, on which she demonstrated a knack for shamelessly exploiting the families of victims across the country in return for healthy ratings. She clearly gets her jollies from giving local officials, suspects, and their lawyers a faceful of microphone in front of millions of viewers, who prejudge the issue of guilt in reliance on her slanted views and purported expertise in the field of investigative journalism.

Today, she says, her guest is Carlie Douglas. Live via satellite from Honolulu.

Carlie Douglas is Shannon's mother. A picture of her flashes on the screen. She is attractive, as her daughter was, younger than I would have expected. Early forties, I would guess. She was a single mother, that much I knew. Hurst also tells us that Carlie has traveled to Hawaii from her home in Knoxville, Tennessee, seeking justice for her daughter.

Gretchen Hurst goes to commercial and I turn my whiskey upside down till the ice hits my teeth. The case of *State versus Joseph Gianforte Jr.* has just gone national.

The national news media have been hungry for island murder after a missing-girl fiasco on an island in the Caribbean. This case has all the necessary ingredients: sex and violence involving a beautiful young woman, a tropical-island setting, and a white man accused of murder. Sure, they have the body, which takes away some of the mystery and intrigue, but the Caribbean case is growing stale. Aloha, Waikiki.

I don't watch television. I don't have one in my home. I get my news from newspapers and the Internet. So this is the first I'm seeing of this. *All Ears* returns with the large words at the bottom of the screen: SLAIN IN PARADISE.

Hurst gives some background on the case. The body of a beautiful law student was found five days ago on the world-famous Waikiki Beach in Honolulu. She had been bludgeoned to death and left on the sand. Charged with her murder is her ex-boyfriend, a New Jersey man with a history of domestic violence against the victim.

"I realize this is a very difficult time for you, Carlie, and I thank you for taking the time to talk to me," says Hurst.

"Thank you for having me, Gretchen."

Carlie Douglas has the moist eyes of a grieving mother, the voice of someone who has spent the past few days crying, the southern accent emphasized by the strain in her voice. She wears little makeup, and she needs none. She has green eyes and auburn hair, wears a flower behind her right ear and a tiny smile, a likely look for someone's first time on camera.

"Carlie, can you tell us why you have gone to Honolulu?"

"My only child is gone," she says, her first sentence no doubt as difficult as any she has ever spoken. "After the funeral, I knew I had to come here to Oahu to seek justice for Shannon. She was a law student, she wanted to go into law enforcement. She believed in justice and the American criminal justice system. She would've wanted me here."

"Are you satisfied with the police investigation into your daughter's death?"

"I am satisfied, Gretchen. They have the killer behind bars and they tell me they have all the evidence they need to obtain a conviction. Unfortunately, Hawaii does not have the death penalty, so true justice can never be achieved for my daughter."

"The man they have behind bars awaiting trial is Shannon's ex-boyfriend, Joseph Gianforte Jr., isn't that right?"

"Yes, it is, Gretchen."

"They were in a relationship for almost two years as I understand it. Did you know Mr. Gianforte, Carlie?"

"I knew *of* him. I had never met him. She never brought him home for Thanksgiving or Christmas. I only knew about him through my conversations with Shannon."

"Had you known he was convicted of domestic violence due to an incident involving your daughter?"

"Yes, I did, Gretchen. The incident occurred the night I told Shannon something about her boyfriend that she had not known about him. She wouldn't tell me exactly what happened that night, but I'm sure Shannon told him what I told her, and he struck her."

"What is it you discovered about Shannon's boyfriend? What did you tell her that would cause him to strike your daughter?"

"I'm sorry, Gretchen. I'm not at liberty to say right now. I was told by the police and prosecutors not to discuss issues that may directly relate to the case."

"I understand. But you're convinced that the police have the killer behind bars, that it was Joseph Gianforte who murdered your daughter, isn't that right?"

"Absolutely. I know it was him."

"How long do you plan to remain in Hawaii, Carlie?"

"I have no immediate plans to return home to Knox-ville. As far as I'm concerned, my business is here, helping ensure that some semblance of justice is brought to Shan-non's killer."

"Thank you, Carlie. We'll be watching this story very closely as it unfolds. We hope you'll join us again soon."

"Thank you, Gretchen."

"When we come back, we'll go to local correspondent Mike Oliver in Honolulu with the latest on the case against Shannon's accused killer, Joseph Gianforte Jr."

I start in on my second whiskey and wonder what the weather is like in New York. I can check it out on the Inter-net when I get back to my apartment if I'm not too drunk to work the computer. Who am I kidding? I'm going to make sure I'm too drunk to work the computer. I drain my glass and order up another.

"Easy, cowboy," says Jake. "It's not yet noon. You're gonna wake up tomorrow with the brown-bottle flu and you've gotta question that doorman in the morning."

"It's almost six in New York, Jake. Remember?"

Seamus is quick on the trigger. My third drink hits the bar as Mike Oliver comes on.

Oliver tells us that Joey has been indicted on first-degree murder. He's being held in lieu of $3 million bail and he's likely to plead not guilty when he's arraigned on the charges in the indictment next week.

"Mike Oliver," Gretchen says, "we've spoken a bit about the defendant in this case. What do we know of his attorney, Kevin Corvelli?"

"We haven't yet been able to reach him for comment, Gretchen. We're told he's actually very new to the islands, having been admitted here just over a week ago, coming by way of New York. He's a young attorney, a former protégé of Milt Cashman of the Cashman Law Firm in Manhattan."

"Would that be Not Guilty Milty, the criminal attorney who represents all those rap artists?"

"That's right, Gretchen. Since then, Corvelli has been in private practice in Manhattan. He ended his career there on a very sour note, a fairly high-profile murder case, which he lost in spectacular fashion."

"Tell us what happened, Mike."

"Well, Gretchen . . ."

I ask Seamus to mute the volume and change the channel. The image of Mike Oliver is replaced with that of Jon Stewart, a journalist with real integrity and a show even I could watch.

The Irish whiskey has lost its flavor, which is a good

thing for someone who prefers Scotch. I drink it down and order another.

"Jake, do you know a good investigator?" I ask.

"Of course, I do. A good fella. His office is just down the block."

My head is swimming. I should eat, but nothing on the board looks appetizing. Corned beef and cabbage with a side of poi? Kalua pig and Tater Tots? I don't think so. I'll eat my ice.

I think back to three days ago when I first met Jake. I think back to what he warned me about. I have placed myself in a position to repeat the mistake that led me here, this time on a national scale. Thanks to Gretchen Hurst and Mike Oliver, that which I escaped from has followed me here to Oahu. Now, with four whiskeys soaking my mind, I am about to forget where I am. *Malihini* or not, I want to run the table.

"Would you mind calling your investigator, Jake? Having him meet us here if he's available?"

"Of course not, son. May I ask what for?"

"Carlie Douglas is here to help the prosecution try Joey in the press," I say. "I intend to level the playing field."

CHAPTER 9

Ryan Flanagan, or Flan as Jake calls him, is a gruff-looking native of New Orleans who had nothing to lose when he decided to call Honolulu home. He walks into the Sand Bar with a cigarette dangling from his lips, chest hair creeping out of his mostly unbuttoned aloha shirt. He is middle-aged with salt-and-pepper hair, at least two days' scruff but not a beard. He is thin and wiry but solid. Billy Bob Thornton with different tattoos.

His hand is coarse like sandpaper and I instinctively pull mine back at the touch. I'm used to shaking lawyers' hands. Flan's hands are no lawyer's hands. Not a private investigator's hands either. He's got a broad smile on his face, but his eyes don't hide the hand in life he was dealt.

Flan, Jake told me, was blue-collar by blood, a steel cutter who never bitched about a life cutting steel. He loved it, took great pleasure in earning a good day's pay for a hard day's work. He cut steel for just over two decades, waking at the crack of dawn and quitting at the cusp of dusk. He followed orders. He cut steel. He went home dirty and went to bed clean. Woke up the next morning and did it all again.

Flan was thirty-four, on a job just outside New Orleans, when he met Victoria, a twentysomething princess from the suburbs. Her daddy was the owner of the property Flan was working on, and she decided to check out the property, not to mention the men working on it, late one September afternoon. It was ungodly hot for autumn, and Victoria strutted over to Flan and offered him a bottled beer. As Flan will tell you, a woman brings a workingman an ice-cold beer on a damned hot day, he falls in love with her instantly, no questions asked. It didn't hurt none that Victoria herself was hotter than the August sun.

They married and Flan soon learned that Victoria was as spoiled as she was gorgeous. Or as Jake put it, she was a bigger pain in the ass than a Texas-size hemorrhoid. Three years and two children after he said "I do," he was out on his ass, cutting steel eighty hours a week just to pay alimony and child support.

A year after his divorce, Flan was working on his day off for a subcontractor hired to refurbish a bulkhead at the pier of a large beverage importer when a wake from a tugboat caused him to fall from the floating stage he was working on. He grabbed hold of a small anchor hole just large enough for his hand to keep himself from falling into the creek and drowning. His weight, along with the fifty-pound tool belt he was wearing, was too much. After tear-ing his rotator cuff and nearly ripping his right arm out of its socket, he dropped into the water, the tool belt pulling him to the bottom.

Freeing himself of the tool belt, Flan escaped with his life. But his life wasn't much after that day. Permanently injured, he couldn't work, so he couldn't pay his bills, including the hefty monthly amounts for alimony and child support. Victoria cut off contact with him, thus effectively severing his ties with his two lovely young daughters. He declared bankruptcy and contemplated suicide.

Rather than kill himself, he decided to try his hand in paradise. He'd been to Waikiki on his honeymoon, and it surely beat the cemetery, with the exception of the company he'd had. He escaped his life in New Orleans and all the shit that came with it, but for one thing. He could not escape the physical pain caused by the accident. To this day, he eats Vicodin the way baseball players eat sunflower seeds, and he wears at all times a fetanyl patch, which releases morphine into his body just to get him through the day.

Jake and Flan moved to the island within a month of each other. They met at Margaritaville two months after Flan arrived. They told each other their stories. Flan had made it off the mainland, but he didn't know where to go from there. Because of the endless pain, he couldn't perform hard labor, the only kind of labor he knew. Jake suggested Flan become a private investigator. Flan looked into it, but to get licensed, he needed four years experience in the field. Jake told him, to hell with the license. He brought Flan in as an investigator on some cases and referred him to other attorneys on the island. Thanks to Jake, Flan had found a new career, albeit a bit of a shady one.

We take a booth away from Seamus and his ears. The bar is empty, but in criminal law, one person hearing your business is one too many. Flan orders a bourbon from the waitress, and Jake and I go another round with the whiskey.

"Flan, Kevin here has some work for you if you're interested," Jake says. "He represents the Jersey kid charged with murdering that young girl on the beach in Waikiki."

"I'm familiar with it," says Flan, taking a drag on his cigarette.

The smoke floats across the table and I swat it away. I'm ready to get up and walk away. One thing I can't stand is smoke. I celebrated for a month when Mayor Bloomberg banned smoking in bars and restaurants in New York. I think I read somewhere that they banned smoking in public places here in Hawaii, too. You can make a bet I'll check that out on the Internet as soon as I get the chance.

"Saw the girl's mama on television this morning," says Flan. "Excuse me," he adds, pulling his chirping cell phone from his pocket.

That's another thing I can't stand. Cell phones. Yeah, I carry one because I have to in my business. But I keep the ringer off, and I never pull it out when I'm in the middle of a conversation. It's rude and obnoxious. Flan is chatting with someone on the other end, about the New Orleans

Saints, no less. I'm growing annoyed at him, what with the cigarette smoke and the cell phone conversation. His fucking car alarm goes off and I'm out of here. Don't get me started on car alarms.

Fortunately for everyone, the drinks arrive.

Flan folds the phone and doesn't apologize. I ask him how he is at making friends.

"If they drink like ol' Jake here, makes it pretty damn easy," he says.

Flan and Jake clink glasses, another annoying ritual. At least they didn't toast.

"Well, I'm not sure about that," I say, "but if you can get some liquor in her, it'll make your job that much easier."

"Her?"

"Yeah, her."

"You mean the girl's mama?"

"I do, indeed."

I don't slur my words when I get drunk. I do, however, start talking like Doc Holliday in *Tombstone*. I tell people I'm their huckleberry and remark at how everyone's so cosmopolitan. This behavior has not yet led to my getting my ass kicked, but I'm sure I've come close.

"I'd like you to find her," I tell him. "Get close to her. I want information about her daughter, things my client either doesn't know or won't tell me. I want her version of the background on the relationship between Joey and Shannon. I want information on the people Shannon spent time with, from high school on up."

I see Jake out of the corner of my eye, shaking his head

but saying nothing, staring into his empty glass, wishing it full. I signal for another round, even as I feel myself getting sick.

"I don't have much experience interviewing witnesses, Kevin. Jake and the other lawyers usually have me track down documents, run papers to the courthouse, that sort of thing. You might wanna handle something as important as this yourself or hire someone with better credentials."

"She may have seen my picture by now," I say. "She'd spit in my eye. Besides, she's probably lawyered up in preparation for a wrongful-death civil lawsuit against my client. I wouldn't be permitted to speak to her without going through her attorney."

"Nor would your agent," Jake adds helpfully.

"That's why I need someone off the radar," I say. "Someone without a license. Someone invisible."

"What makes you think she'll talk to me if she'd as soon spit in your eye?" Flan asks.

"Your backstory. You're going to play a role, do a bit of acting. You're going to comfort her, sympathize with her. You're going to tell her that you also lost a daughter."

"I lost two daughters," he says gruffly. "I'll probably never see them again."

"That will make it that much easier for you," I say. "It's called Method acting. You borrow from your real emotions to act more convincing in the role you're playing." At least I think that's what it is. I don't know. Too much whiskey on an empty stomach.

"I'll let you know as soon as I find her," Flan says, finishing off his bourbon.

"Do you want Flan to talk to that third bartender over at the Bleu Sharq?" Jake asks me.

"No. If Flan is seen speaking to anyone else connected to the case, all the wells will dry up at once. I'll handle the barkeep."

Flan pulls out his wallet to pay. I tell him to put it away, that I've got the tab covered. I hand him a modest roll of cash and tell him to use it to buy Carlie Douglas some cocktails.

"Always pay cash," I tell him. "You're not going to be giving her your real name, so you can't pull out a credit card. Carry your wallet with pictures of one of your daughters, but leave all of your identification at home."

"I appreciate the business, Kevin," Flan says, pocketing the cash quickly, as if we just transacted a drug deal.

I nod, and Flan turns to walk out.

Before Flan reaches the door, Jake asks me, "Did you learn this kind of shit from Not Guilty Milty?"

"No, Jake. I learned it from my mistakes. If I had bothered to do some background on Moss and Reese, Brandon might be alive today."

"You don't know that."

"Maybe not. But at least I could've lived with myself, knowing I overturned every stone."

"Well, son, just bear in mind that this isn't New York. People have very different notions of fair play on the islands."

I raise my hand and make the international signal for the check.

"How about one more round, son?" Jake pleads.

"No, thanks. I'm going home to throw up. Besides, I've got an early day tomorrow. I'm going kayaking."

"Kayaking? I thought you said you were gonna track down that Palani fella and ask him some questions?"

"Why, indeed, Jake. That is precisely what I intend to do."

CHAPTER 10

Contained in Palani's statement to police was the tidbit that on mornings he isn't working at the Waikiki Winds he kayaks from Lanikai Beach, on the windward side of Oahu, to the twin Mokulua Islands. He brings breakfast in a dry bag, according to the statement, and enjoys it leisurely, sprawled out on the pristine stretch of sand in complete solitude. He then paddles his way back before the tourists are out and about, fumbling with their rented equipment and gear. This information seemed extraneous at the time I first read it, but would ultimately prove quite useful for my purpose of finding him alone.

At dawn I park my bright orange Jeep Wrangler a half mile down the road from my intended launching point. I had always wanted a Jeep, but figured it would look rather silly sitting in traffic in Manhattan, especially in winter. I zipper up the soft top, lock the doors, and finger a nick I've already put in the side panel. Hell, it's not my Audi. It's a Jeep. The nick adds character, makes it look tough.

I begin my walk to the launching point and immediately wish I'd parked closer. I do a lot of walking these days, especially compared to the amount I walked in New York, where I took taxis and subways all day every day. It wasn't that I didn't like to walk back then. It was that in New York I always felt that if I could get somewhere faster, be somewhere sooner, I was dutybound to do so. I don't quite feel that way here. I'll get there when I get there.

I breathe in the morning air, and it smells strange. Strike that. There is a *lack* of strange smell. As my mind drifts back to commuting to work in New York, I realize just how different these two worlds are. The Pacific doesn't give off the ugly scent of the Hudson River. I don't smell tar or hear jackhammers. No smoke or steam emanates from manhole covers in the street. No taxis bear down on me as I cross the street, no skyscrapers block the rising of the sun. I hear no horns. I hear no shouts or sirens. I hear nothing, nothing at all but my own footfalls. It is peaceful, like nowhere I have ever before known.

I reach the beach and kick off my sandals. After calling the Waikiki Winds yesterday and learning that Palani had this morning off, I made reservations for a kayak rental and arrangements to have one waiting for me on the beach before the rental shop opened. It's sad and amazing what a lot of money can do.

The kayak is there on the grass, hidden between two trees, covered in a drop cloth. I undress it and find a dry bag and paddle, but no life jacket. The kayak is yellow and large and much heavier than I anticipated. I drag it along the sand of Lanikai Beach toward the launching point. I looked up kayaking on the Internet and thought I knew everything I needed to know. Now I realize I don't have a fucking clue what I'm doing.

No matter what the temperature, the ocean is always chilly at first touch. I ease into it with the kayak banging against my shins. As the water gets deeper, the kayak stops banging against my shins and starts banging against my knees. When it starts banging against my hip, I know it's time to somehow get in.

The sun is up, illuminating the crystal clear water. The ocean is balmy now that I've ducked my entire body under, nearly getting knocked unconscious when the kayak came at my head. I am finally out past the breakers, though the waves weren't cooperating, rushing into the shore as if they had some party to go to.

I let go of the kayak's leash and the kayak immediately starts to float back to shore. It's no doubt as frightened of me as I am of it. I grab the kayak, and in one great feat of athleticism, I hurl my body on top of it. The kayak immediately capsizes, sending me to the ocean floor. I surface and spit out an ounce or two of seawater, choking out every curse I can. Son of a bitch. Practicing law is hard work.

On the third try I'm in, paddling like a master, yet heading in the wrong direction. Through trial and error, I somehow turn the kayak around and face the Mokulua Islands, sitting as they are like two large breasts, jutting above the sea. In the distance they wait for me but a mile away. I figure it'll take me a week and a half to reach them. Luckily, I took into account my inexperience and Palani's probable prowess and gave myself an hour's head start.

My destination is the northern island, the only island that is visitable. The southern island is a bird sanctuary. The current is strong and against me, and I consider giving up and heading back. Mother Ocean is fierce around these islands. It seems every day I am reading in the *Honolulu Advertiser* a story about someone swallowed whole by the sea. Experienced surfers and swimmers and kayakers, even people standing on rocks waiting to have their picture snapped, are sometimes snatched away by a hungry, ferocious wave. And here I am, a novice with no life vest, paddling out to sea.

In the midst of my great struggle, I am passed by a giant native sea turtle, half the size of my kayak, gliding effortlessly toward the Mokulua isles. I remember seeing a sign somewhere prohibiting riding these animals, and only now can I see how the temptation can arise. I name my new friend Sammy and flash him the *shaka*. When he doesn't reciprocate, I flip him the bird.

An hour after launch I wash ashore. I am proud of myself, yet sickened by the thought of traveling back. My arms are tired, my neck and back stiff and sore. I drop like a rock onto the sand and leave myself to bake under the sun.

After only ten minutes, I observe another kayak coming in, its occupant a deep bronze, his paddling fluid and clean. I try to look nonchalant, not like the crazy son of a bitch who nearly killed himself coming here. Just another avid kayaker come to soak up the sun and solitude.

As he lands, I acknowledge him with a slight nod of the head. His face is youthful, even for twenty-eight, and he's blessed with the symmetry of good looks. He tosses his gear onto the sand and plops down next to it, approximately forty feet from where I sit. I am grateful that he seems at least somewhat winded, though not nearly as close to puking up a lung as I was. He removes his wet T-shirt, revealing a muscled frame and a small tattoo of a weeping tiki god just above his left pectoral muscle. He sees me acknowledge him, yet much like the sea turtle, doesn't acknowledge me at all. It's all I can do to keep from flipping him the bird, too.

I know little about Palani other than that he speaks pidgin and curses a lot. Pidgin is spoken by hundreds of thousands of people all over the Hawaiian Islands. It is a different language, although most of the vocabulary is borrowed from English. English speakers first referred to it as pidgin English and considered it a simplified or broken form of English. I bought a book on pidgin along with the *Complete Idiot's Guide to Understanding Conversational Japanese* when I first moved to the islands, but I haven't opened either book. When trying to gain someone's trust, it helps tremendously to speak, or at least understand, their language. To that end, I did take a crash course on pidgin on the Internet when I looked up kayaking. I can only hope I'll fare better at the former than I did at the latter. At least I can't drown trying to understand Palani's pidgin. Besides, although I can't speak pidgin, I sure as shit can curse.

"Fucking strong current today, yeah?" I shout over to him, making my way slowly toward a dollar bill I let fly in his direction.

He nods without looking at me.

"Fucking near capsized paddling out here," I say. I don't mention I capsized six times.

"I seen. You paddle like a *wahine.*"

"A *wahine?*"

"A woman, brah. Just like a girl."

"Well, *mahalo,*" I say, proud of my advanced Hawaiian.

"Why *mahalo? Mahalo* is tourist talk for 't'anks,' eh?"

"I'm *malihini.* I'm still learning. My name is Kevin." I extend my hand. "You're *kama'aina,* a local?"

He grudgingly takes my hand, as if he just saw me reach into a stopped-up toilet and forget to wash.

"Howzit, Kevin? I am Palani. But *kama'aina* is tourist talk, too."

Sometimes the Internet just has it all wrong.

"I just moved here," I say. "This is my first time on Mokulua."

"This here is Moku Nui," he corrects me again. Palani cuts off his *r*'s and his *th*'s are really *d*'s so that it sounds like *Dis heah is Moku Nui.*

"First time, eh?" he says. "Well, welcome to my island, brah."

"Your island? Shit, I didn't know. Am I supposed to pay you admission?"

"No, that's okay, no need. That's how I get you hooked. Just like this."

Palani pulls from his dry bag a Ziploc filled with green herb and a pipe. He evidently neglected to mention the marijuana to police when he told them about his little morning excursions.

"We throw one party, yeah?" Palani says, as he pulls the pipe from the Ziploc and packs the bowl. He pulls a lighter from his pocket and cups his hand to thwart the breeze from ruining his fun. A plume of smoke wafts overhead. "You want some *pakalolo?*" he asks, reaching to hand it off.

It was one of Milt Cashman's ten commandments. *Thou shalt get high with neither client nor witness.* But the commandment was something like number eight. The latter commandments couldn't be nearly as important, right? Besides, it is another opportunity to help me gain his trust. And get high. Anything for a client.

I take the pipe from him and he tosses me the lighter. I light the bowl and take a hit.

"That's Maui Wowie," he says. "Heavy-duty Valley Isle smokes."

I hold it in my lungs, blow it out, choking like a seventh grader on his first cigarette.

"You like or what?"

I nod, coughing, handing him back the pipe. I was hoping the weed would loosen his tongue, get him to talking. But I can't ask him any questions if I can't stop coughing. My eyes are watering, my throat burns. Finally, I catch my breath.

"So," I say, "is running this island a full-time job, or do you work for a living?"

"I work, brah. I'm a doorman over at the Winds in Waikiki."

"No shit," I say, watching him take another hit. "You wouldn't happen to know a guy works over there with the last name Kanno, would you?"

He exhales. Hands me the pipe with an incredulous smile. "That's *my* name, brah."

"You're shitting me!"

"No, brah. Palani Kanno." He nods his head in celebration of the fact. Nodding like a bobblehead doll in a hurricane. Boy, those bobblehead dolls must be fun when you're high.

"The funniest fucking thing," I say, lighting the bowl. "I was going to come see you at the hotel, ask you some questions."

I take a hit, watching him stare at me from the corner of my eye. His smile is gone. Suddenly he's unsure whether to celebrate that his name is Palani Kanno.

"For what?"

"Oh, no big deal," I say, handing off the pipe. "I'm a lawyer. I represent the guy who got picked up by the cops in connection with that girl in Waikiki." I avoid the words *murder, killing,* and *death,* acting as if the whole discussion were to be about nothing more than a local beach-volleyball competition. "I just want to talk to you about a few things."

"I don't think so. I don't want no *pilikia*. No trouble."

"Palani, you're not in any trouble. You're a free man.

My client is the one in trouble. I just want to find out a little about that night, a little about the girl, about what she might have said to you."

"You think you're one sly mongoose, eh? One clever bugger, yeah? I already told the police everything."

I hold my hand out for the pipe, reminding him that we're still friends. Reminding him that I'm not a cop. That I'm on his side. The side that's not the law.

"I'm sure you did, but they don't always write everything down. And even when they do, they don't always share it with the defendant's lawyer. You know how it is, how the cops operate."

He takes a hit, hands off the pipe. He stares off into the distance at the bright blue ocean, as if a sea turtle, Sammy maybe, might just pop its head out of the water and tell him what to say. If Palani is half as high as I am right now, perhaps he's seeing and hearing just that. Finally he shakes his head. Sammy has spoken.

"Whatevahs. I don't have to talk to you."

"No, you don't," I say. "At least not here, not now. But eventually you will."

"How you figure?"

"If you don't speak to me now, I'll have to subpoena you, bring you to court, have you testify under oath before the judge. If you do talk to me now, help me out, I won't have to do that. In other words, you can testify in court before a judge or you can do your talking here on an isolated beach while smoking some Maui Wowie with me, basking in the sun. The choice is yours."

The beach clearly sounds more agreeable to him than court. What I don't tell him is that the prosecuting attorney will inevitably call him to testify at the time of trial anyway. And even if by some miracle the prosecuting attorney doesn't call him to testify, I certainly will.

"What you wanna know?"

"Tell me about that night, how you met Shannon Douglas."

"That night I go *holoholo*. To the Bleu Sharq. I saw one sharkbait. That's one with really white skin. That's this girl, Shannon, eh?"

"What was she doing when you first saw her?"

"Dancing. Dancing all up against some guys. She was *keke*, all drunk, loaded."

"You were single?" I ask, trying to make it more conversation than interrogation.

"I just broke up with my girl one week before. I just wanted to trip, but she wanted to go steady, like. She got real *huhu*, real upset. Then she told me she *hapai*, knocked up."

"So what did you do when you saw Sharkbait Shannon?"

"I went for broke. I rolled up, told her, 'You like dance with me or what?' She told me she has one boyfriend, back on the mainland, like. I told her, since he not here, it no matter to any of us. So she danced with me, real close like, eh? I became *mane'o*, real turned on."

"What happened after the dance?"

"Then I went to the bathroom to smoke one joint.

When I walked out, one haole gave me the stink-eye. I told him, 'I owe you money or what? You like beef?' Then he bagged, he split. I go look for her, but no can find. I figured some moke cockroach her.'"

The Hawaiian term *haole* (pronounced HOW-lee) once meant "foreigner," but today is reserved for Caucasians. It's as often endearing as it is disparaging, and I don't take offense.

"But you found her before you left?" I ask.

"Just before closing time. She told me, 'You wanna go for one walk?' I told her, 'Hell yeah.' "

"Where did you go?"

"Down Kalakaua along the beach. No one was round, so we sucked face. Then when we were going at it, we heard one sound. She got all crazy, started hitting me, like. I hit back just to get her off. But she was alive after that when I left her there on the beach."

"Back up just a bit," I say.

Palani slides his ass up the incline on the sand.

"No, I mean in your story. What was it that you heard?"

"Some kine noise, like one clank."

"Where did it come from?"

"No idea," he says. "I was just trying get my nut off, eh?"

"Was there anything strange or unusual that she said to you that night that sticks out in your mind? Maybe something you forgot to tell the police?"

"Nah. Nah, not really," he says. "Oh, she did say something funny kine."

"What was that?"

"Early on she said she no can gimme her number at the hotel. She told me she was meeting one guy next day, one haole from New York. She told me she'd be with him for the rest of her trip."

"What did you say?"

"I told her, fuck him. Call him, tell him he no need come. Tell him stay fucking mainland, yeah?"

"How did she respond to that?"

"Funny kine, I tell you. She told me, 'That be bad for my grades.'"

CHAPTER 11

Exhausted from this morning's kayaking adventure, I sit tonight alone at the bar of the Bleu Sharq, my arms barely able to lift the pint glass to my lips. My head, finally clear of marijuana, is now being bombarded with beer as I wait for Nikole Kapua to find some spare moments to speak to me. It seems each time four drunken tourists exit the bar, five new ones walk in. Nikole steps over to the newest band of brothers and asks them what they want. Then, she produces a tray of carved-out pineapples and coconuts, fills them with rum and fruit juice, and sticks in crazy straws and tiny umbrellas for good measure. The guy who ordered for the group hands her some money. She smiles her smile, and he hands her some more.

The music is loud, the bass high, such that I can feel it in my stomach, a not-so-good vibration made that much worse by the shoulders I take in the back, as people who shouldn't be dancing dance.

"I'm really sorry, Mr. Corvelli," Nikole shouts above the music. "It looks like I won't be free to talk until closing time. It's just too busy. Will you wait?"

I raise my glass and nod. As I watch her bend over to scoop some ice, I feel fortunate I chose not to send Flan on this interview. Nikole is a picture postcard, a perfect representation of my Hawaiian-girl fantasy. At first look, my mind undressed her of her tight T and shorts and put her in a grass skirt and coconut bra, a lei around her neck, and laid her on a white-sand beach in the bliss of sundown. Yeah, I'll wait. I'll wait until she tells me to wait no more.

Like the drink Nikole is mixing up, the Bleu Sharq is a unique blend: Hollywood meets Hawaii. There are the token tikis, surfboards, hula girls, and Polynesian plants. But among them are the Fonz, the A-Team, Charlie's Angels, and the Incredible Hulk. Signed pictures from Sinatra, Ray Charles, and the Duke. The décor is busy but in a fun sort of way. The Sharq *would* be fun, I'm sure, if only it were a little bit bigger and a lot less crowded.

I turn my chair to watch the dance floor. I try to picture the scene Palani so vaguely described. I see not a single local, only tourists complete with their Hawaiian shirts, Bermuda shorts, digital cameras, and third-degree sunburns. I try to picture Shannon dancing provocatively, rubbing up against drunk guys, sucking down daiquiris and mai tais as if they were going out of style. I picture him going to the bathroom, smoking a joint. That part is easy. The rest doesn't seem to make much sense.

A few minutes after last call, as a sea of open aloha

shirts makes for the door, Nikole steps over to me with a small handbag draped over her left shoulder, a white flower tucked behind one ear. "Are you ready to go?" she asks me.

"Yes," I say. "Let me just settle up."

I pay the tab and hand each of the bartenders a generous tip, courtesy of Joseph Gianforte Sr. Each of the other two women give me funny little smiles, looks that tell me Nikole has let them in on why I'm here. I already know that neither of these women were working the night Shannon was slain.

We walk outside and sidestep the human tide. We slip past a bearded panhandler asking for spare change, then past a familiar prostitute seemingly glued to the street. Past men and women from the mainland and Japan, energized by the light tropical air. Past the rows of tiki torches that help the moon light up the night.

Nikole, who asked me to call her Nikki, steps into the crosswalk and waits for the light. As soon as it changes, she crosses Kalakaua and I follow like a puppy dog chasing treats. I trail her to the beach, where she kicks off her sandals, her bare feet hitting the sand. She keeps going until her toes are touching the surf.

"Is this a good spot for us to talk?" I say.

"Depends on what you want to talk about."

I drop down onto the sand and she drops down to her knees beside me.

"I want to talk about Shannon Douglas. About the night she was murdered," I say in my best Joe Friday voice. I'm all business, yes, I am. I'm looking for the facts, ma'am, just the facts. I don't even notice that your taut, nicely tanned knee is touching my leg.

"That's the girl from New York, right? I saw her picture in the paper," she says. "I served her drinks Sunday night."

"What was she drinking? Do you remember?"

"Yeah, she was downing zombies like there was no tomorrow."

Her hand flutters to her mouth as she catches her faux pas.

"That's okay," I say. "I didn't know her personally. Besides, there's no padding the fact that for her there was no tomorrow. Do you remember how many zombies you served her?"

"Not exactly. I cut her off toward the end of the night, but I think someone else was buying her drinks by then."

"Did you see that someone else?"

I've lost my Joe Friday voice. I think I saw it swim out to sea. Yes, I want more than just the facts. I shift in my khakis. Luckily, it's pitch-black out here, or else Nikki would be asking me if there is a palm tree in my pocket, or if I just get a really big kick out of doing my job.

"Yeah, I saw her talking up some local guy," she says.

"Did you see her talking to anyone else that night?"

"Not that I remember. But we were pretty busy for a Sunday night. I wasn't really paying attention."

"How did she react to your cutting her off for the night?"

"Not well. Tourists particularly don't like to get cut off.

They figure they are here on vacation, they can do what-evah they please."

It's the first hint of Hawaiian I hear in her singsong voice. I wonder if she's watching her words, trying to speak American English for my benefit. I wonder if it's because she likes me. Little does she know, she could speak to me in gibberish and I'd sit here and listen all night.

I am trying to think of more questions, to extend the conversation in any way that I can. Although this will be billed to the Gianfortes as a witness interview, it is difficult right now to see it as such. What would I say to this girl if she were just a girl and not a witness? I'm drawing a com-plete blank.

Back in New York, I would no doubt tell her lies when it suited me, the truth when it would help get her into bed. What should be so different here? Why has the cat taken my tongue? She is sitting here, staring at me, waiting for my words to come. But I have nothing, not a single, solitary one. Even the beer is silent. And the beer seldom is. This interview is over.

I stand, take her hand in mine, and help her up. She is petite, at least six inches shorter than my six feet.

"Where do you live?" I ask.

"Kailua."

"Do you have a car here?"

"No. A couple of the bartenders live right near me. I usually catch a ride home with one of them."

Sufficiently sobered up, I say, "I can drive you home if you'd like."

"Are you sure?"

"It's the least I can do. You've been very helpful."

"T'anks. I'd appreciate that."

I lead her to my Jeep, parked not three blocks away. I deftly unzip the soft top and open her door. I help her in and hold on to her hand maybe a moment too long.

I walk around to the driver's side and get in, all the while thinking about what to talk about on the half-hour ride to Kailua. I start the engine. I put the transmission in reverse and slowly release the brake. That's when I do it. That's when I make the rookie mistake of telling her to tell me all about herself.

And, for the love of God, that is exactly what she does.

CHAPTER 12

I can picture Nikki Kapua as an eleven-year-old girl, content with life as only an eleven-year-old girl can be. I can picture her on the island of Kauai, the Garden Isle, so named for its natural beauty. I can picture her under one of Kauai's waterfalls, wet and smiling at the lush landscape all around. I can picture her in her small hometown, so beloved by its members for its simplicity and quaint allure. I can picture her playing hopscotch in the schoolyard with friends, local kids having local fun, already developing the sense of place, of community, so often lacking on the mainland, particularly on the coasts. I can picture her posing for a photograph with the beauty of Kauai as her backdrop. I can picture her with her younger brother, Alika, making funny faces for the camera. I can picture her and Alika standing stoically with their parents, Kanoa and Maru, all smiling broadly with their arms draped across each other's back, counting down from three, while a friendly local snaps the shot.

I can picture all this because she describes it all so vividly, in ways I could never describe New York. Then again, she calls Kauai "home," and I call New York "New York."

They struggled, she tells me, her family did. Kanoa was a laborer, like many locals. A long day for little pay. It was a fact of life, a fact her folks accepted, yet dreamed to live without.

Nikki remembers the day her father came home, minus the exhaustion and sadness she usually caught on his face. She remembers the skip he had in his step that day, a skip she had never before seen. She remembers that his voice was different. Not the voice of a man who spent his day in dirt, laboring in the heat. It was more like the voice of a child, a child sliding down a slide or swinging on a swing. It was a voice devoid of despair and filled with hope.

I can picture Kanoa and Maru sitting in the kitchen. I can see them as Nikki did through the crack of her bedroom door. I can hear Kanoa telling Maru that a friend of a friend of a friend had told him of a job, a job with twice the pay for half the work. I can see the reluctant look on Maru's face. I can hear her warning Kanoa about how things that sound too good to be true always are.

I know Kanoa. I know Kanoa because Nikki knows Kanoa, and Nikki needs someone else to know him, too. I know Kanoa is stubborn but well-intentioned. I know that he wants more for his family. I know he wants to spend more time with his children. I know he wants for them everything he grew up without.

I hear the yelling back and forth. I can see Kanoa put his foot down, but nothing more, because that's when Nikki saw fit to close her bamboo bedroom door. I can feel Maru relent. I can feel the twinge of fear of an eleven-year-old as she packs to leave the only home she ever knew.

I can picture the Kapua family setting out in search of the so-called better life.

"And so off to Oahu we went," she says.

Enter the blond-haired, blue-eyed man Nikki knew only as M.

She would learn it all years later, the terrible truth of what her father became when he went to work for the man called M. Kanoa never knew quite what he was getting into, of that much Nikki is sure. Ice, after all, was a quiet epidemic. There were no bloody turf wars in Hawaii. On the islands, even death peddlers peddled death with the spirit of aloha. Nikki knows that once the family was on Oahu, Kanoa had no choice in the matter at all. He either sold ice or he watched his family starve.

Ice is the smokable form of crystal methamphetamine. In the early nineties, the family-run Mexican cartels took advantage of the opportunity to seize control of the Hawaiian drug trade while Hawaii law enforcement cracked down on Asian gangs. Ice was growing wildly in popularity on the islands. After all, Hawaii is a smoking culture, and the transition from *pakalolo* to ice was hardly difficult at all. Pounds of meth manufactured in labs in Mexico were smuggled into California and then carried to Oahu by couriers, mules who, for a paltry sum, used their body cavities like duffel bags, giving new meaning to the term *fanny pack*.

M, masquerading as a legitimate businessman, was in charge of meth distribution on the island of Oahu.

Nikki remembers the day her father was arrested, taken from their home in Pearl City in handcuffs while she and Alika watched. I can see Kanoa looking back at them, mouthing an apology while being hauled down the concrete steps. I can see Maru crying in a corner, holding the pot in which she was about to cook her husband's breakfast. I can see Nikki holding Alika back from grabbing hold of the police.

I can hear Kanoa's lawyer advising him to turn state's evidence against the man called M, because I would do the same. I can hear Kanoa's protests, because I've heard them all before. He feared for his family, as well he should. M, he was sure, would kill them all, one by one by one.

I can hear Kanoa pleading guilty, taking his medicine like a man. I can hear the judge sentencing him to six years imprisonment, a sentence that would be carried out in a prison on the mainland. Hawaii prisons were already filled to capacity and couldn't hold Kanoa for even the first leg of his six-year stretch.

"And so off to Colorado he went," Nikki says.

Enter M again.

In return for Kanoa's loyalty and his silence to the end,

M promised Maru he'd take care of them. After all, he was a friend. True to his word, he helped Maru. He helped by supplying her with ice, by getting her so fiercely addicted to the drug that in three years' time, she was unrecognizable.

I can picture Nikki at age sixteen. I can picture her running home from school to call her friend, whom she had just left, to gossip more about the boy in algebra class, a transfer from a school on the Big Island. I can picture her picking up and putting down the phone, deciding first to pee. I can picture her opening the bathroom door, thinking it strange that it was closed. I can picture what she must have seen. Her mother, the top of her head barely visible above the crimson bathwater. No note. Just the razor, the pipe, and a plastic bag with a quarter gram of ice. The surreal aftermath of a literal bloodbath.

"And so off to heaven she went," Nikki says.

When she and Alika needed each other most, they were split apart, sent to separate foster homes. Alika to Kaneohe. Nikki to Ewa Beach.

Nikki heard that her father was released, but all she knows for certain is that he never returned home.

When Alika turned eighteen, Nikki asked him to move in with her. And they live together now, in a cozy cottage in Kailua, complete with shutters and a brightly painted red front door.

We stand at that red door in silence, Nikki and I, our hands intertwined. At some point during the ride to Kailua, at some point in her unfortunate tale, I developed the un-controllable need to touch her, and so my hand found its way into hers.

"It was nice meeting you," I say lamely.

She smiles in the glow of the porch light. Her face defies the fact that she's lived a difficult life, such that one would never guess to look at her that she's the author of the story she's just told. Perhaps it's just the luxury of youth. Perhaps, in time, the calamities of her past will catch up with her and make her but a shadow of the girl that stands before me right now.

"Would you like to come in?" she asks.

The butterflies turn to bats. My free thumb goes straight to my mouth and offers it a snack. My leg trembles, and suddenly my face feels flush. I want to get away from under the glow of the porch light, but I am frozen in place with nowhere to go.

I nod silently.

"We need to be very quiet," she says. "My brother will be asleep."

She quietly unlocks the door, the jingle-jangle of the keys doing nothing for my nerves. The door creaks open, as I knew, of course, it would. We step into the small foyer, and my sandals sound like gunshots upon the hardwood floor. Nikki navigates in the pitch-blackness like the blind, guiding me past furniture and walls. Finally, I feel carpet, and behind me she closes a door.

"We'll have to keep the lights out," she whispers, her sweet breath tickling my left ear. "I hope you don't mind."

I shake my head silently, though I know she cannot see.

She guides me to the bed, pushes me lightly on its spread.

It was another of Milt Cashman's ten commandments. *Thou shalt have sex with neither client nor witness.* It was number six, I think. A little bit higher on the totem pole, yet all the more tempting. Back in New York, I lived by Milt's commandments. I never considered breaking a single one.

Thou shalt not take a case without being paid up front.

I would never dream of it.

Thou shalt not be held in contempt of court.

I came close, but never sinned.

Thou shalt not drink before court.

No need to. There's plenty of time to drink right after court.

Honor thy magistrate and judge.

Always have, always will.

Thou shalt not go into business with a client.

Never have, never will.

Thou shalt not count your money until the check has cleared.

Goes without saying.

Thou shalt not call the prosecutor a cocksucker to his face.

A little less clear-cut.

Thou shalt live and die in the press.

Well, we all know how that turned out.

And here I am about to break two of Milt's commandments in a single day.

I hope.

Her lips press against my own, her tongue searching deftly for a dance partner. Her hands work at my belt.

"On the Hawaiian Islands," she whispers as she works, "it is very inconsiderate to leave your shoes on when you enter someone's home."

"I'm sorry," I manage to say between deep breaths. "I didn't know."

"I can forgive you that, but on the islands, it is absolutely forbidden to leave your pants on when you enter someone's bed."

"I wouldn't dream of doing that," I say, lending her a hand.

I pull her shirt over her head, her hands reaching for the skies as if I'd told her this were a holdup. Her left breast falls into my mouth as my pants slip off my feet and fall to the floor.

There is no pretense. She refrains from offering me the usual drivel. She doesn't say, "I never do this on the first date," or push away my hands until I try a second time. She allows it all to happen without hesitancy, assuring us only pleasure with complete freedom from guilt and second-guessing.

She slides her panties down over her legs and climbs on top of me, reaching with her hand around her back, putting me inside. She moans, a soft, gentle purr, and reminds me what I need not be reminded of.

"We. Need. To be. Ve. Ry. Quiet."

CHAPTER 13

The ad I placed in the *Honolulu Advertiser* is no bigger than a postage stamp, but it has netted me my second client, a small-time, large-framed pusher named Turi Ahina. I handled a great deal of drug cases back in New York. They are, Milt taught me, the criminal defense attorney's bread and butter. It doesn't get much better than being handed an envelope filled with tattered twenties with white powder flavoring the edges of each bill. And there is no shortage of dealers in Manhattan. You have pushers downtown on Wall Street selling big-time brokers eight balls of coke during their lunch hour. You have low-life peddlers inside Manhattan's hippest nightclubs selling ecstasy and other designer club drugs to club kids from New Jersey. You have stereotypical minorities dealing crack up in the Harlem ghettos. You have bicycle messengers delivering marijuana to customers from Greenwich Village to the Upper West Side. You have NYU students peddling hallucinogens such as shrooms and LSD to other NYU students looking to expand their otherwise not-so-expanded minds. You have gangs on street corners waiting for pale, malnourished skeletons with rotten teeth and tracked-up arms who are looking for one more hit, just one more goddamn hit, of heroin before going clean. And, of course, you have the good ol' New York City Police Department—the NYPD—watching over all of them, making arrests, bringing them all to your office door with their envelopes filled with tattered twenties.

Here on the Hawaiian Islands, we have ice.

Ice is made of highly volatile, toxic substances melded in differing combinations, forming what many describe as a mix of laundry detergent and lighter fluid. Smoking ice results in an instantaneous dose of almost pure drug to the brain, providing the user with a cocainelike rush, followed by up to sixteen hours of euphoria. Exhilaration and sharpening of focus can lead the user to any erratic behavior from obsessive cleaning or tidying to mad, abandoned sex for hours, sometimes days, on end. With a quick and lasting high that is easy to get and relatively cheap, ice is now to Hawaii what crack was to New York City in the eighties. Ice has attached itself like a leech, particularly to impoverished people of Hawaiian ancestry.

The ice epidemic has led to a crackdown here in Hawaii, the ice capital of the nation. Although the epidemic has been building for over two decades, public officials decided to take action only recently, when Gerry Maltese, a young, sharp trial lawyer who headed the narcotics division of the

Honolulu Prosecutor's Office, got himself pinched for selling a gram of ice to an informant. An "Ice Summit" quickly convened at the whim of the lieutenant governor. State authorities were ordered to seek out and capture the enemy by any means necessary, one of the enemy combatants being the short, rotund man standing before me, smiling like a child about to get himself a big red balloon.

"Howzit, Mistah C?" he says by way of introduction.

The first time I saw a client facing serious charges smiling at me from across my desk, I thought he was a psychopath. I now distinguish it for what it is, the cockiness of a young guy familiar with the system. Familiarity goes a long way in extinguishing fear.

He holds out his hand, and I look at it for a long while, hoping he'll get the hint and pull it back. Who started this fucking handshaking business to begin with? I'll have to check that out on the Internet. Why not just bow and have it over with? Or wink? At least we wouldn't be spreading any germs. But, noooo. We've got to shake hands to let people know we're pleased to meet them, even when we aren't in the slightest.

His hand is still out there, waiting for me. I take it. And shake it. I hope it was at least good for him.

Turi takes a seat in one of my two new client chairs, and I fear he's too much for it. I listen for the sound of snapping wood, but it doesn't come. It's a good thing I took the Gianforte case or I'd be conducting this interview on the floor. The fifty grand allowed me to furnish my office last week. I bought a large cherry desk and immediately cluttered it with client files, calendars, bar journals, half-used legal pads, and unpaid bills. When it arrived, it was just a desk. Now, it's a lawyer's desk. A genius's desk, some might say.

I start with some preliminaries and learn that Turi is a local from the windward side whose speech flutters frequently from pidgin to English and back. He is twenty-two years old and this is his third arrest. Turi has one misdemeanor conviction for possession, but he is not presently on probation. He has been unemployed since being fired from Taco Bell three years ago for eating a few too many tortilla shells without paying.

"Okay, Turi," I say, reclining in my new leather chair, "tell me what happened."

"I sold some ice to one undercover cop."

"How much did you sell him, Turi?"

"Just a forty-dollar bag. That's all I had on me, Mistah C."

It's a small case. A simple buy and bust. The trick now is to gauge how much money is in his pocket. He's familiar with the system; his smile and his rap sheet tell me as much. If I quote him too high a price, he'll walk. If I try to lower my price as he waddles out the door, I'll look inexperienced and desperate. If I quote him less than what's in his pocket, I'll have failed myself. So, what's it going to be, Kevin? How much green is your new plump pal carrying in his pocket?

"Okay, Turi, I'll need you to provide me with a thirty-five-hundred-dollar retainer, and I'll be at your side at your next court appearance."

I wait for the song and dance about the money, how he'll pay me over time. Instead of singing and dancing, he reaches into his pocket and pulls out a white envelope stuffed with cash.

He takes out a stack of twenties and counts out $3,500. The rest go back into his pocket. Son of a bitch. My chubby new buddy had at least five grand.

Turi lays the money atop one of the files on my desk. I begin to count it out, unable to hide my disappointment at having lost the other $1,500. Milt can always tell how much a client is carrying down to the nickel. Milt is a truly gifted lawyer.

"I can't be taking no plea, Mistah C," he says as I count.

"No plea," I say, thinking about the money I left in his pocket.

"We need to go over some evidence or something?"

"Nah," I say. "We're not going to need to deal with evidence in this case."

I finish counting the bills and I know exactly where they came from. Directly from the top, the kingpin, whoever that is. The money is meant to assure Turi that the organization will take care of him, so long as he keeps his fucking mouth shut. It also assures the organization that Turi won't get stuck with some incompetent public defender who would have Turi singing like a canary before the first court appearance. Give Turi the money to give to the lawyer and everyone is happy. Any lawyer with any sense and a lick of self-preservation would know he can't flip this client like a pancake on the griddle. The client will either get off on a technicality or do his time like a man. As far as all parties involved are concerned, there is no organization. Turi is a freelancer, and the ice, it fell from the sky.

I hand Turi a receipt and I thank him. The interview is over, but he doesn't stand. Maybe with all that girth, he simply can't.

"You new to the islands, brah?" he asks.

For a paltry thirty-five hundred bucks he wants to chat. For the full five grand, I'd take him over to Sand Bar for some afternoon karaoke, but fifteen hundred is still sitting in his pocket instead of on top of my desk where it belongs. Instead of paying my rent, it'll no doubt end up with Turi in McDonald's, assuming he can still fit through their door.

"Yeah," I say. "I recently moved here from New York."

Although I didn't think it possible, his smile widens.

"Welcome to my island, Mistah C."

Moku Nui belongs to Palani. Oahu belongs to Turi. I better plant a flag somewhere before all the good islands are taken.

"I see you live in Kailua," I say, looking over his client intake form.

"Yeah, brah. All my life."

I recognize the address, too. It is only a block away from Nikki's cottage, where I spent this past Saturday night after driving her home from Waikiki. She consumed much of my thoughts on Sunday, such that I missed much of the Giants kicking hell out of the Cowboys.

"Have you ever left Oahu?" I ask.

Turi smirks, motions with his head to the window behind me. I swivel in my chair to face, briefly, the mountains like powerful giants reclining to look deep into the heavens.

"Why would I ever do that?" he says.

I open my desk drawer and retrieve a stack of freshly printed business cards with THE CORVELLI LAW FIRM embossed above my name at the top. I hand him a stack of fifty or so.

"These are for your buddies."

"T'anks," he says. "I'll make sure my brothers get these."

Turi reaches into his back pocket, the client chair creaking under him as he shifts his weight. He pulls out a card of his own and hands it to me.

"You ever have any problems, you ever need anything, you give me a call. I got your back, Mistah C."

I take the card and thank him. It reads only T, followed by just six numbers.

"The last digit," he says, "is one."

"One?"

"Yeah. One. That's for how many people I trust, including myself."

CHAPTER 14

Not five minutes after Turi trucks his wide load out the door does Jake walk in with a file folder tucked under his arm.

"I just got off the horn with Flan," he says, dropping into the client chair vacated by Turi. "He was able to get the information you asked for."

After my Saturday-morning meeting with Palani on Moku Nui, I telephoned Flan and asked him to obtain a list of Shannon's professors at the law school. I look at my watch. Not yet noon on Monday. I'll give Flan this, he works fast.

Shannon's remark to Palani that her grades would suffer if she stood up the man she was scheduled to meet in Waikiki the following day may have been a brush-off. Then again, it may have been more. It's a stone Palani dropped in my path, and for once, true to my word, I intend to overturn it.

Jake flips through the contents of the folder and finds what he's looking for. He squints at the page as I wait.

And wait.

I consider reaching across my cluttered desk and plucking it from his hand. Why the hell doesn't he get a pair of glasses? Is he too vain? Does he fear they will not go well with his wrinkled skin and rosy gin blossoms? I pull a nail off my index finger, spit it into the nearby wastebasket, and continue to wait.

"Shannon's most recent professors are all at the law school lecturing as scheduled," he says. I sigh and crack my knuckles. So much for my new theory.

"But," he says, raising that one finger in the air, "one of her first-year professors is on sabbatical."

"Tell me it's a male," I say.

"It's a male. And there's more."

My ass literally moves to the edge of my seat without my realizing it until I nearly fall off.

"This morning, Flan called the girl's hotel, the Grand Polynesian. He's there."

"He's there?"

"He's there. And what's more . . . You're gonna get an erection when you hear this, son."

"I doubt I'll get an erection, Jake."

"Flan checked with a friend of his at Continental Airlines. The professor arrived at Honolulu Airport seven hours before Shannon was last seen alive."

"Jake," I say.

"Yeah?"

"I have an erection."

"I knew you would, son. I knew you would."

Jake hands me the file folder containing the hand-written notes from his conversation with Flan, and just like that I have another suspect in the murder of Shannon Douglas, albeit a law professor. The professor's name is Jim Catus, and I suspect he'll have a squeaky-clean history. Nevertheless, Catus clearly now shares the same motive as my client. And if he doesn't have an alibi—a tremendous *if* in this world of hotel video surveillance—he is the walking incarnate of reasonable doubt.

If Shannon truly did not expect the professor until the next day, and he arrived early, it is possible, in a world of infinite possibilities, that he, and not my client, stumbled onto her and Palani's little game of hide-the-sausage on the beach. And if that is possible, then it is possible, too, that he killed her in a fit of jealous rage. I'm not sure I would buy it were I sitting on the jury, but I'll not have to. I'll be the one selling it.

I'm jumping the gun, I know. The way I jumped the gun in the Brandon Glenn case. Professor Catus is my new Carson Reese. I have to slow things down. I have to trap Catus under a glass and make sure he can't wiggle his way free like Reese. The burden of proof hasn't changed. I don't need to convince a jury that Catus killed Shannon, just that it is possible he did. The question now seems to be, of what do I need to convince myself?

"Do you have any idea of when the professor is split-ting?" I ask.

"He has a return ticket for next weekend, but with all that's going on, who knows?"

"I'll get to him tonight, see what he has to say. As far as we know, the police haven't even looked in his direction, so I might just catch him off guard."

"What if you scare him off, son?"

"All the better. It'll make him look guilty as hell."

"By the way," Jake says, "how did your two interviews go on Saturday?"

The heat is rising in my face. I can feel it, and I try with futility to hold it back. I am blushing the way I did under the glow of the porch light in front of Nikki's cottage, and once again I've nowhere to hide.

"One went better than the other," I say. "In fact, one went very well, indeed."

"Well, son," Jake says, rising slowly from his chair, "let's hope your interview tonight goes at least as well as that."

"Somehow," I say under my breath, "I doubt that."

CHAPTER 15

I am prepared to pull the fire alarm on the fifteenth floor at the Grand Polynesian hotel. I am prepared to smash the headlights on his rental car and alert the valet. I am prepared to call in a bomb threat, really I am. I am prepared to do just about anything to get Professor Jim Catus out of his room and downstairs so that I can pull him aside and speak to him alone.

As it turns out, I don't have to do anything. I recognize him immediately from his photographs on the law school's Web site. I recognize the sharp profile, the thinning gray hair. I even recognize the clothes. Apparently, he didn't get the memo on the dress code here in the tropics. He's wearing a sport jacket with suede patches at the elbows, a pair of charcoal gabardine slacks.

It's not so much luck, my spotting him. I have been sitting here in the lobby of the Grand Polynesian for nearly three and a half hours contemplating which clever stunt I should pull to get the professor out from his room. I had pretty much settled on the fire alarm when I caught sight of him stepping out of the elevator with a copy of the *Honolulu Advertiser* in hand.

It is fortunate I marked him. I was less than thrilled with the idea of causing such chaos at this immense resort. Sure, there was that nervous excitement, like the time Milt and I swiped the city attorney's briefcase containing his entire legal file right before the civil trial in a police brutality case and chucked it in the garbage. We watched the city attorney squirm before the judge until finally he caved, making us a high six-figure offer to resolve the case. Ah, the good old days.

But this would have been different. The Grand Polynesian is the largest resort in Waikiki, with over three thousand rooms, six swimming pools, fourteen restaurants, and nearly a hundred shops. The thought of seeing five thousand guests and two thousand employees scampering out of the hotel gave me pause. But the whole point is now moot, and I can think myself quite cool for having devised the scheme and for having the willingness to follow through with it. Whether I would actually have or not.

Here I am now, watching my subject. I am James fucking Bond, 007 himself.

I duck behind a Polynesian plant and see my subject stop to view the menu outside the Rainbow Restaurant in the main lobby. A leaf from the plant tickles my nose. I push it out of my face, but it's rubbery and it bounces back, hits me in the eye. Goddamn, it hurts. I rub my eye and scratch my nose. I look back toward the Rainbow Restaurant and my subject is gone.

When I eye Catus again, he is heading for the door. I take four strides toward him before my right foot slides out from under me causing me to crash onto the marble floor. My spine is just one great length of pain as three bellhops rush to my aid. Two of them assist me to my feet while the third helpfully points to the yellow sign ten yards away reading CAUTION: WET FLOOR. I look past them to see Catus looking back toward the commotion before exiting to the street.

What would 007 do? I decide not to file a report, although I'm sure I could've made at least ten grand off the fall. I brush myself off and tell the bellhops I don't need any medical attention. One of them attempts to hand me a Band-Aid for my fractured vertebrae. Another informs me there's karaoke tonight in the Sunshine Lounge. The third son of a bitch is still pointing at the sign.

I push them all aside and continue to the door, making it without incident.

I step into the night and think the sport jacket might not have been such a bad idea after all. It's chilly, but I never heard James Bond say it's chilly, so I push the thought aside. I follow Catus from Kalia to Kalakaua, where he window-shops here and there. While I watch him standing outside an art store eyeing up a large wooden dolphin, I decide that tailing suspects is much more exciting in the movies than it is in real life.

I am hoping he'll stop at a restaurant, or better yet, a

bar. I could use some drinks, some liquid courage before beginning my inquisition.

He walks up a block to Kuhio, and I keep pace about eighty feet behind.

My cell phone vibrates in my right front pocket and I curse the person who invented them. I pull the damned thing from my pocket and the caller ID reads JAKE.

"Speak," I snap into the phone.

"Kevin? May I speak to Kevin please? Kevin, is that you?"

I just don't get it. I could understand it if Jake were calling someone's home and more than one person could have picked up the phone. But this is my cell phone. He knows it's my cell phone. Who the hell is going to answer it besides me?

"Yeah, Jake, it's me."

"How did it go with the professor?"

I don't tell him that I spent three and a half hours trying to decide how to get him out of his room. I don't tell him about the incident with the plant or that I nearly broke my neck on the wet marble floor.

"I have him in my shights," I say in my best Sean Connery voice.

"Your *shights*? What the hell are you talking about?"

I snap the phone shut. He sounded drunk anyway. I'll let him know how it went in the morning. I've known him but a week, and he's already growing on me like the ivy up the brick wall at Wrigley Field. I'm starting to like the son of a bitch.

Catus finally ducks into the Whale Watcher Bar & Grill. I stop outside and wait, giving myself a manicure, biting what's left of my nails and some of the skin around them.

I wait outside for ten minutes because I think that's what they do in the movies. It'll lessen the chance that he'll make me when I walk through the door.

When I step inside, I see him bellied up at the bar, his head buried in the *Advertiser*. Next to the paper sits an empty Collins glass begging to be filled.

The Whale Watcher is a dismal blue with a nautical theme that's making me seasick already. I am surrounded by models of boats, photos of boats, paintings of boats, toy boats, sailboats, girl boats, and boy boats. Even the salad bar is shaped like a boat.

I find a stool away from Catus at the opposite end of the bar, fearing he will recognize me from the unflattering photo displayed by Gretchen Hurst on her cable news show, *All Ears*. I make a mental note to make an attempt at getting the "before" photos of Hurst from her plastic surgeon. But right now, I'm all business.

"A martini," I say to the bartender when she asks me for my order. "Shaken, not stirred."

She turns to grab the shaker, and I add, "Bone-dry. Three olives and a lemon peel."

She gives me a look and nods. Maybe it's the Connery voice. Maybe I need to cut that out.

"Make that a vodka martini," I say. "Grey Goose if you

have it." James Bond or no James Bond, there's nothing I hate worse than gin.

My plan, if you can call it a plan, is to let him drink a few before I go in for the kill. It'll give me a chance to drink a few, too. It'll make the whole night a lot more fun.

As he takes the first sip of his third Tom Collins, I take down the last of my fourth martini. As they say, one martini is just right, two is too many, and three is not enough. Or some shit like that.

I head off to the pisser.

I'm standing at the urinal, draining the lizard, more than slightly dizzy from the drinks, when who stands next to me but the professor himself.

Hey, you. Yeah, you. Who the hell is following who?

I hold my tongue, not saying a word. I turn to look at him, and up close in this light I can see the age around his eyes, the loose skin where tight skin used to be. I've turned too far, such that I nearly pee down his leg. I turn back and finish the job where I should.

As I wash my hands at the sink, I watch his image in the mirror. He exits without washing at all. Another solid reason for me to never shake hands with anyone under any circumstances ever again.

I head back to the bar and spy an empty stool right next to him. I'm drunker than I'd like to be, but what the hell.

I take my seat next to him and motion toward the paper. "Are you through with this?"

"Help yourself," he says without looking at me.

I take the *Honolulu Advertiser,* a prop on the stage I'm about to set. I turn to the sports section.

"That Eli Manning is turning into one hell of a quarterback," I say. "What a difference a few years make."

The photograph of the professor on the law school's Web site was taken in his office, a small room cluttered with Giants football memorabilia.

A clever way for me to break the ice, is it not?

He's not taking the bait, not acknowledging me at all. Now I'm getting pissed that he's ignoring me, so I continue, "Manning's been patient in the pocket. Using the whole field. Looking more and more like his big brother every game."

"I'm not a fan of football," he says abruptly.

First he ignores me, now he's lying. I never liked any of my own law professors and I sure as shit don't like this one. My clever little Jedi mind tricks aren't working, so I decide to go at him directly, take him head-on.

"I suppose," I say, "teaching law doesn't leave one much time for leisure activities like following professional football."

The professor's jaw drops to the floor and he doesn't bother picking it up. The tan he's worked on for the past week disappears without a trace.

"Who the fuck are you?" he asks.

The name's Bombed. James Bombed.

"I'm the fucking Welcome Wagon," I say. "Sorry I'm late, but you never told anyone you were here. Luckily though, I found you." I wink at him. "Aloha, Jim."

CHAPTER 16

Catus looks around, probably fearing I'm a cop, that every patron in the bar is a cop, including the scruffy old man dressed like a one-eyed pirate three stools down. I allow him time to think before speaking again. Catus is smart. He knows the law. He knows that some conversations can be adjourned, but not escaped. He reaches for his Tom Collins and takes a hit. He's decided to stay.

"My name's Kevin Corvelli," I say, trying not to slur my words. "I represent Joseph Gianforte Jr. in connection with the charges brought against him for the murder of Shannon Douglas."

I look for a reaction, any kind of reaction, but he knew what was coming as soon as I said my name.

"Did you know Shannon Douglas?" I ask.

"Don't play dumb with me, Mr. Corvelli. You know damn well I did, or else you wouldn't be sitting here."

Questioning other lawyers is no fun. They know what

you're looking for and they're tougher to trick. They anticipate your questions and have answers at the ready. Truth be told, I fucking hate lawyers.

"Fine. Then let's stop pissing in the kiddy pool and get right down to it. You came to Waikiki to spend two weeks alone with Shannon, isn't that right?"

I take his silence as an admission. I suppose it could've been one wild coincidence, but now I know it's not.

"Why didn't you go to the police when you found out Shannon had been killed?" I ask.

He takes another gulp of Tom Collins as the bartender sets another Grey Goose martini down in front of me. I didn't order it, but I'm not one to complain.

"I'm irrelevant to their investigation," he says. "I didn't want to sully Shannon's name."

"Sully her name how?"

"I'm fifty-nine going on sixty. I'm a divorced father of three. I'm a grandfather for Christ's sake. Hell, I'm older than Shannon's parents."

I want to ask him what the hell he thought she saw in him, but if I get too far under his skin early on, he'll walk out. And probably stick me with the tab.

"Why the two rooms at the Grand Polynesian?" I ask.

"That was at her insistence, of course. She wanted to keep up appearances."

"But you had a sexual relationship with Shannon?"

He nods and drains the Collins glass.

The thought of him atop that beautiful young girl makes me angry. I can count on its making the jurors angry, too.

"And Shannon's insisting on two rooms didn't bother you?"

"Of course, it bothered me. I was paying for both rooms. I put mine on my credit card and I gave her cash for the other."

"If it bothered you so much, why did you do it?"

He looks at me as if I'd sprouted a second head. I suppose if he's half as drunk as I am, he's already seeing double. Then he smirks as if the question I posed to him were funny.

"How old are you, Mr. Corvelli?"

"Thirty-one," I say, taking a hit off my martini.

"Then ask me again in another thirty years."

Some guys even my age will do just about anything for a piece of ass. I suppose it only gets worse as they get on in years. From the look on his face, Shannon could probably have made him reserve an entire floor.

"When did you arrive in Honolulu?" I ask.

"Late that night, the night she was killed."

"Was she expecting you, Professor?"

He shakes his head and signals the barkeep for another Tom Collins. Then he points to my glass, too. I hope I'm not already blacked out, or the entire night will be for naught.

"Shannon wasn't expecting me until the next day."

"How did you come to arrive earlier?"

"I wanted to surprise her," he says. "I conjured this fantasy of arriving early, decorating the hotel room with rose petals and scented candles, ordering a couple bottles of champagne and fresh strawberries from room service, and surprising her with it all. I loved her."

Catus regrets saying that last sentence the second it escapes his lips. It's too late. He's said it, and if I'm not blacked out, I'll remember him saying it. He takes a healthy sip of the fresh Tom Collins, trying to wash his words back down.

"What did you do when you got to Waikiki?" I ask.

"I checked in at the Grand Polynesian. I called her room from my cell phone just to see if she was there. She wasn't, so I dispensed with the preparations and set out to find her."

It all sounds a little too rehearsed, right down to the rose petals. I know he's about to tell me he never laid eyes on her that night.

"Did you have any luck finding Shannon when you went looking for her?"

He's silent for a moment, then surprises me with a "Yes."

"When and where?" I ask, suddenly somewhat clear-headed.

"Around one a.m. or so. At a bar. The Bleu Sharq."

I might just be about to hear a full confession pour from the professor's lips. Some people are compulsive confessors. Some cannot help but confess. Some know the consequences, but are guided by an irresistible impulse to confess. The same goes for killing.

"Shannon was with someone when I saw her," he continues. "A local boy. They were dancing, rather provocatively, in fact. I stood at the bar awhile, waiting for her to blow him off, but she didn't. So I was reduced to hoping that she'd see me. But she never glanced in my direction. Not once.

"The place was crowded, and I tried to get closer to them. I couldn't bear to approach her under the circumstances, but I figured if I could just get close enough for her to see me, she'd stop doing what it was she was doing.

"Then, I watched them kiss. I felt disgusted, sick to my stomach, in fact. I felt like I was a teenager again, at a dance at the high school gym, and the girl I really, really liked was making out with some other guy.

"Just after last call, I decided to leave, wait until the next day, and meet her as planned. I figured she'd never know I arrived early, and we could both pretend as though nothing had happened."

It all comes down to whether Catus has an alibi. I try to put myself in his shoes. I fly thousands of miles to meet a lover less than half my age. I pay for two rooms for two weeks because she'll have it no other way. Although she tells me it's for appearances, I'm not at all naïve. I know that she's ashamed of me. I arrive early to surprise her, to help myself win her heart. And maybe because I cannot wait to have her, not another single day. But the surprise is on me. I witness her taking advantage of our night apart, allowing herself to be molested at some local bar by some local boy, the polar opposite of everything I am. I leave the bar barely able to withstand the ache in my gut. Do I return to my hotel? Not a snowball's chance in hell.

"Where did you go after you left the Bleu Sharq?" I ask.

"I went for a walk."

No alibi.

"Alone?"

"Yes, alone."

No alibi.

"Where did you walk?"

"Along Kalakaua, along the beach."

No alibi.

"When did you get back to the Grand Polynesian?"

"Around six thirty in the morning."

No fucking alibi.

I have Catus right where I want him. I have him alone near the scene of the murder, from last call until sunrise. I take a long sip from my martini. There's no way I'm forgetting any of this. My only regret is that I didn't bring Flan. He could've testified to what Catus is telling me tonight. But I never expected Catus to come completely clean the way he is. There must be more. There's something the professor isn't volunteering. He wants me to extract it from him like an impacted wisdom tooth.

"Did you speak to anyone between the time you left the bar and the time you arrived back at your hotel?"

"I didn't want to spend the night alone."

It all comes rushing back. Just like Carson Reese. He's about to lay something on me. Something big, as if he, too, spent the night with a priest.

"I solicited a prostitute," he says.

If I were one of these fucking sailboats in one of these fucking pictures on one of these fucking walls, I'd stop dead in the water. The wind has been knocked out of my sails. But a prostitute does not a concrete alibi make. Nor will it gain the professor any favor with the jury. Besides, it may not even be true. He could've conjured the harlot just as he conjured the scented candles and rose petals. My boat's still afloat, and I'm not jumping overboard just yet.

"What time did you hire her?" I ask.

"Approximately two thirty."

"How long were you with her?"

"Until sunup."

I rattle off my questions like machine-gun fire, hoping to catch him in a lie. But he's prepared for all this. He knew it was only a matter of time before someone came around asking these questions. He swats my questions away like Superman. The bastard thinks he's bulletproof.

"How much did you pay her?"

"I gave her six hundred for the night."

"Did you use an ATM?"

"No," he says flatly. "I often carry that kind of cash."

He's thought this all through. I have little doubt that were I a cop, he'd pull from his pocket his wallet and produce no less than $900 in cash.

"Did you have sex with her?" I ask.

"I didn't pay her six hundred dollars to play Scrabble with me all night."

If I were a cop, I'd crack this wiseass across the jaw. I finally understand why police brutality is not uncommon and how I picked up so many civil cases in New York. Hell, right now, I'm all for it.

"Where did you have sex with her?"

"She had a room at the Leilani Inn."

I breathe a small sigh of relief. The Leilani Inn is not the type of establishment to have video surveillance, considering its clientele. I'm satisfied I can punch enough holes in the professor's story to make him suspect in the eyes of the jury. I'm still convinced Catus might be my client's ticket out of jail.

I take a long pull off my martini, finish it off. This interview is over. I pay my tab and stand up to leave. Catus almost seems sad to see me go. He's one lonely sack of shit.

"A hooker?" I say, right in his face. "That's your alibi?"

"Yes. Her and three bellhops. They made a stink about me not being a guest at the inn. So, I paid them each fifty dollars to allow me entry and to be discreet."

He smirks, proud of himself.

"Clever lads," he says. "It must be a little scam they run to get themselves in on the hooker's action."

CHAPTER 17

"Best seven hundred and fifty bucks he ever spent," says Jake, taking a nip from his flask. "Only thing I ever got from a hooker that I didn't pay for was crabs. This guy gets a fucking alibi circus."

"These witnesses will never testify, Jake," I say from behind my desk.

"The prosecutor will subpoena them, son."

"These kinds of people, they wipe their asses with subpoenas. They'll disappear if they ever get served."

"The prosecutor will grant them immunity if they agree to testify," says Jake, a little whiskey dribbling down his chin.

"I'll have Flan check out their backgrounds. If they do show up in court, I'll make them wish they never had."

"Well, I suppose we should get to work on our much tougher witnesses this morning."

"Who's that?" I ask.

"The video surveillance discs from the hotels."

"Not today, Jake. I've got a date this afternoon."

"A date? May I ask with whom?"

"Let's just say our first night together was billed to the Gianfortes."

"The bartender? You son of a bitch," Jake says, as I toss some extra clutter on my desk. "Shit, the only witness I ever slept with was the prostitute who gave me crabs."

"I'm going to the jail to see Joey tomorrow morning. I'll call you on my way back to the office, and we'll get together to sort through this mess."

"Have fun, son," Jake calls to me, still sitting in my client chair as I walk out the door. "Have fun."

My shrink in New York thought it less than wise for me to model my career after that of a man the likes of Milt Cashman. He thought it downright criminal that I should model my love life after Milt's. After all, when I last left Milt, he was putting the finishing touches on his fourth divorce. Each separation, of course, was initiated by the female on the grounds of Milt's relentless infidelities.

With women, as in my career, I've always felt like a fraud. I'd enter relationships with good intentions, but somehow they always turned out bad. I never trusted my own feelings, let alone a woman's feelings for me. I'd question their motives, and then I'd inevitably question my own.

Manhattan produces a certain kind of woman. The kind of woman who consults *Sex and the City* for love advice, not just fashion tips. The kind of woman who thinks finding the right man is anticlimactic to the joyous struggle of looking for him. The kind of woman who drinks too much and has too little to say. Of course, my universe in New York centered around me, and more than likely these generalities ring true only for the women who populated the circles in which I ran.

It's too soon to tell what the women of Hawaii are like, but if Nikki is any indication, then I'm in for a real treat. I'm meeting Nikki at the entrance to the Honolulu Zoo, where Kalakaua Avenue becomes Monsarrat. The day is brilliant, as just about all of the days on Oahu are.

I do a double take when I see her, radiant in a white sundress with a neckline that dips low on her chest. The contrast of the white cotton against her caramel skin is mesmerizing and I allow myself a hearty pat on the back. The sunlight does her a certain justice that a forty-watt porch light never could.

"Aloha, Kevin!" she says, waving one supple arm when she sees me. She approaches me as I exit my Jeep and plants an enthusiastic kiss square on my lips.

I was expecting that awkwardness that comes after first sleeping with someone, but there's none of that. She grabs me by the arm and leads me to the zoo. She selected the setting for our first real date during our two-hour telephone conversation Sunday night. I've always loathed the chitchat between girl and boy on the phone, but our talk didn't consist of the usual grade-school drivel. She told me what she loved, what she lived for, what she'd die for, all with a fervor that stirred even the most abstruse passions in me. She cherishes writing, she said, and animals, hence the zoo. She adores Alika, the only family she has left, and admires with every ounce of her being the endearing spirit of Hawaii's people.

The Hawaiians received a raw deal, there is no doubt about that. Their land was stolen by western businessmen, and their language and culture soon followed. The Hawaiians share much with the Native Americans on the mainland, and as on the subject of the American Indians, little is being said and even less is being done to rectify the wrongs inflicted upon them. Nikki knows that a single haole named M did not orphan her and Alika, but rather a collective endeavor by a contingent of Caucasians begun about a century and a half before she was born.

I pay the discounted *kama'aina* admission price and we enter the zoo. My last visit to the Bronx Zoo was as a small child, and I wonder as I step through the gate why I'd never gone back. Then it hits me. The pungent odor of animals and their excrement. I gag and nearly vomit from the combination of the stench and my five martinis last night. A zoo person I am not.

Nikki puts her hand upon my back and whispers softly in my ear the ever comforting words "You'll get used to the smell."

I thank her and we move forward.

Our first look is at flamingos, feeling underwater for fish and insects with their spoon-shaped bills, stepping

elegantly in every which direction, their pink feathers demanding to be photographed.

I'm anxious that it's daytime and I'm not at work, even
though much of my work of late has been done at night.
I want to be with Nikki, but I'd prefer her at my side as I
pecked away at the keyboard, drafting Joey's motion to
suppress. I always saw leisure time as time to get ahead,
and leisure activities as cutesy fun for the unambitious and
lazy. I take a deep breath and look past a pair of giant Indian
elephants toward Diamond Head. Nothing impedes my
view of the incredible crater on the horizon. No ugly skyscrapers or tacky video billboards. I'm not in New York, and
perhaps I need not work every waking moment of the day.

Nikki holds me close to her as we walk around a bend.

"We didn't wake Alika the other night," she says.

"I'm certainly glad of that."

An only child, I don't pretend to fathom the relationship between brother and sister. But had I a sister, I would
fear for the man she brought into my home. I don't know
Alika and I've little desire to know him. These connec-
tions I'm unable or unwilling to make have contributed to
my remaining so utterly single this first decade of my adult
life.

"Alika never came home that night," she adds.

I ask her why not, not because I want to know, but because I know she wants to tell me.

"He was working all night," she says.

"What is it he does?"

Nikki gives me a look as if she'd rather not say, but were that the case, she wouldn't have led our conversation down this path. She had ample opportunity to discuss her brother's whereabouts over the phone, but she chose to do so only now, in person, where she can gauge the reaction on my face.

"He sells ice."

I remain stoic. Six years in the criminal courts in New York City have desensitized me. I can tell by her face that this is a big deal to her, and thus, I know, it should be a big deal to me. But I'm no good at hand-holding, at comforting the sad and hurt. I am, however, a fucking champ at changing subjects.

"Monkeys!" I shout. "My favorite!"

Swinging from branches on a single tree are three white-handed gibbons, Southeast Asian rain-forest primates with no tails. The tree rests on a small island surrounded by a moat replete with turtles, some swimming while others rest leisurely on logs.

"I hate that he sells ice," she says.

Much like the gibbons, the topic is here to stay.

"How did he get into it?" I ask, turning toward a group of spur-thighed tortoises, all standing stone still like rocks, heads popping out only to gnaw the leaves of fallen branches.

"How do you think? M."

Nikki's voice is shaking. I put my arm around her shoulders and lead her to the vacant herpetarium, the reptile house. Alone, in the darkness, standing before tanks of toads, lizards, frogs, and geckos, she leans into me and I feel her tears soak through my shirt and onto my chest.

I am new to this. I wonder how she can cry on the shoulder of someone she hardly knows. I wonder, too, if it's terribly wrong that I'm so turned on.

"I'm so afraid of losing Alika like I did my mom and dad."

It's often said that lawyers like the sound of their own voices, and I suppose I'm no exception. But this is one of the rarest of times when I am at a complete loss for words.

I lead her by the hand back into the light.

We are met by Jun, a Malaysian sun bear with poor eyesight. At least that's what the sign reads. The small bear ambles toward us to Nikki's delight. I'm relieved that there's someone to shoulder the load, to help take Nikki's mind off the ruination of her family.

Unfortunately, Nikki finds another sign that reads that Jun was just a cub when her father was carted off to the mainland to live in captivity at the Oakland Zoo. The look on her face tells me she's thinking of her own dad, of the time he served on the mainland. And that he never came back.

I'm thinking, *Of all the goddamn luck.*

We walk to the entrance of the African Savanna, where an East African tribesman made of copper stands guard, bidding us *karibu* or welcome.

Nikki's mood switches from somber to chipper and she apologizes if she brought me down.

"Not at all," I lie. "I want you to be able to tell me everything that troubles you," I lie again.

"You're so sweet, Kevin."

Nikki and I walk the length of the zoo, watching the animals be animals. We see two seven-thousand-pound hippos, who spend the warm days resting underwater, coming out to play only at night. We pass all kinds of creatures, from gazelles, dainty and alert and graceful, to warthogs, ugly and fat and smelly. A rhino, brown and dirty, swats flies with its tail, while zebras and giraffes mingle like old friends.

Chipper Nikki makes for great company, and the date makes for one great afternoon. As we wave good-bye to a chimpanzee, I regret my inability to console and decide to take one last lick.

"It's nice that you stuck together, you and your brother, despite everything that's happened. I'm sure with you at his side, everything will turn out all right for him. In my business, I deal with a lot of youths who get mixed up with the wrong crowd and make some bad mistakes. But those that have the right family support are able to turn the corner and change their lives for the better."

It sounds lame and melodramatic even as I say it, but it makes her eyes a little moist.

"The only *ohana*—the only family—Alika and I have left is each other. I would do anything for my brother, and I know he would do anything for me."

Nikki holds me and invites me back to her place to spend the night. Over her shoulder I watch a Komodo dragon pacing back and forth in its cage. Some living things would rather die than live a life behind bars. I have an appointment to meet with Flan this evening. And I am scheduled to meet Joey at the jail come morning. So, as tempting as her offer is, I ask for a rain check.

Just as I'm about to give Nikki the long, hot kiss goodnight, we hear the merry melody of the cell phone in my pocket. I apologize and pull the damned thing from my pocket. I cup my hand over the screen to shield it from the glare of the setting sun. The caller ID reads FLAN.

"Speak."

"Kevin?" Flan asks. "May I speak to Kevin please? Kevin, is that you?"

Here we go again.

"Yeah, Flan. It's me."

"Are we still meeting tonight?"

"Yeah. Sand Bar, seven o'clock."

"I just left Carlie Douglas at her hotel," he says.

"You have some news for me, Flan?"

"Yes, I do, Kevin. I recommend you get to the Sand Bar early and have a few drinks before I get there."

"Why's that, Flan?"

"Because you're not going to want to be sober to hear what I have to say."

PART II

ALL IN THE OHANA

CHAPTER 18

"Why the hell didn't you tell me that your family is part of the New Jersey mob?"

I am livid. Even this concrete tomb can't contain my anger. The echoes ricochet off these walls like bullets, hitting Joey from every which direction. The room is supposed to be completely soundproof, yet a guard pops his head in after I smash, with a deafening bang, my metal folding chair against the floor. He pops his head right back out as soon as he sees the red in my face and the venom in my eyes. Were I the Incredible Hulk, I'd be green, and this beige linen suit would be in shreds, such that I could wrap it around the throat of this lying son of a bitch and squeeze until he couldn't breathe.

That something that Carlie Douglas told her daughter that night that led to the incident that led to Joey's misdemeanor conviction was this: Joey Gianforte Jr. is the son of the underboss of a northern New Jersey Mafia family.

Flan extracted this bit of information from Carlie Douglas with the help of peach schnapps and his natural charm. After hours of soothing talk and a dozen Fuzzy Navels, Carlie was happy to finally get it off her chest, having been warned by police and prosecutors not to share that bit of news with the media. At least not for the time being. I have absolutely no doubt that come time for jury selection, Senior's mug will be plastered all over the news right next to Joey's. A healthy dose of pretrial poison for which there is no antidote.

Joey sits silent, avoiding both my gaze and the question on the table.

"If you don't answer me, I'll file a motion to be relieved as counsel this afternoon."

I confirmed what Flan told me last night with a late-night call to Milt Cashman in New York. Milt verified the information with a couple telephone calls of his own. The time difference between Honolulu and New York is evidently irrelevant to the city that never sleeps. What Milt said was what I most feared: Senior is, indeed, second-in-command to Louis "Louie the Screw" Fiordano, the fearsome head of the Fiordano crime family, which operates out of Newark.

"I'm sorry," Joey says lamely. "I have absolutely nothing to do with my father's business, so I didn't think it was relevant."

"*I'm* the lawyer. *I* ask the questions. *You* give the answers. Then, *I* decide what is relevant and what is irrelevant. Am I making myself clear?"

"Yes."

"What?"

"Yes!"

Joey wants to move on, but I'm not letting this go. Not after Brandon Glenn. Brandon's dead, partly because he didn't share with me that he was gay. Now Joey has tried to keep from me his family ties to La Cosa Nostra.

I somewhat blame myself. Ordinarily, my first order of business would have been to ask the parents what they did for a living in order to gauge how much they could afford for their son's defense. But when Jake told me about the $50,000 check sitting underneath the prepared retainer agreement, how Senior made his money became, well, irrelevant.

"Had I asked him, what would your father have told me he does for a living?"

"My father would've told you he's in construction."

Good. Now I can go back to blaming Joey.

"Last week, when we first met, I told you, unequivocally, that I need to know *everything* you know. 'My father is a cross between John Gotti and Tony Montana' should've been the very next fucking words out of your mouth. Now we're past the lies and the lame apologies, past the pleasantries and half-truths. If you hold anything else back from me, you might as well save it for your memoirs, which you'll have twenty-three hours a day to work on in your eight-by-ten cell over the next fifty or sixty years of your life. Do you understand what I'm telling you?"

"I do."

"Good. Now tell me about Jim Catus."

I wait for the reaction. It's one of complete confusion. I suspected Joey knew, that he came to Hawaii to pull the professor's wrinkled, old ass off from atop his girl. That Cindy DuFrain had known and let slip the details of the tryst. That the professor was another secret Joey somehow saw fit to keep from me. But the look on his face says otherwise. The poor bastard had no idea.

"The law school professor?" he asks.

"Yeah. Tell me everything you know about him."

"He taught constitutional law to our first-year section. He gave me a C-minus both semesters."

"Did you know that Shannon was meeting Professor Catus in Waikiki the day after she arrived?"

Joey's face is frozen in a blank stare as he computes what I just said. His is the reaction one would expect of someone just informed of their dead love's ultimate betrayal. Either he is one hell of an actor, which I think not, or the Catus-Shannon sex romp is news to him. News that hits him like a rock. A poor analogy, I suppose, considering how Shannon was killed.

"Are you sure?"

"I am," I say, my anger subsided, my sympathies returned. "I met with Catus myself."

Joey looks as though he may become sick, a look that tells me that had he known about Catus, he might never have come. His hands drop onto the table, his head drops into his hands.

"Do you think Catus killed her, Kevin?"

"His story is thin. His alibis are weak. He's someone we may be able to use to cast reasonable doubt."

Joey's head stays buried in his hands as I remind him that his arraignment tomorrow is a mere formality. He will plead not guilty and bail will remain out of reach at 3 million bucks. Senior does not have that kind of cash, he tells me. Evidently, in this economy, even organized crime doesn't pay all that well.

Joey doesn't lift his head until I stand up to leave.

"Is that it?" he asks.

"Unless there's something you haven't told me yet."

Joey shakes his head. He looks at me like a puppy who doesn't want his master to leave. I can tell he's trying to think of something to say, to keep me here, even if only for a few extra minutes. Brandon Glenn used to do the same thing, by trying to force small talk about the New York Knicks.

"I'm going to level with you," I say. "I wasn't hired to hold your hand. I'm not being paid to keep you company. My job is to do everything I can to get you acquitted. You can make both our lives easier by telling me everything I need to know. If you insist on keeping things from me, then I've got to go out there and learn what I need to know on my own or wait until the prosecutor starts piling this shit in my lap on the eve of trial."

"I'm not keeping anything else from you. I promise."

That and eighty-five cents will get me a can of Diet Coke.

"You see, now that I know that the press will eventually

label you a real-life Sonny Corleone, I can prepare for it and exercise some damage control."

"I understand," he says. "I promise I'll do anything you ask."

"Good, because I have something else to ask of you."

"Anything. What is it?"

"I see your father's name is on the approved guest list for later today."

"Yeah. He's coming to visit me this afternoon."

"That's fine, so long as you keep our little conversation today between the two of us."

"I won't say a word. May I ask why?"

"Because, Joey, I don't want to wake up to find a fucking horse's head at the foot of my bed."

CHAPTER 19

Just as I set the telephone receiver back into its cradle, Jake enters my office without knocking. His hands are orange from the bag of Doritos or Cheetos or whatever the hell he's holding, and the flask sticks out of his left hip pocket like an appendage. As he takes a seat in the client chair in front of my desk, he licks his fingers one by one with orange lips and tosses the crumpled bag on my desk. He sees me eyeing the bag and quickly thinks better of it, removing the bag from my desk and depositing it in the waste receptacle on the floor. I'm not used to this kind of familiarity. Milt and I have known one another for over a decade, and neither of us would even think about entering the other's office without knocking. Yet I've known Jake for a week and a day and here he comes strutting into my office like Chester the Cheetah, turning everything in his path a crummy and ugly orange.

"Who was that?" he says, pointing to the phone with

an orange finger, while cheesy projectiles spew from his 80-proof mouth across my desk.

"That was Milt Cashman," I tell him, grabbing the paper towels and the bottle of Fantastik from my bottom desk drawer.

Milt works fast. When I spoke to him last night, I briefed him on the entire Gianforte case. He said he was intrigued and offered to help. Since I'm not shy when it comes to accepting favors, I asked him to start by getting me some background on the victim, including the Newark law firm where she worked.

"What did Not Guilty Milty have to say?" Jake asks, unscrewing his flask.

"I had asked him to check out Shannon's employer, the law firm of Carter, Backman and Knight."

"They're the personal injury lawyers, right?"

"That's what Joey told me."

"Was he lying to you, son?"

"I don't think so, Jake. I think that's what Shannon told him."

"But it isn't the truth?"

"Apparently not," I say.

Milt Cashman informed me that the law firm of Carter, Backman & Knight is a front. All of the partners on the firm's charter are former FBI, but Milt's sources say none of them are really very former. The law firm is a cover. Shannon didn't *want* to work for the FBI. Shannon *was* working for the FBI.

Finished with the Doritos, Jake begins to chew on this.

"Does Cashman have any idea what Shannon may have been working on specifically?"

"No," I say, "but if I had to hazard a guess, I would say organized crime."

"Hell, that could be helpful to us, son."

"Apparently, you haven't spoken to Flan."

"Not for a couple days," he says. "Why?"

I tell him about Senior, about how the $50,000 check was written to me by the underboss of the Fiordano crime family. If Joey knew that Shannon was working for the Feds, it would give him even further motive to kill her, or so the state would argue. Claiming that Joey's association with the Mafia goes to show motive would also allow the prosecution to explain that association to the jury. The not-so-subtle message to the jury about Joey would be simple: killing is in his blood.

"Do you think Shannon was working this kid the whole time?" Jake asks.

"I don't know, Jake. It's a crazy post-9/11 world. The bolder the Justice Department becomes on the terrorism front, the bolder they're going to become on other fronts, like organized crime. Times have changed. Donnie Brasco sure didn't have to fuck the information out of his crew, but nowadays, who knows?"

"Are you gonna tell Joey about this?"

"I'm going to have to tell him at some point. But I'm going to give it some time. I just this morning dropped the information about Professor Catus on him. All this news on top of the stress of life behind bars could put him over the edge. Tomorrow's his arraignment. We'll go through the motions and I'll tell him I'll visit again next week."

Jake takes a nip from his flask and shakes his head. "This case is taking on a life of its own. Sure as hell glad I'm not lead counsel."

Taking on a murder case is a lot like getting a pet. When you're deciding whether to go through with it, you focus on the negatives. Mainly, whether you can handle cleaning up all the shit that comes with the territory. Once you decide to go through with it, cleaning up the shit becomes just another part of your daily routine. The case or the pet quickly becomes a major facet of your life. Before you know it, you find yourself wondering how you would've ever lived without it, shit and all.

I swivel my chair around to face the mountains. When you're knee-deep in shit, it's easy to forget where you live. Even here in paradise.

From behind me, Jake's voice takes me out of the moment and back to reality.

"Since *I* didn't have a date at the zoo yesterday afternoon, I took it upon myself to view the hotel surveillance videos. Would you like the good news first, or would you like the bad news first, son?"

I swivel my chair back around to face him. "I could use some good news."

The good news, he tells me, is that Palani left his post for some time after taking over for his fellow doorman at the Waikiki Winds on the night Shannon was murdered. However, he was gone for less than fifteen minutes, barely enough time to get to the beach and back, let alone enough time to find Shannon, get into another argument, and kill her.

"I'll pace it off, from the hotel to the beach and back," I say. "But why would he leave work to go back to the beach?"

"Maybe he still wanted to fuck her."

"Must've been one hell of an erection."

"Hell, haven't you ever taken Viagra?" Jake says.

I give him a look and shake my head.

"Well, we're not all thirty-one, son."

"So, Jake, aside from your needing Viagra to get it up, what's the bad news?"

"I have to get up to piss a dozen times a night."

"Anything else?"

"You bet," he says. "Let's go into the conference room. I think it's best you see it for yourself."

Jake asks Hoshi to set up the DVD player in the conference room. We pull the shaded film over the windows to reduce the glare and take our seats.

Hoshi seems to know even more about the discs than Jake. She puts one in and fast-forwards as she looks down at notes she has scribbled on a yellow legal pad. She hits play and a minute goes by before I see Joey stepping off the elevator and into the lobby of the Hawaiian Sands hotel.

"At first," Jake says, "I was only focusing on the time reference at the bottom right-hand corner of the screen."

The image of Joey disappears as he exits the hotel. Jake nods and Hoshi fast-forwards again. Minutes pass here in the conference room as hours pass on-screen. Finally, Hoshi hits play again. Another two minutes go by before Joey steps back into focus.

"The second time I watched it," Jake says, "I focused in on Joey himself."

Jake squints, and I find myself squinting, too. Joey's face is fuzzy, so I can tell nothing about his mood. His clothes seem clean, and I'm thankful for that. He sways like someone who has been drinking all night. In other words, like everyone else stumbling into their Waikiki hotel at that time of night.

Then, I see them. A pair of flip-flops on his feet.

"Oh, shit," I say.

There is absolutely nothing out of the ordinary about stumbling into your Waikiki hotel at four thirty in the morning wearing a pair of cheap rubber flip-flops.

Except, that is, when you left your hotel nine hours earlier in a pair of bright white Nike sneakers.

CHAPTER 20

The arraignment was uneventful. However, hearing our application for bail reduction denied still brought Joey to tears. He grabbed hold of me in a desperate embrace and left snot on the shoulder of my new navy blue suit. In that moment, I pitied the both of us. I chose to spare him, at least for some time, the news of Shannon's employment with the Justice Department and our discovery of his unfortunate change of footwear. I'll speak to Joey about these items next week. After all, there's really no rush. He's certainly not going anywhere.

That was yesterday. Today is Friday and the beginning of what I hope will be a long weekend. In New York, I wouldn't have dreamed of taking a Friday off. Or even a Saturday, come to think of it. But Nikki insisted, and so I caved. And here we are, the two of us, at the entrance to the Waikiki Aquarium.

Nikki is dressed in a sexy, colorful midriff and tight,

short shorts, which quickly extinguish every bit of excitement I had mustered for looking at fish. Nevertheless, hand in hand, we make our way inside. I pay the reduced *kama'aina* admission, and we are handed a pair of audio wands. The wands are black, about a foot in length, and I feel silly carrying one in my hand. The wands, we are told, serve as a virtual tour guide throughout our walk through the aquarium.

At Nikki's insistence, I put the silly wand to my ear. We step in and stop at the first tank. The woman in the wand tells me that I am looking at coral, a hard substance built by sea creatures, taking the shape of lettuce leaves, rosettes, or solid stones. Magnificent. But I'd prefer to be having sex.

"Alika is upset with me for dating a haole," Nikki tells me out of the blue.

"Really? Why is that?"

"He hates haoles. He doesn't trust Caucasians after all that's happened. He thinks haoles don't belong here on the islands."

"I can't wait to meet him."

We make our way left, and the woman in the wand tells me we're looking at angelfish, butterfly fish, and puffer fish, all swimming in the protection of a sea anemone's stinging tentacles. It's all so beautiful and peaceful. I promise myself to get to know the sea.

"Do you have any brothers or sisters?" Nikki asks me.

"I'm one of a kind. An only child."

"Do you enjoy what you do? Being a lawyer, I mean."

That's a good question, one I haven't really reevaluated since I moved to Hawaii. I thought I enjoyed practicing law in New York, but I didn't. I enjoyed telling people what I did. I enjoyed the attention. I enjoyed the money. I enjoyed playing the role of a criminal defense attorney, but I didn't enjoy the actual practice of law. I hated my clients. I hated my adversaries. I was told by my shrink that I even hated myself. It was like that for a long, long time. And it all culminated with the death of Brandon Glenn.

Most lawyers will tell you that they hate being lawyers, and just about all of them are full of shit. You don't get trapped by the law. You can leave it at any time. Sure, I sometimes feel like an indentured servant with the insurmountable school loans looming over my head. But I'm lying when I tell myself that's why I practice law. I could do a lot of things to earn a living. But it's like Milt always told me. Some people are just made for this shit.

And practicing law seems different in Hawaii. Or maybe it's me that's different. I'm certainly handling the Gianforte matter in a way different from the way I handled any other. I'm handling it the way a good lawyer should. Taking it apart piece by piece, instead of playing for the media and looking ahead to the next retainer. I feel good about myself. For the first time in my career, yes, I am enjoying the practice of law.

As I inform Nikki of my newfound contentment, the woman in the wand informs me that the rainbow of colors moving gracefully in the tank to our right are blue devils, cardinal fish, and lemon peels.

"How come a sexy lawyer from New York City doesn't have a girlfriend?" Nikki asks.

I wince at the question. I don't want to talk about relationship history. Not hers, and sure as shit, not mine. Of course, there is my standard response.

"I just hadn't met the right girl."

The woman in the wand saves me from any further talk on the subject. She tells me the next community of fish is more diverse. Convict surgeonfish, blotched foxface rabbitfish, flame angelfish, all swim about giant clams and coral.

As we turn the corner, two small children run into us, nearly knocking Nikki over. In my short time on the islands, I've already grown quite tired of tourists.

Nikki notices a sign for the ladies' room and excuses herself. After watching her backside dance away, I turn to see something not quite so pleasant. A giant tank filled with some of the largest and meanest-looking fish I have ever seen. I make myself a promise not to get to know the sea all that well after all.

As I stand up against the tank, I feel the presence of tourists milling about behind me. Despite the packed subways and busy city streets, New Yorkers have the least tolerance for people who invade their personal space. I am certainly no exception. I press myself up even closer against the glass as the bastard tourists behind me move about. They are standing so close, I can feel their sickening breath on the back of my neck.

"That's some ugly fish," I hear from over my right shoulder, as a large threadfin jack passes across the glass. The voice is a deep, noxious baritone, coming from a man taller than my six feet.

"Yeah," agrees a shorter man on my left. "Fucking hideous."

"How 'bout you, kid?" says the voice on my right. His voice is lower now, but close to my ear, such that I can smell his foul cigarette breath. "You're the opinionated sort. What do you think of the fish?"

I attempt to turn around, but my body's pressed against the glass. They're not letting me move an inch.

"Don't turn around," says the voice to my left. "We seen enough of your face in the *Post*."

"Yeah," says the voice on my right. "Sure hope you do a better job for little Joey Bangs than you did for that fag in New York."

My heart is thumping so hard I fear it will shatter the glass on the tank. My first thought is of my son-of-a-bitch client. I should've known his promise would be good for shit. My second thought is for my safety. With my peripheral vision, I can see a crowd in the next room. My pulse slows just a fraction, until I remember my college class on organized crime. My paper was on the subject of mob hits, and I was fascinated by the boldness with which they were often carried out.

"We hear you been asking questions bout Mr. Gianforte's business," says the voice to my left.

I say nothing.

"Mr. Gianforte respectfully requests that you cease and desist, Counselor," he says. "That's lawyer-speak for 'cut it the fuck out.' *Capiche?*"

I nod but say nothing.

"And that goes for your friend, too," he says. "The Jew lawyer back in New York. Got it?"

I nod but say nothing.

A reflection of the three of us is in the tank. I study their faces, starting with the one on the left. I have about an inch on him. His right eye is on me, but his left is looking out into space. He's got thinning black hair, a wide nose, and pockmarks all over his face. The one on the right is broad-shouldered with curly black hair slicked in grease. His face is heavy, he's missing a tooth, and he's got three chins, at least. I take a mental snapshot.

"You got yourself a cute little girlfriend," says the son of a bitch on my left. "I wouldn't mind giving her a *lei.*"

"Yeah," says the prick to my right, midguffaw. "I betcha her *poi* tastes pretty fucking good."

I say nothing.

When they're through with their laugh, the fucker on the right reaches between my legs from behind and grabs my balls. He squeezes, as the bastard on the left covers my mouth with one of his foul-tasting hands. The other hand is behind me digging his wand into the small of my back. I feel faint, and I wait for everything to turn a bright white.

"Consider yourself on notice, Counselor," one of them says.

And with that, they are gone.

Nikki returns not a minute later as I stand stone still, eyeing the threadfin jack.

"Sorry I took so long," she says. "Some guy asked me and another girl coming out of the ladies' room if we would come outside with him to help feed the sea lions. Then when we got to the tank, he couldn't find the food. He went around the side and never came back."

I look at the wand in my hand. "Nikki, my wand isn't working. I have to run up front and get another."

I push past the tourists and head for the front desk, where the chubby woman who distributes the wands is eating a Hot Pockets and sipping a supersize Coke.

"Excuse me," I say, "do you recall two Italian-looking men purchasing admission? One was very large and the other had a lazy eye."

"Yes," she says between bites. "As a matter of fact, there were three. They just walked out."

"Did they return their audio wands to you?"

She sets down the Hot Pockets and sweeps the area with her eyes.

"No," she says with her hands on her generous hips. "As a matter of fact, they didn't. They must have walked right out with them."

She's clearly displeased with this. She's not the only one. Without their fingerprints from the audio wands, the only means I have of identifying them is the mental snapshot I took. The snapshot is of unquestionably poor quality and the picture's fading fast.

I head back to Nikki, thinking of lame excuses along the way.

"I hate to do this," I tell her, "but I have to end our date."

Nikki doesn't look pleased. A sadness in her eyes makes it almost impossible for me to lie to her. Almost.

"Hoshi just called," I say. "Jake is really ill, and I've got to take him to a doctor."

Nikki had made it clear to me that she wouldn't tolerate a man who put work before her. I certainly can't tell her I'm being threatened by the northern New Jersey Mafia for obvious reasons. I don't consider myself a liar anymore. But sometimes women are so damned demanding that they leave men with no alternative but to lie. This is one of those times.

After safely tucking Nikki away in a taxi bound for Kailua, I race back to my Jeep, back to downtown Honolulu, back to South King Street, back to my office. I am through the door and past reception before Hoshi can manage an aloha.

I drop in my chair and dial Milt's cellular phone number in New York.

"Speak," says Milt. A lot of background noise is on his end.

"Did I catch you at a bad time, Milt?"

"No, Kevin," he yells into the phone, "it's never a bad

time for you. I'm waiting on a jury verdict at One Hundred Centre Street. The DA's offer was twenty-five years. I'm going to have my client home eating supper with his baby mama by six p.m. tonight."

"Good for you, Milt. Listen, I need to see some photos related to the Fiordano syndicate. I'm looking for a couple of soldiers."

I tell him about my run-in at the aquarium. About the threats made about both me and him.

"What is it with you goddamn guineas?" he says. "I'll have the photos faxed to your office by later tonight."

"I don't want to put you at risk by having you poke around, Milt."

"Me? At risk? C'mon, Kev. I'm a fucking Superman. Besides, these will be coming directly from the FBI."

"You have friends in the Justice Department?"

"I have friends everywhere. Actually, my source in the Bureau and I have a mutual friend. You may have heard of him. His name is Benjamin Franklin. He's deceased, but I always keep a few pictures of him in my wallet."

I think back to when I first met Milt Cashman. I was a first-year law student, and Milt was lecturing at a seminar called "Making Crime Pay." At lunch, we got to speaking. I wanted to learn something, but all he did was boast about his latest female conquests.

"I know what you're thinking," Milt had said to me. "I'm a short, bald Jew with big ears and rotten teeth." He reached into his pocket and flashed a roll of bills as big as his fist. "But when I take this out at the bar, I'm six foot three with blond hair and blue eyes. Just like that, I'm Robert fucking Redford."

I hear Milt ask the assistant DA if he's ready to offer up time served and a plea to disorderly conduct in lieu of first-degree murder. A second goes by, then Milt laughs.

"What did he say?" I ask.

"He told me to go fuck myself."

"Good for him."

"So, Kevin, I thought you left New York to get away from this shit. Now, from what you're telling me, you're balls deep in a murder case that's getting national attention, and you got the New Jersey mob threatening to put you to bed with the fish. What the hell happened?"

"I guess, Milt, that what you told me ten years ago is true."

"What's that, Kev?"

"Some people are just made for this shit."

CHAPTER 21

This early Monday morning, I am standing in a courtroom at the district court in Honolulu, which differs little
from my legal haunts in New York City, except that the
female court officers wear flowers in their hair. I'm not
sure exactly what I was expecting before I first stepped into
a Hawaiian courtroom for Joey's arraignment last week.
Maybe palm trees where flag posts usually stand behind
the bench. Tiki torches lighting up the gallery. Maybe pris-
oners shackled with fresh flower leis in lieu of handcuffs.
But there's none of that. It's all business here in paradise.

The courtroom, any courtroom, is a welcoming place
for few. But I am one of those few. I revel in hearing the
sound of my voice as it echoes through the gallery. I relish
in being pit against a foe. I delight in the duel, in landing
blows from the podium and parrying with my objections
like a valiant English knight. But, usually, I'm not so valiant.
Usually, I sneak up on my adversaries from behind, pull

out my sword, and strike them down cold. Indeed, that lawful underhandedness, I confess, provides me the greatest pleasure of all.

I am standing at the counsel table with the robust Turi Ahina at my side. He's glowing like a candle, displaying for all who look upon him his bright, big signature smile. Ordinarily, I would tell my client to wipe that smile off his face before the judge does it for him. But I notice for the first time today that it's not the show of cockiness I first took it for. The man is simply merry. He is a jolly, big fellow as some big fellows tend to be. He's happy, and I can't fault him for that. Though what in the world he has to be happy about is fucking beyond me.

The case of *State versus Turi Ahina* is called. I pull Turi's file folder from my briefcase, File Number 00002. I considered using for Joey's case the next available file number from my New York practice, but that wouldn't allow me the fresh start I came here looking for. The Corvelli Law Firm was not the name of my firm in New York either. It was the Law Offices of Kevin D. Corvelli. But the Law Offices of Kevin D. Corvelli were the attorneys of record in the case of *People versus Brandon Glenn*. Anything I can do to distance myself from that case, I will. Even if it means legally changing my own name altogether.

Luckily for me, Turi didn't seek private counsel immediately after his arrest. Otherwise, he wouldn't have found me, since I wasn't yet licensed to practice law in the State of Hawaii. It wasn't until after his court-appointed lawyer began pressuring him into taking a plea bargain that Turi jumped ship and sought out some paid for. Yes, *paid for* is a term usually reserved for harlots, you know, hookers, whores, women of the night. But when you think about it, is there really that much of a distinction between our two professions?

Luckily for him, he found me. I have no intention of attacking this case on the merits. If I did, I would walk out of the courtroom with a slash in the L column, and I don't like to lose. Turi was caught in what is called a buy and bust. Simply put, an undercover officer makes a hand-to-hand purchase of narcotics from the suspect, then waiting officers move in for the arrest. A search incident to arrest will yield from the suspect the marked currency used by the undercover officer to purchase the narcotics. The testimony of the undercover and arresting officers, along with the marked currency and whatever else the suspect is found to be holding, will just about always be more than enough to obtain a conviction.

Enter Rule 48.

"The state is not ready, Your Honor," says the young female prosecuting attorney from the table across the aisle. "We request a brief adjournment."

Rule 48 is Hawaii's speedy-trial statute. The U.S. Constitution guarantees a criminal defendant's right to a speedy trial under the Sixth Amendment of the Bill of Rights. Maybe it's the Fifth, I don't know. That's what the Internet is for. The states set forth their own speedy-trial rules, which are often broader than the rights granted by the U.S. Constitution. In New York, the speedy-trial statute is known as

Criminal Procedure Law 30.30. In Hawaii, it's known as Rule 48. The statutes are designed to promote justice and fair dealing. I like to think that they are designed for clever lawyers such as myself to manipulate the system and make a quick buck.

"Is the adjournment on consent, Counselor?" the judge asks of me.

"Absolutely not, Your Honor," I say. "The defense is ready, and we are prepared to select a jury this morning. Our witnesses are all present and accounted for."

In fact, we have no witnesses, not a single, solitary one. And we never will. But technically, it's not a lie, since I could call Turi to the stand if I so wished. And he's here, standing next to me, grinning like the cat that ate the blond canary.

You see, Rule 48 says that the state has 180 days from the time of arrest to bring this matter to trial. A violation of Rule 48 entitles the defendant to have the trial court dismiss the charges against him for want of prosecution. It's what many outside the legal profession would consider a technicality. It's what I consider a game. A game I like to call Beat the Speedy Trial Clock.

"Very well," says the judge, a Filipino male in his mid-sixties. "Ms. Raffa, is there any way for you to proceed today?"

"No, Your Honor," says the prosecuting attorney. "The arresting officers are unavailable to testify at the present time. We need at least another two weeks."

Testifying in court is part of a police officer's job, a

part most of them do not like. Sitting in court, waiting to be called upon to take the stand, is less than adventurous. Being criticized and having your integrity put into question by some sleazy criminal defense lawyer is no day at the park. Being told where to be and when by some stuffed shirt with a law degree and a badge is no picnic either. Hence, police officers are frequent no-shows at the time of trial, particularly in misdemeanor drug cases, where the payoff for law enforcement is slim.

"Very well," the judge says. "I am setting a new trial date for three weeks from today."

"Thank you, Your Honor," Ms. Raffa and I sing in unison.

It's another reason I'm lucky Turi waited to seek private counsel. Ninety days are already chargeable to the state, meaning we have only ninety more to go, including the twenty-one days just ordered by the judge. Should the officers appear in court three weeks from today, I'll answer, "Not ready." Our witnesses will suddenly have disappeared. I'll request an adjournment, and the time until the next trial date will be excluded. However, the chances are that the officers who appear ready to testify will not appear again the next. If they do, I'll request yet another adjournment. The object of the game is simple: play until you win.

Turi and I exit the courtroom together. I explained the entire strategy to him before we stepped up to the counsel table so that he wouldn't look surprised when I mentioned our nonexistent witnesses or that we were ready for trial.

He is dressed in the odd way criminal defendants dress for court. With varying degrees of success, they wear the best they own of everything. A worn black sport coat over a brand-new yellow T with silver denim jeans and a pair of brown Timberlands. He looks like a giant bumblebee that ate a small bear, landed on a metal trash can, and took a dump. But his smile, really, is all I see.

Turi pulls me close to him and traps me in a giant bear hug. It's a brotherly embrace that makes me think of Brandon, and a similar hug we shared just before the start of trial.

"T'anks, Mistah C," Turi says to me.

"Thank the founding fathers who drafted the Constitution, Turi. I'm just helping you exercise your rights as a citizen of the United States of America."

His chubby cheeks lift even higher, illuminating the hallway the way few smiles ever could. All things considered, I've had relatively little to smile about in my career. Financial success did not bring with it the happiness I thought it would. Outside of Milt, I did not sustain a single friendship that lasted past my move. Not a single colleague, adversary, or client has bothered to keep in touch. I stand here lonely in a courthouse corridor envying a client charged with possession and sale of ice. I have no choice but to ask.

"Turi, why are you always smiling?"

He points toward the glass door leading outside. The sunbeams are beating it down, trying to break in. "Brah, the sun is shining. The birds are singing. The waves are hitting the shore. The land, it's mine. And it's waiting for me just outside that door."

I nod my head, looking past him to the outside world. I wish, for just a moment, I could completely comprehend.

"Smile, Mistah C. It's one beautiful day, yeah?"

And with that, he's gone.

Still jittery from the incident at the aquarium, I shudder when I feel a firm hand grip my left shoulder. I breathe a sigh of relief after I turn to see Flan, a file folder tucked under his other arm. "How did you find me?" I ask.

"I called your office. Hoshi said you'd be here."

I'm already alarmed. The look on Flan's face tells me this is not a social visit. Yesterday, I provided Flan the names of the two goons I picked from the photo array sent to me by Milt's friend in the Bureau. To better gauge the seriousness of the threats, I asked Flan to gather for me whatever information he could, including the date and time the bastards arrived in Honolulu.

"Kev," Flan says, "we need to talk."

CHAPTER 22

The two New Jersey men I picked from the photo array were identified as Salvatore "Lazy Eye Sal" Lopardi and Anthony "Tony Bitch-Tits" Antonazzo. Joey, who is apparently known to them as Joey Bangs, probably told his father every word I said, right down to the crack about Sonny Corleone. Now, I have two goons by the colorful names of Lazy Eye Sal and Tony Bitch-Tits threatening my life. It just proves further what Milt Cashman always said: aside from Frank Sinatra and Lou Costello, nothing good ever came out of Jersey.

Flan and I have moved down the hall to the Lawyers' Room. It's set up like a grade-school cafeteria, complete with folding tables, metal chairs, bulletin boards, and vending machines filled with crap. It smells more like a toilet than a cafeteria, but precious few places in the courthouse are as private as this, so we sit our asses down on the metal folding chairs to talk.

"I checked with my guy at Continental Airlines," says Flan. "Sure enough, Lopardi and Antonazzo took a flight from Newark Liberty International to Honolulu Airport together."

"I already know they're here, Flan. I need to know when they got here."

"I'm getting to that. Boy, Jake was right. You really need to calm down."

I apologize, real genuine-like. I suppose it's too much to ask of someone to get to the point. It's one thing I miss about New York. The fast-talking, curt manner in which I could dismiss everyone throughout my day. There's a certain attitude in New York. Give me what I need and let me be on my way. Here in Hawaii it's different. Someone sells me a diet soda, and I'm supposed to kneel down and kiss their ass cheeks on both sides. Then I'm supposed to sit down for an hour and a half and listen to them talk story.

Talking story, Nikki told me, is part of the Hawaiian culture. It's sitting down, talking, gossiping, shooting the breeze. Everything I live for.

"You are going to shit your pants when you hear this," Flan says.

"I doubt I'll shit myself."

"Lopardi and Antonazzo arrived in Honolulu on the same day as Shannon Douglas and your client. Their flight touched down in Honolulu less than an hour after Joey's."

"Flan," I say.

"Yeah?"

"I just shit myself."

"I warned you. I knew you would."

My mind is spinning clockwise with hope, counter-clockwise with fear. If I can show that members of the Fiordano crime family knew that Shannon Douglas was working for the Feds, then we've just discovered two more viable suspects in Shannon's murder. But I've been put on notice. To pursue Lopardi and Antonazzo as suspects will place me in grave danger. My personal stakes in this case have just been raised. One wrong move and I'll be facing more than just some cameras in my face. If I fuck up, the least I'll have to worry about is a few humiliating head-lines. One mistake, and this time I won't just be leaving Manhattan. I'll be kicked off the goddamn planet.

We know that the police and prosecuting attorney are aware that the Gianfortes are connected to the mob, thanks in whole to Carlie Douglas. What we don't know is whether they know about Lopardi and Antonazzo. We can't let them know I was threatened because we'd be tipping our hand. They would quickly locate the duo and learn that they arrived on the same day as Shannon and Joey. If Lopardi and Antonazzo do have alibis, they'd find them, too. And we'd be back to square one. It's diffi-cult when those charged with the responsibility of protect-ing you are also the enemy.

"Do you want me to tail these guys?" Flan asks.

"No," I say. "It's too dangerous. If you get made, you'll end up doing a face plant on Waikiki Beach same as Shannon."

"They can't be any scarier than my ex-wife."

"Still. For the time being, just find out where they're staying and learn whatever else you can from Carlie Douglas."

"You're the boss," he says, sounding somewhat disappointed that I won't let him lay his life on the line just yet. "Now that you have two plausible suspects, it seems like things are looking up, aren't they, Kev?"

"I don't know," I say, shaking my head. "Besides the fact I'd be placing my life in jeopardy, there's something else bothering me about fingering Lopardi and Antonazzo as the killers."

"What's that, Kev?"

"Back in New York, Milt and I represented a good many members of the Tagliarini crime family. The family was in the midst of a war with two other syndicates. Bodies were surfacing around the five boroughs just about every other week for two years."

Flan narrows his eyes. "And?"

"And," I say slowly, flashing back through the thousands of crime-scene photos I examined during that span, "Shannon's murder has neither the look nor feel of a professional hit."

CHAPTER 23

Back at the office I find Jake in the conference room, the contents of the Gianforte file and an empty six-pack spread across the long cherry table.

"I thought you were too old for this shit," I say.

"I am," he says, taking a last swig from his Sierra Nevada. "Still, there's something about this case that draws me in like a moth to a flame. The victim is as complex as any I've ever seen or even heard of. A law student, working undercover for the Justice Department, dating the son of a Mafia underboss. She's a beautiful brunette, clearly intelligent, yet promiscuous as all hell. She has sex with a local on the beach the night before she's supposed to meet her law school professor for a two-week-long fuckfest. She drinks like a fish, she does drugs."

"Wait a minute," I interrupt him. "What did you just say?"

"About the fuckfest?"

"No. About the drugs."

Jake scans the table. The file I kept so well organized looks as if it were hit by a tornado. I don't see a Doritos bag in the room, but orange fingerprints are all over my meticulous notes. He has clearly used the pleadings as a coaster and the retainer agreement as a place mat for his Doritos and pale-ale snack. He finally finds the document on the floor under his feet.

He tosses it to me. Despite the footprint I can see that it's a toxicology report.

"Shannon tested positive for marijuana," Jake tells me.

"Son of a bitch. How did I miss this?"

"Actually, you didn't. I noticed the toxicology report wasn't attached to the autopsy records. I figured you being so organized and all, if you had it, it wouldn't dare be anyplace else. So I telephoned the prosecuting attorney's office. A secretary faxed it over to us an hour ago. They must have forgotten to give it to you when you picked up the file."

"I wonder what else they forgot to give me."

"Like a shiny new pair of Nike sneakers?" he says.

I nod. Defense attorneys typically have to fight tooth and nail with prosecutors to obtain discovery. I was naïve to think it would be any different in paradise. Just because Barbara Davenport handed me some preliminary discovery with a smile on her face doesn't mean they're not holding back the good stuff. Law enforcement can utilize many tactics to keep the defense lawyer in the dark. If police found the footwear, they may have had it analyzed, then neglected to hand it over to the prosecuting attorney's office. The police are under no duty to provide us with discovery. Only the prosecuting attorney is. Thus, the police and prosecutors usually have their own little "don't ask, don't tell" policy.

Back to the marijuana. The *pakalolo*. Immediately, my thoughts turn to Palani.

"Palani has already admitted to police that he bought marijuana at the Waikiki Winds after he left Shannon on the beach," I say.

"Don't forget, son, the weed could have been in her system for up to thirty days."

"It could have. But remember, Jake, she worked for the FBI. She wasn't calling it a day and rushing home to smoke a joint. The Justice Department tests its employees on a regular basis."

"Another fine reason not to become a Fed."

"Practically speaking, I'm sure we could also elicit testimony from Shannon's mother, who would assure us all that her darling little girl never touched the evil weed in her entire life."

"Okay, son, let's assume, then, that Shannon smoked the ganja the night she arrived in Waikiki. Where does that leave us?"

"Well," I say, "let's assume she didn't smoke it at any of the bars. Even though Palani says he smoked a joint in the bathroom at the Bleu Sharq, I'm sure the owner and manager of the bar will call him a liar and say that sort of stuff doesn't go on in there. The same goes for Margaritaville."

"That would mean she smoked the weed sometime after she left the Bleu Sharq."

"Exactly."

"But Palani has the video surveillance camera at the Waikiki Winds as an alibi, son. Even assuming he was able to get back to the beach, kill her, and return to the hotel in the fifteen minutes or so that he left his post, he sure as hell didn't have time to sit down with her to puff on a joint."

"Right," I say. "But what about his buddy, the other doorman? This J. J. Fitzpatrick. The guy who gave Palani the weed."

"I hope you're not talking about a coincidence, son. Juries don't buy into coincidences."

I shred some skin off my thumb and wince at the pain.

"No, Jake. No coincidences. Perhaps Palani was in a giving mood after his buddy J.J. lit him up. Perhaps Palani told his friend and colleague that there was a drunk, horny, half-naked girl down on a deserted stretch of Waikiki Beach."

"You think you'll be able to sell a jury on that, son? That the local boy wanted his friend to have a go at her?"

"As fucked up as it sounds, there's precedence, Jake. Think about it. If Palani told his friend about the girl—which he probably did given the scratches on his face—then, at the very least, we have another suspect, one who doesn't have an alibi in the form of video surveillance."

"So what you're surmising is that this friend of Palani's walks down to the beach, finds Shannon, has a chat with

her, smokes her up, then hits her with a reef rock when she
won't put out?"

"That's one possibility," I say, rising from my chair.

I walk down the narrow hall to my office. I step inside
and close the door behind me. I step out of my shoes. I remove my suit jacket and pants, hang them neatly on the
hook atop the cherry door. I remove my tie and my button-
down shirt and fold them over my chair. I change my socks.
I throw on a T-shirt and shorts, slip on a pair of sneakers.

On my way out of the suite, I pop my head back into the
conference room and say good-bye to Jake.

"Where are you heading off to, son?"

"I'm going for a run. And I have a sudden urge to try to
score some *pakalolo*."

CHAPTER 24

No law bans the use of cellular phones while operating a motor vehicle in Hawaii. I read an article in the *Honolulu Advertiser* just a week ago stating that the latest bill to ban cell phone use was shot down in the state legislature. Ironically, the article was situated directly below the graphic photograph of a stomach-turning motor-vehicle accident, in which the driver of one of the motor vehicles admitted he was distracted by his conversation on his Nextel cellular phone. Any group of learning-disabled eight-year-olds could tell you that fiddling around with a cell phone while operating a motor vehicle at sixty-five miles per hour will cause accidents and inevitably lead to serious injury and death. Yet the Hawaii legislature doesn't quite get it. Kind of makes you wonder just what kind of people are writing our laws.

As I navigate my Jeep around a hairpin turn, I flip open my cell phone and dial information. I request to be connected to the Waikiki Winds hotel on Kapahulu. I am connected with the front desk, and a woman named Irene graciously asks how she can help me. I tell Irene that I stayed at the Waikiki Winds two weeks ago. I was incredibly satisfied with the exceptional service. The doormen were particularly helpful in carrying my bags, providing directions, and assisting my pregnant wife and invalid mother. Irene tells me she is delighted to hear that.

I nearly flip my Jeep as I try steering with one hand through the heavy Waikiki traffic. I tell Irene that I feel terrible because I lost my wallet early on in my vacation, and I wasn't able to tip the doormen what I felt they deserved. I would like to make up for it by sending the fine fellows a check. Irene assures me that, although it isn't necessary, the doormen would undoubtedly appreciate my good-hearted generosity. I tell Irene that one of the fellows was named Palani, and I ask if he's working today. She tells me no, she's sorry, he's not.

I am cut off by some tourist as I turn onto Kuhio, and I have to momentarily release the wheel to give the son of a bitch the finger. My Jeep swerves and nearly strikes a pole. I regain control and tell Irene that another fellow was just grand, but I didn't catch his name. I describe the individual I saw on the video from the hotel's surveillance camera, the one whom Palani later relieved. Irene tells me yes, she knows him well. His name is James Joyce Fitzpatrick. Everyone calls him J.J.

"That's the one," I tell her. "I knew he went by initials. Is he working today?"

"As a matter of fact, he is. He's working a double shift, so right now he's on an hour break. But he'll be here the rest of the afternoon and all evening."

"Thank you, Irene. I'll call back."

I snap the phone shut, then reopen it to check for missed calls. When I close it again, I look up and see a line of cars stopped at the traffic light. I slam on my brakes, and the Jeep skids fifteen feet to a halt, no more than two inches from a Land Rover stopped in front of me. Goddamn legislature.

After twenty-five minutes of driving around, I find parking in front of the zoo, a mile away from the Waikiki Winds. At least Honolulu resembles Manhattan in *some* ways. I turn onto Kuhio Avenue and go against the tide of tourists. After a couple of blocks, I stop at an athletic-wear store called Niketown.

I first head over to the sneakers and immediately spot a shoe resembling the pair on Joey's feet in the video taken from the Hawaiian Sands hotel. The cross-training shoes are sparkling white with the silver Nike Swoosh insignia. They are endorsed by a superstar professional athlete, who recently got kicked off his team for running his big, fat mouth, the only thing on him that is terribly out of shape. I pick the shoe up, check the price tag, and wince: $169. Plus tax.

I have the inventory of what was found in Joey's hotel room, and the sneakers aren't on it. I checked his feet last week, and Joey definitely isn't wearing them in jail. So where the hell are they? Wherever they are, it can't be good for the defense, since they are already immortalized on video. Even if they are never recovered, the case will be made to the jury: Who would discard a $170 pair of shoes unless he had something to hide? I put the shoe back on its shelf. I'm appalled at the price, but I do take some pleasure in that I earned myself the cost of a pair of these shoes out of the Gianforte retainer in the time it took me to find a parking space.

I purchase for myself a stopwatch, a pair of sunglasses, and a Los Angeles Dodgers baseball cap. I step outside and choose one of the countless ABC Stores littering Waikiki. I go inside and purchase a pack of Kools, the state cigarette of Hawaii.

When I reach the Waikiki Winds, I go to the rear of the hotel. I pull out my new stopwatch and place it around my neck. I put on my sunglasses and pull the Dodgers cap low across my eyes. I take a deep breath, then take off in a sprint.

I run past joggers and bicyclists. I am hit in the grill with barbecue smoke as I run past the park. Less than two minutes into my run, my legs feel like rubber and my chest begins to ache. Exhaustion and bikini-clad women conspire to slow me down, but I push on. I run past palm trees and unlit tiki torches, past statues of surfers adorned with fresh flower leis. I am stared at by swimmers and sunbathers as I eventually reach the spot of beach where Shannon was killed.

I pull out the stopwatch and check the time. Seven minutes and twenty-eight seconds at a full sprint. I rest with my head down and my hands on my knees. I feel as if I might die as I try to catch my breath. So this is why my paralegal bought me a gym membership last Christmas. Maybe I shouldn't have regifted the membership to my receptionist. Chasing ambulances may not be the best idea for me after all. Hell, after this, I may need a ride in the back of one. Shit. The return trip would take days if I tried to run again at full sprint.

Palani is not the killer. Unless he is also secretly the Flash.

As I walk back to the Waikiki Winds, I drip with sweat. The tropical sun beats down on me like an angry, old woman chasing a scared, little mouse with a broom. When I get close to the hotel, I remove the stopwatch from around my neck and place it in my pocket. I pull out the package of Kools and pack it the way I've seen done so many times at bars. I rip open the package and pull a lone cigarette out.

I adjust my cap and sunglasses and place the unlit butt between my lips. It's what I'd imagine shit might taste like. Fortunately, I see J. J. Fitzpatrick standing at the hotel's entrance looking bored.

I make my way over to him, trying not to gag from the cigarette in my mouth.

"You gotta light?" I ask him.

"Sure," he says, digging into his pocket.

J.J.'s face is covered in freckles, something not readily discernible from the surveillance video. He is dressed in a full gray, long-sleeved uniform, something I'd imagine causes him a great deal of discomfort standing hours on end under the hot Hawaiian sun.

J.J. lights me up, and I almost puke. I didn't really think this through.

"Are you a Dodgers fan?" he asks.

"Hell yeah," I lie.

I bought the hat and sunglasses to help hide my face from the hotel's video surveillance cameras. The hat also served to soak up the sweat from my seven-and-a-half-minute bout with death that I called a run. Now it's serving a third purpose.

I try to recall the Dodgers' roster from the dozen or so times I watched them play my New York Mets this past season.

"They need some starting pitching," I guess. What team can't use some strong arms to add to their rotation?

The conversation goes from the Dodgers to the Lakers to the Oakland Raiders, and I can tell he's pleased to have someone with whom he can shoot the shit and pass the time. Guests of the hotel constantly interrupt by asking him for directions and restaurant recommendations, making it difficult for me to segue from sports to cold-blooded killing.

A band of Japanese tourists asks J.J. to take their picture, and I decide that when he is done, I'll ask him to join me for a beer at the Bleu Sharq after he gets through with work.

The sound of screeching tires causes me to turn around. That's when I see him, coming at me from behind. Palani's eyes target me like a sniper setting his sight.

"Ey!" he shouts at me. "What the fuck you doing here?"

J.J. looks back toward me, confused.

"I just—"

"You just what?" Palani yells.

The Japanese tourists look on in wonder as Palani grabs me by the collar of my T, lifting me a half inch off the ground. His head moves in as he eyes me down, knocking the Dodgers cap off my head. So much for my brilliant disguise.

"You ask more questions? You talk stink, haole?" he shouts.

Before I can answer, he throws me backward onto the ground. I land hard on the cement, my back bearing the brunt of the fall. He hovers over me as I twist my body to rise. As I try to get to my feet, Palani hits me squarely in the left eye. My head slams backward and bounces off the cement. He drops down on top of me and lands another strike, this one to my jaw.

My vision blurs and I begin to lose consciousness. Through the white fog washing over me, I can make out three men pulling Palani off my chest. I hear his voice as if through a phone. It tails off as he curses me, warns me away. Away from him. Away from his friends. Away from his job.

I feel nauseous as I spit some blood onto the pavement beside me. I can already feel the knot forming at the back of my skull. The pain washes over me like a twenty-foot wave up North Shore. I try to smile but it hurts too damn much. If I can get him to do this to me at trial, if I can cause him to lose his temper on the stand, the jury might just suspend disbelief and think him the killer of Shannon

Douglas after all. I may not need to prove he could run back and forth to the beach in less than fifteen minutes. I may not need to prove he's the Flash. I may not need to show that he's capable of any spectacular athletic feats at all.

Then I see what lies at Palani's feet. As he looks back at me where I lie bloodied on the ground, I'm finally able, despite the pain, to manage a smile.

I need not prove he could run back and forth in fifteen minutes. I need not prove he's the Flash. I need not prove he's capable of any spectacular athletic feats at all.

The fucker drives a moped.

CHAPTER 25

Less than two hours after my ass-kicking, I find myself on the road to Kailua. I am sore, light-headed, and more than a little concussed. Yet somehow I am certain Nikki can provide me more comfort than the entire staff at the Queen's Medical Center.

I use my time on the road to recount the suspects. That way, I can bill the Gianfortes for my travels. There is Palani Kanno and J. J. Fitzpatrick, Tony Bitch-Tits and Lazy Eye Sal. And, of course, there is Professor Jim Catus. I have learned that the Hawaiian word for "teacher" is *kumu*. Ironically, it is also the Hawaiian word for "lover." Sure, that tidbit might be a bit extraneous, but since I may eventually use it in my opening statement at trial, the time I took to find it out is billable all the same.

The New Jersey Mafia is watching me, and a local doorman wants my head. Yet I am in a delightful mood. You see, after having my head pounded into the cement,

I stopped in to see Flan at his office downtown. I was none too comforted to see that he keeps a copy of the *Complete Idiot's Guide to Private Investigating* faceup on his desk. Nevertheless, I told him what happened, expecting him to urge me to a hospital. But he did no such thing. Instead he pulled from his desk drawer a bottle of prescription pills. He opened the bottle and emptied a half dozen Vicodin into his hand. He turned them over to me with instructions to take one pill every six hours that I experience pain. He has been taking them ever since his accident in New Orleans. They are heavy-duty, he told me. Be careful how many you take.

Well, I'm not one to take much care. So I ate half of them in the elevator heading back downstairs to my Jeep. It's now forty-five minutes later, and I'm so giddy, I'm inclined to gather Flan and Nikki together for a party at Pearl Harbor. We can call Jake and Hoshi and invite them both, too. Hell, we'll ring the Waikiki Winds and see if Palani and J.J. would like to join us. And while we're at it, why not Tony Bitch-Tits and Lazy Eye Sal?

As I pull into Nikki's driveway, I hear shouting coming from inside her cottage, and I'm suddenly aware that I'm arriving unannounced. I shut off the engine and jump out of my Jeep, eyeing the red front door and trying to imagine what's transpiring behind it. My first thought stings, though it's entirely unfamiliar to me: what if it's another guy?

Just as I reach the welcome mat the door swings open and a young Hawaiian man pushes past me, nearly knocking me over. "Out my fucking way, haole," he says, heading toward the street in a hurry.

I turn back toward the door and see Nikki, soaking wet, wearing a thin, white robe, clearly angry but not sobbing.

"What happened to your face?" she cries.

My head swings back toward the street, my eyes following the man who just barreled past me.

"My brother," she says, then steps aside and motions me in.

A wave of relief rushes through me as I step inside.

I thought about what to tell her during my drive here. I haven't told her much of anything about Joey's case, and she's been kind enough not to prod. So I have decided to repay that kindness with yet another lie.

"Road rage," I tell her, pointing to my bruised eye.

She tells me to wait in the small foyer as she runs into the kitchen. She brings ice from the freezer and a pink towel from the linen closet and applies them gently to my face. She sprinkles me with kisses, warm and wet, and, I must say, much more effective than the ice.

Nikki brings me to her room, this time illuminated by a lamp. She motions me to the bed and apologizes for the room's disarray.

"It's a sign of genius," I tell her.

She seems unconvinced. She works furiously to return clothes to her closet, ledgers and loose papers to their drawers. She sweeps away hair and beauty items, mementos, and carefully cropped photographs, undoubtedly of lovers past.

As she continues to tidy, her robe comes open, and it's all I can do to stay seated on the bed. "My mother," she says, "rest her soul, used to keep everything so neat and clean. When she first started using ice, she became compulsive about cleanliness. After a few hits off the pipe, she would tidy and scrub for hours on end. Then as the addiction grew worse, she stopped doing everything. Except getting high."

Nikki looks so amazing, I'm not listening to a word she says.

"What was that scene with your brother?" I ask, hoping I won't discover four slashed tires when I leave.

"Nothing," she says, avoiding my eyes. "He hasn't come home the last few nights. He says he's only selling, but I'm pretty sure he's using. He seems wired whenever I see him. And he's growing more and more paranoid."

Finally finished tidying, Nikki takes a seat next to me on the bed. I push aside her wet, jet-black hair so that my lips might find her neck. She smells like a sweet spring day. Any worries I had about how the Vicodin would affect me downstairs quickly diminish as my left hand reaches into her robe. We fall back on the bed, our bodies melting together like wax. And in the quiet of the Kailua night, we make love with the lights on, not once but twice.

Nikki falls asleep at my side, and I wait a half hour before awakening her with my kiss good-night.

"Stay," she purrs. "Please stay the night."

"I wish I could, Nikki. But I have a long day ahead of me tomorrow. I'm meeting Jake and Flan at nine in the morning to go over the Gianforte case. I requested an initial pretrial conference to discuss some discovery issues, and it's been scheduled for this Thursday. We have to get all of our ducks in a row before then."

"Just stay," she begs. "You can leave early in the morning."

"Sorry, Nikki, but traffic into Honolulu during rush hour is murder."

CHAPTER 26

It is difficult to become completely lost on an island of merely six hundred square miles. Yet somehow I have managed to do just that on my way home from Nikki's cottage in Kailua. I am searching, so far in vain, for signs for the Pali Highway, but none are in sight. The narrow two-lane road I am cruising on is illuminated by nothing but the headlights of my Jeep, and I am growing more and more anxious and frustrated as time passes. To make matters worse, not a single decent song is playing on the radio at this late hour.

As I curse at myself for getting lost, another pair of headlights become visible in my rearview mirror. I slow my Jeep, hoping the other vehicle will pass me. At least I'll have someone to follow, hopefully back to what passes for civilization here on the islands. Only the vehicle behind me seems to slow down, too. Then, on the roof of the car, a flashing blue light begins spinning like mad.

A mixed blessing, I suppose.

I pull my Jeep to the side of the road, and the other vehicle pulls up behind. In my rearview mirror, I can make out two men exiting from either side of an unmarked car, a dark blue midsize sedan. Both men are dressed in suits, and one of them carries a flashlight.

I pull my wallet from my back pocket and find my Hawaii driver's license, registration, and insurance. I know the drill. When I turn to roll my window farther down, the flashlight glares in my face.

"Step out of the vehicle."

Before I can move, my door is opened for me, and a firm hand grasps me by the left arm, tugging me out of the Jeep. I stumble and nearly fall as my feet hit the gravel.

"What the fuck?" I say.

"Keep your mouth shut!"

I struggle as I'm pulled from one side and pushed on the other toward the hood of the dark blue sedan. One of them grabs me by the back of my hair, just above the knot on my skull, and slams my face onto the hood, causing a loud thump. My nose stings with pain and my eyes immediately tear. I see blood dripping on the hood and know that it's mine. Fear courses through me. I am suddenly aware of just how dark and secluded this roadway really is.

My right arm is twisted even farther behind my back, and I yelp in pain. I've changed my mind about police brutality. I am so completely and utterly against it. It is cowardly and morally reprehensible. I see the error in the conclusions I came to at the Whale Watcher Bar & Grill.

"We're going to do you a tremendous favor, Mr. Corvelli," says a deep voice hovering just above my right ear. "We're going to narrow down your investigation into the murder of Shannon Douglas."

My right arm is at its limit. Something must be broken or torn inside. Blood continues to spew from my nose onto the hood. I am feeling faint.

"You can stop looking at Lopardi and Antonazzo beginning tonight," continues the voice. "This will allow you to focus your attention on more viable suspects. In the end, you'll thank us for it. We're helping you avoid another debacle like Brandon Glenn."

The mere mention of Brandon Glenn gets my adrenaline pumping. I spit some blood on their hood and speak.

"Are you gentlemen associates of Mr. Lopardi and Mr. Antonazzo?"

"No," says the voice with a sinister chuckle. "We're a slightly higher species. We're with the Bureau."

My first feeling is one of relief, however slight. Milt Cashman's inquiries must have generated some buzz within the Bureau. Perhaps the late Ben Franklin isn't as loyal to Milt as he once was. Whatever the case, the Feds have entered the fray. And I want to know why.

"What's your interest in the Gianforte case?" I manage.

The grip on my right arm is slightly released.

"We have an open investigation into the Fiordano syndicate, and you're jeopardizing it. Not only that, you're putting agents' lives at risk."

So that is what this is. An interagency struggle. The

Feds are close to taking down Senior, maybe even Louis Fiordano himself. They don't want the Honolulu Police Department barging in and mucking it all up.

"Lopardi and Antonazzo can be taken down for the Douglas murder," I say. "Once they're in custody, you go to work on getting them to flip. If they're facing life, one of them will sing, and you'll have your target, whoever it is."

"We can't do that."

"Why the hell not?"

"Because Lopardi and Antonazzo didn't commit the Douglas murder, Counselor."

"How the hell do you know?" I say.

"Because they have alibis."

"Who? Each other?"

"No," he says. "Their alibis are a little stronger than that."

"Let me guess. Priests?"

"Close. Federal agents."

"Are you telling me agents have been tailing Lopardi and Antonazzo since they came to the island?"

"We've already told you more than you need to know."

"If you want me off their tails," I say, "I need to know what the hell they were doing here in the first place."

He tightens the grip on my right arm, and a shrill sound escapes my mouth. If I want any more information, it'll come, if it comes at all, with a price.

"We're not here to satisfy your idle curiosity, Corvelli. But, if you must know, they came to follow the Gianforte boy, to make sure he didn't go and get himself into any kind of trouble."

"Well," I manage through deep breaths, "they did one hell of a job."

"The boy spotted Lopardi and Antonazzo tailing him, and he lost them. Instead of trying to find him, Lopardi and Antonazzo decided to go to a strip club and get tanked. The boy's father doesn't know that part, or Lopardi and Antonazzo would probably be floating facedown in the Pacific by now."

"Shannon Douglas was killed because of her role in the Fiordano investigation, wasn't she?" I say, fear still evident in my voice. "Don't you have an interest in helping to find her killer?"

"The Honolulu Police Department already found her killer, Counselor. It's your client."

"Bullshit."

"You saw the photos, Corvelli. You know how she was killed. Does that look like a professional hit to you?"

"Not all professionals do things by the book," I say. "Otherwise, I wouldn't be in this goddamn armlock, having this conversation with you with my face buried in the hood of your car."

He loosens his grip. But not by much.

"You're not looking for the killer, Corvelli. You're looking for reasonable doubt. And you better start looking elsewhere, because Lopardi and Antonazzo are off-limits. Do you understand me, you fucking shark?"

Anything other than a yes and my arm would be snapped in two.

He lifts me off my feet and drags me to the side of the

road. He throws me to the ground, and I have some dirt to wash down the taste of their hood. I feel a steady, warm trickle down from my nose and onto my upper lip. I touch it, and my finger turns a familiar shade of crimson.

Their headlights smack me in the face as they turn back onto the blacktop. As I watch their taillights speed away down the dark roadway, I realize I forgot to ask one more question. One question, the answer to which would have solved the greatest problem I now face. The one problem that, if left unsolved, renders all other problems in my life and law practice utterly meaningless.

I am still lost.

CHAPTER 27

"Well, that wasn't very aloha of him," says Jake, eyeing the bruises Palani tattooed on my face. Jake has a look on his own face as if he just discovered a long, black hair in his soup. "That shiner will get worse before it gets better," he adds helpfully.

This morning we sit in the conference room waiting for Flan. I've told Jake about my entire yesterday, from the point I left him here to go out for my run.

"Let Flan interview the professor's prostitute," he says, taking a hit off his flask. "He's doing a fine job with Carlie Douglas so far as we know. Besides, at the rate you're going, she and her pimp will be bitch-slapping you all the way down Kuhio if you show up at the Leilani Inn for a chat."

"Fine," I say. "I'll let him interview the bellhops, too. And J. J. Fitzpatrick. We'll need to know where he went after he left the Waikiki Winds that night. Or at least, where he'll say he went."

"So, we have the professor, who has four alibis. We have Evil Knievel and his moped. We have J. J. Fitzpatrick, who has no discernible motive or opportunity. I've got to tell you, son, it doesn't look good."

"And we have the mob."

"Are you kidding me? After what the Feds told you? The agents were watching Lopardi and Antonazzo like hawks. You can't finger those two as suspects anymore."

"There was a third man," I tell Jake, "one the agents didn't mention last night."

"You said there were only two goons at the aquarium."

"Someone else pulled Nikki away by asking her for help feeding the sea lions. Then he disappeared. That's how Lopardi and Antonazzo were able to get me alone for so long."

"How do you know it wasn't just a coincidence, son?"

"There are no coincidences. Right, Jake?"

"I believe I said *juries* don't buy into coincidences."

"Well," I say, "this was no coincidence. In fact, the woman at the front desk at the aquarium also said she saw three men leave together."

"Your girlfriend, Nikki, saw this third guy. Can she identify him from the photographs Cashman had sent to you?"

I pause at the mention of her name, but more so at her being labeled my girlfriend. I haven't thought of her as my girlfriend; I simply don't think in those dimensions. I don't want Nikki to become involved in Joey's murder case. She knows I represent Joey and she knows what she has read in the papers, but that is essentially all she knows. I never talk to her about the case. She doesn't know about the Mafia soldiers at the aquarium. She doesn't know Palani roughed me up. She doesn't know about my late-night run-in with the Feds. But she may be the only one who can identify this third man.

I nod my head solemnly. "I'll ask her."

The mood in the conference room has suddenly shifted, and Jake's voice takes on a serious tone. "Kevin." It is, perhaps, the first time Jake's used my first name. Not that I mind him calling me *son*. He puts the flask to his lips to help him say whatever he has to say. "I'm sorry I got you involved in all of this."

"You have no reason to apologize."

"Yes, I do."

"What is it, Jake?"

"I owe you a tremendous apology, Kevin." He finishes off his flask. His eyes are moist, his voice strained. "When you walked in here two weeks ago today, you breathed new life into this office. There I was, on the brink of retirement, handling petty crimes, misdemeanors, traffic tickets, jaywalking citations. And I saw in you a possibility, a possibility to get back in the game. I knew I couldn't do it myself. Not at my age. Not with my drinking."

"Jake, you didn't hold a gun to my head."

"I might as well have. The way I dangled that fifty-thousand-dollar check in front of you."

"You were right to do it. I needed the money, Jake. Joey's

parents came to you, and you were good enough to offer them to me."

He eyes his empty flask, wishing it full. "That's not quite how it happened, son."

"What do you mean, Jake?"

"Before we left for Sand Bar with Hoshi that first day, I told you I had to make one phone call. The phone call I made was to a friend of mine at the jail. A deputy sheriff. I had read about Joey's arrest in the newspaper. I asked my friend if the Gianforte boy was lawyered up yet. He told me no, the boy's parents had just arrived at the jail. I told him to give the parents my number, to tell them that there's an aggressive, young attorney from New York in town. A hotshot that specializes in violent felonies. I told my friend to tell the parents that his name is Kevin Corvelli."

I sit stone still, silent as a tomb. He waits for my reaction, his eyes holding back tears, his face full of regret. I lean forward on the conference-room table. I stare him dead in the eyes.

And let out a long, hearty laugh.

"Jake, the reason I wanted to forgo felonies for misdemeanors wasn't that I disliked the work. I disliked myself. And I disliked the way I handled the work. In New York, I was a criminal attorney for all the wrong reasons. The money and the spotlight were all that mattered to me. The client was nothing more than a means to an end. I felt like a fraud. Hell, I *was* a fraud. I wanted to win only so I could say I won. I was scared to pick up here in Honolulu right where I left off in Manhattan. But I don't think I have.

"My priorities have changed a lot, even in the past two weeks. Just as you said they would. I am handling Joey's case in a way I'm comfortable with. I made a promise to him, and I'm sticking to it. I am glad that I took this case. And no Mafia soldier or federal agent or local punk with a good right hook is going to change that. And they sure as hell aren't going to succeed in scaring me off. My greatest fear was that Joey Gianforte was my next Brandon Glenn. But I think Joey is more like me than anyone else. So I suppose my utter selfishness will be an asset to him. Because I don't think either of us deserve to spend the rest of our lives rotting in prison."

Jake fiddles with his empty flask. I sit back and get comfortable in my conference-room chair. Despite everything that's happened, I feel oddly at ease.

"I admire you for that," says Jake, "and I sympathize with your plight. But you can't let your own future hang on the fate of this case. The cards are stacked against us. The circumstantial evidence is overwhelming, and we'd be fools to think some physical evidence is not forthcoming. Prosecutors can be crafty sons of bitches, whether in New York or in Houston, or even in Honolulu."

"I realize that, Jake. We're conferencing the case before the judge the day after tomorrow. In all likelihood, that's when we'll see their hand."

Jake and I push the file aside and wait for Flan. We take the time to talk about the things men talk about when they're not talking about homicide. We talk baseball and beer, starlets and hard liquor. In the middle of a full-throttle belly laugh over Buckner's error in '86, we are interrupted by Hoshi's voice over the intercom.

"Mr. Corvelli, Mr. Flanagan is here to see you and Mr. Harper."

"*Mahalo,* Hoshi," I say. "Send Mr. Flanagan directly to the conference room."

Sixty seconds later, the conference-room door opens and a somber Ryan Flanagan steps in.

"Gentlemen," he says, "we have a serious problem."

CHAPTER 28

The courtroom is silent. It's the kind of silence that looms in the principal's office as your less-than-exemplary conduct report is being reviewed. You could hear a pin drop. And if I had one, I'd drop it to prove just that. But I don't. So I stand silent, biting my nails, while Judge Hideki Narita mulls over, with great displeasure on his face, the news he just heard.

Judge Hideki Narita, I've learned, is a former prosecuting attorney from the Big Island of Hawaii. A paunchy Japanese man in his midsixties, he has been on the bench for more than eleven years. His face is framed by short, jet-black hair, and he wears glasses three times the size of his face. Standing five foot five with the absurdly large spectacles, he would make a comic figure if not for his no-nonsense demeanor and quick trigger-finger when it comes to charging lawyers with contempt.

"Mr. Corvelli," Narita says from the bench, "am I hearing this correctly? Your investigator, a Mr. Ryan Flanagan, befriended the victim's mother under the guise of a griev-ing father in order to obtain from her information about the victim herself?"

I am in trouble. Jake was right. The practices that were acceptable in the Wild West courtrooms of Manhattan do not necessarily fly here in paradise. This is the serious problem Flan brought to my office two days ago. Luckily, we had forty-eight hours to devise some sort of strategy. Luckily, too, I am heavily skilled in the art of bullshit.

"Your Honor," I say, "the issue is not as cut-and-dry as that."

"Judge, if I may," says the prosecuting attorney, cutting me off. "Ms. Carlie Douglas discovered in Mr. Flanagan's wallet evidence of his true identity and his relation to Mr. Corvelli's law firm in the form of business cards and tele-phone messages."

The prosecuting attorney is Donovan Watanabe, a tall and lanky Japanese man in his late thirties, who is believed by many to be the most dynamic and effective prosecutor in the state of Hawaii. His meticulous style and superex-pensive wardrobe have earned him the nickname Dapper Don in legal circles around the islands.

"How did Ms. Douglas come to observe the contents of Mr. Flanagan's wallet?" asks Narita.

In New York, I often felt like an outsider not being Jew-ish. I was sure that judges were conversing with my adver-saries in Yiddish behind my back. Here, now, I feel much the same way. The Japanese culture, I've read, is based largely on honor, something I know nothing about. And it seems unfair that my Japanese adversary and I have drawn a Japanese judge.

Dapper Don Watanabe takes a deep breath and pauses for dramatic effect. He exhales slowly, turns to me, and asks, "Would you like to tell the judge or shall I?"

"Be my guest," I tell him. Although I'm not exactly sure what the hell he's about to say.

"Mr. Flanagan," Dapper Don says, "was taking a shower in Ms. Douglas's hotel room, Your Honor, after he engaged in sexual relations with her."

This Flan did not tell us. He told me he got made but nothing more. And, yes, I'm certain he said *made,* not *laid.* My poker face vanishes from the room, and my eyes dart to Flan, who is seated alone in the front row behind the defense table. Luckily, the judge cleared the courtroom for our appearance. I look at Flan in disbelief, mouthing the words, "You *slept* with her?"

Flan shrugs as if to say he's guilty as charged.

I turn back to the bench, where the judge seems as shocked as I am.

"You mentioned 'his true identity,'" says the judge. "You mean to say he lied to her about who he was?"

"Your Honor," says Dapper Don, "he told the victim's grieving mother his name was Benjamin Dover."

Ben Dover? Are you shitting me? I look back at Flan, whose face seems to have contorted into a permanent grimace. That's the last time I let an investigator choose his own fake name.

"Your Honor," I say, trying to clean the shit from the fan, "even if these allegations are true, they have no bearing on this case. I submit to you that they are brought before the Court by Mr. Watanabe in an effort to cast dispersions on the defense, and on me in particular. Frankly, I am outraged by Mr. Watanabe's conduct in bringing this matter to the Court's attention. He knows as well as anyone that the defense has every legal right to hire investigators to interview witnesses and obtain information by any lawful means necessary. As Your Honor well knows, some witnesses are less forthcoming than others, and certain strategies must be employed in order to extract vital information that is crucial to the defense."

Narita holds his right hand in the air. He's heard enough bullshit. He wants me to reholster my shovel. If I get through this one unscathed, I'll send a copy of today's transcript to Milt Cashman in New York. He'll get a real kick out of something like this.

"Enough, Counselor," says Narita. "While the actions taken by the defense are appalling to this Court to say the least, they are not, to my knowledge, unlawful. The ethical issues concerning Mr. Corvelli's so-called strategies are not for this Court to address. This Court will, however, remind Mr. Corvelli that this is *not* New York City, and that whatever tactics he employed on the island of Manhattan may not be well received here on the island of Oahu. If this charade is indicative of the way you practice law, Mr. Corvelli, then you not only risk becoming a fast outcast in the legal community here on the islands, but you risk becoming the subject of inquiry by the state's ethics committee. Is that understood, Counselor?"

"Yes, Your Honor."

"Good," says the judge. "Then let's move on to more pressing matters."

Judge Narita leafs through his file, no doubt searching for the recent motion I filed.

"Mr. Corvelli, you have requested a gag order in this case. Tell me why I should grant it."

"Your Honor," I say, "cases of this nature are not news. The media exploits them not for the benefit of the public, but for the benefit of their own ratings. They are intended to appeal to the public's voyeuristic proclivities and serve no redeeming social purpose. This case in particular is being buoyed in the national news media by comparing this case with events in the Caribbean. In fact, much of the commentary on this case has been prefaced by videos and photographs connected to other island fiascoes. Before long, the commentators will be questioning the Hawaiian system of justice."

"Mr. Corvelli," interrupts Narita, "enough of the rhetoric. You said in your motion papers that this attention is negatively affecting your client's ability to gain a fair trial. Tell me how that is so."

"Firstly, Your Honor, the public here on Oahu will inevitably fear the backlash of the negative national attention that would come with an unpopular verdict. Simply put, the media's continued coverage of this case will all but assure a verdict of guilty against my client."

"Well, Counselor," says Narita, "even a gag order will not prevent the media from covering this case."

"Of course not, Your Honor. But it *will* prevent all parties involved from adding fuel to the fire. When defense attorneys, prosecutors, and victims' families are permitted to give constant interviews, it allows for endless around-the-clock coverage that could not otherwise occur if everyone were ordered silent."

"You said in your papers that there was specific information about your client's associations that was in imminent danger of being released."

"I did, Your Honor. Which brings me to my second point. Upon information and belief, Ms. Carlie Douglas is alleging that my client is associated with a northern New Jersey Mafia family. In fact, she alluded to this allegation in an interview with Gretchen Hurst two weeks ago. Obviously, this allegation would be highly prejudicial to my client, and should the allegation be made public, it would make it utterly impossible for my client to receive a fair trial."

"Mr. Watanabe, what say you on this matter?"

There is little Dapper Don can argue. Clearly, he would love to try this case in the press. It is a prosecutor's wet dream. A Mafia son accused of killing a bright, beautiful, young girl in a tropical setting. But Dapper Don can't tell the judge that. All he can argue is that my allegations are unfounded.

"Judge," Dapper Don says, "the prosecution has no intention of trying this case in the press."

I haven't heard a crock of shit like that since I last spoke.

"We are only vaguely aware of the defendant's criminal associations," Dapper Don continues, "and we do not intend to inform anyone about these associations, particularly members of the press. We, therefore, see no legal justification for the issuance of a gag order in this case."

"Thank you, Mr. Watanabe," says Narita. "As you know, I do not favor having cameras in the courtroom. If I wanted to be on television, I would have become an actor."

"And you would have been a fine one at that, Your Honor," I say.

The judge continues as if I hadn't spoken. "As you also know, I am very opposed to having lawyers try their cases in the press, particularly when there is so much at stake. Although I have Mr. Watanabe's assurances that the prosecution does not intend to do just that, I am still inclined to grant Mr. Corvelli's request for a gag order. The details will be set out in my order. Any violation will result in a charge of contempt of this Court."

I consider this a major victory on two levels. One, it will spare my client's chance at getting a fair trial. Two, it will spare me the need to go on the record to defend the relentless allegations about my client's family, and about his past. Not to mention, allegations about my own history. Of course, Milt would never have filed this motion. Neither would have the Kevin Corvelli of old.

"Now," says Narita, "I understand there are some evidentiary issues that need to be addressed."

"Yes, Judge," says Dapper Don. "There is some newly

discovered evidence, which we are prepared to hand over to the defense. This evidence would have been turned over in due course without the need for the Court's intervention, but Mr. Corvelli seems to be a less-than-patient man."

"Just proceed, Mr. Watanabe," says the judge.

"There were two discoveries, Your Honor," says Dapper Don. "The first is a latent print found in the abandoned lifeguard station at the scene of the crime."

What the hell is this? I bite my nail and my knees begin to knock.

"How can that be?" I ask. "We were told there were no fingerprints found anywhere at the scene."

"That is correct, Counselor," Dapper Don says directly to me. "There were no fingerprints found anywhere at the scene."

"Then, just what the hell are you talking about?"

"A *lip* print. Your client's lip print was discovered at the scene."

CHAPTER 29

I know all about lip prints. I wrote my final paper on lip prints for my forensic science class at the University of Rhode Island. I received a B on the paper, but it deserved an A. The professor deducted points because I hardly ever showed up for class, and I slept through most of the ones I did show up for. And I don't think he much cared for the title: "Be Careful Who You Blow: How a Misplaced Lip Print Can Land You in the Slammer." Fortunately, I've never had to deal with this pseudoscience in real life. Lip-print identification is rarely used by law enforcement, and lip-print comparisons are hardly ever admissible in court.

"Your Honor," says Dapper Don Watanabe, "the prosecution intends to introduce evidence at trial of the defendant's presence at the crime scene in the form of impression evidence, specifically through a latent lip print found on the inside portion of the Plexiglas at the lifeguard station a few yards away from where the victim's body was discovered."

"Judge," I scoff, "this is ridiculous."

"Allow Mr. Watanabe to finish, Counselor," Narita admonishes me.

Dapper Don clears his throat and continues, "A police-lab forensic scientist specializing in latent-print examination will testify that lip prints, like fingerprints and other impression evidence, are unique and can be used to positively identify an individual."

I can't help but roll my eyes, and Judge Narita catches the gesture. He warns me not to continue with the theatrics.

Dapper Don seems downright insulted. He clears his throat again and continues, "The forensic scientist will further testify that she performed a side-by-side comparison of the lip print taken from the lifeguard station and a sample taken from the defendant. She will testify that upon thorough examination, she concluded that the lip print found in the lifeguard station was, indeed, left by the defendant."

"Thank you, Mr. Watanabe," says the judge. "Now, Mr. Corvelli, what say you on the matter?"

"Your Honor, lip-print identification is novel scientific evidence at best. It is seldom used by law enforcement agencies because it is completely unreliable. Very little research has been conducted in the field. Clearly, this kind of pseudoscience has no place in the courtroom, and any evidence of so-called lip-print identification *must* be excluded."

After some further back-and-forth, Narita raises his hand and speaks loudly and clearly for the record. "The prosecution will be permitted to introduce evidence of lip-print identification through their expert witness upon establishing the expertise of that witness during voir dire outside the presence of the jury."

"Your Honor," I say, my voice raised in anger, "at the very least, the defense is entitled to a full hearing specifically on the issue of whether lip-print identification is scientific evidence at all."

"Mr. Corvelli," says Narita, "I have made my decision. You will be permitted to cross-examine the prosecution's witness in order to attempt to discredit her as an expert outside the presence of the jury. If she qualifies as an expert witness and takes the stand at trial, you will be permitted to cross-examine her in an attempt to discredit her findings. And you, of course, will be permitted to have your own expert testify during your case-in-chief."

"But, Your Honor—," I try.

"Enough, Counselor!" Narita yells, banging his gavel. "Oral argument has concluded and I've given my decision."

Bang your gavel at me, will you? "I want it noted for the record—"

"You have made your record, Mr. Corvelli!"

"This is preposterous!" I yell. "Lip prints aren't admissible scientific evidence! With all due respect, Judge, where are we? On an episode of *CSI: Hawaii*?"

"One more word from you on this subject, Mr. Corvelli,

and you will spend the night in the county jail on an order of contempt of this Court!"

I silence myself. *Thou shalt not be held in contempt of court.*

Narita angrily shuffles his papers. I'd like to pluck his giant glasses from his little face and punch him square in the nose. Instead I bite my nail and wait a full five minutes for him to speak again.

"The next issue raised in Mr. Corvelli's papers," says Narita, "is the defendant's misdemeanor conviction in New York for assault and battery. Mr. Watanabe, what say you on this matter?"

"Your Honor," says Dapper Don, "this conviction is crucial evidence of motive. The defendant pled guilty to a violent crime against the victim, which ultimately shattered his hopes of becoming an attorney. It caused him to drop out of law school, and then, the victim ended their relationship. This perceived betrayal by the victim clearly goes to the defendant's motive for killing her, Judge."

"Your Honor," I say calmly, "introducing evidence of a prior assault by the defendant against the victim would, of course, be highly prejudicial. And that prejudice, of course, would far, far outweigh the limited probative value that the prosecution is contending this conviction has. This conviction *must* be excluded."

Dapper Don has the look of a cat ready to pounce on a tiny mouse. "Judge, a witness will testify that the defendant took the plea only to keep the victim from being charged with making a false statement."

"Firstly, Judge," I say, "the testimony of this witness, whoever it is, would amount to nothing more than hearsay. Secondly, Mr. Watanabe's argument is counterintuitive. He wants to introduce evidence of an assault and then say it wasn't an assault. He can't have his sushi and eat it, too."

Dapper Don pulls a single paper from his file. "Judge, as to the hearsay argument, the prosecution will produce an e-mail communication from the defendant to the witness, one Cynthia DuFrain, which will describe in great detail his motivations for taking the plea. We will concede that in the defendant's mind, he may have felt that no assault took place. But in reality, Your Honor, the hospital records from Lennox Hill clearly show otherwise."

"Judge," I say, "there is absolutely no basis—"

"Enough, Counselor," says Narita, cutting me off again. "I am inclined to allow evidence of the conviction to show motive. Clearly, it is a paradox, Mr. Corvelli. A paradox you will have to address on cross-examination and in your case-in-chief."

I stare at Narita, a pulsating look of anger mixed with incredulousness. I grab my briefcase from the floor and drop it with an echoing thud onto the defense table. I open it and begin to pack away my papers.

"Your Honor," says Dapper Don from across the aisle, "there is one more discovery issue we have yet to address."

Dread slinks down my spine from the sheer tone of his voice. I turn and see Flan exiting the courtroom.

Dapper Don clears his throat and continues, "Police

discovered, near the scene of the crime, a pair of sneakers we believe belong to the defendant in this case."

I turn my head to look at Dapper Don. He's wearing a smile, the first I've seen on his face.

"They are a pair of Nike cross-training shoes," he says. "And they are spattered with the victim's blood."

CHAPTER 30

After being tossed around court like a rag doll this morning, I could use a drink or twelve. Fortunately, Nikki worked the early lunch shift today, and she has agreed to meet me at Aqua Bar in Waikiki for some drinks after she's relieved at the Bleu Sharq. My meeting with Nikki will not be all pleasure today. It will include some business, though I'm hoping a fair share of pleasure will find its way into the meeting, too. With the lip print, misdemeanor conviction, and blood-splattered sneakers all waiting for us at trial, it has become all the more important that I find Shannon's real killer, since it is all the less likely I'll be able to create, in the minds of the jurors, a reasonable doubt. Thus, tonight, I'll ask Nikki the question every girl dreams of being asked: can you identify the man who asked you to help feed the sea lions at the aquarium?

I arrive at Aqua Bar twenty minutes earlier than our scheduled rendezvous time. As one would guess, the bar boasts an overly aquatic theme. The walls are more fish tank than plaster, and the dance floor is some clear gelatinous substance that houses more fish than most lakes. Boat bottoms are above our heads, and man-made coral lines the floor. The only redeeming feature of the motif is the staff's sexy costumes. Every woman working at the bar is dressed like a mermaid, complete with sexy swimsuit tops and fins.

I find an empty clam-shaped stool at the end of the bar. It, like all of my seats of late, faces the entrance. I am far more vigilant since my recent run-ins with Palani and the Feds and my oversize *paisan*.

A green-eyed mermaid swims over to me and asks me what I'll have. "I totally recommend our Shipwreck on Ice," she says. "It's strong, and oh, so good."

I'm in no mood to experiment. I want something I know will get the job done. So I order up my faithful Scotch. "Thank you, but I'll have a double Glenlivet on the rocks."

She gives me a wink and shimmies on over to the top shelf. I grab the knot in my tie and loosen it, so that I can breathe.

The bartender returns with my drink. "Why are you all dressed up?"

That's something you'd never hear in Manhattan. "I'm a lawyer. I had court today."

She leans into the bar, her cleavage inching closer to my drink. "Ahhh, what kind of lawyer are you?"

"A criminal defense attorney," I say, checking my drink for fish.

She takes my silk tie in her hand, pulling me closer to her. Her fragrance is dizzying, and I wonder how long she'll spend working the tip. "Do you like being a lawyer?"

"Not today," I manage to say, my eyes moving from her mermaid lips, down her mermaid shoulders, to her mermaid ti—

Just then I spot Nikki, standing at the entrance, still as a statue, gazing angrily at my Scotch. Or, maybe even at me.

I take back my tie, drop a twenty on the bar, and head over to Nikki. I lead her by the arm to a booth in the corner. She's scoffing at me before I have the chance to slide in across from her.

"Who the hell is she?" Nikki asks without looking at me.

"The bartender?" I ask, donning my mask of incredulousness.

She nods like one extremely pissed-off bobblehead doll.

"She's the bartender," I say lamely.

"Why was she touching you?"

"She wasn't touching me. She was touching my tie."

Nikki tilts her head to one side and glares at me. "Why was she touching your tie?"

"Because she likes it."

A grim smirk plays on her lips. "If she tells you she likes your cock, are you going to let her touch that, too?"

Is this what a relationship is like? No wonder I avoided one for so long. No wonder Milt has gone through so many wives.

"Nikki, what's wrong?" I ask with a sigh.

"What's wrong is that I walked in here and found you flirting with some haole slut."

"She's the *bartender*."

"So. Was. I."

A valid point. I fear I'm losing my second argument of the day. Time for the champ to change the subject. "Would you like a drink?"

"Are you cheating on me?" she asks in a controlled, even tone.

"Of course not."

"Are we even together?"

"Sure, we're together," I say. "We're seated in the same booth."

Nikki doesn't like my joke. "Will you drive me home, please? I'm not in the mood for drinks anymore."

A merman steps up to our table and kills what was left of my underwater fantasy. I tell him we changed our minds, and Nikki and I get up to leave.

We take my Jeep to the windward side of Oahu. Despite several of my attempts at conversation, Nikki refuses to speak more than a word or two. I pull into her driveway and wait, hoping she will still invite me in.

"You don't want to come in, do you?" she finally says.

Close enough. "Yeah, sure, I'll come in for a while."

I step around the Jeep and remove my briefcase from the trunk. We step inside the empty cottage and go directly to her room. It's far more orderly than it was the last time I was here. No clothes are strewn about the room.

No ledgers or loose papers are scattered over her desk. The hair and beauty items are aligned neatly on her dresser. The mementos and photographs are nowhere to be seen.

She doesn't say a word for she does not wish to speak. And she doesn't tear her clothes off, asking me for sex. So with nothing else to do, I ask her if she'd mind looking at some photographs.

"What fo'?" she asks, a hint of pidgin in her angry tone.

"I'd like you to tell me if you recognize anyone, like the man who asked for help feeding the sea lions at the aquarium."

"Why would you have a picture of him?"

"Don't be alarmed, but he may be connected to my case."

She shrugs and takes the photos from me. They are arranged in a makeshift album. She moves through the pages slowly, studying each and every face. Approximately halfway through, she points. "That's him."

The name underneath the photograph is Paolo "Small Paul" Nicoletti. He looks to be in his fifties. One eye is open more than the other, giving him that sinister Lucky Luciano look.

"Will you excuse me while I go outside to make a call?" I say.

"Whatevahs."

Outside, it is evident how windward Oahu got its name. I speed-dial Flan from my cell phone and he answers, but the wind is chopping at his voice.

"Flan," I yell above the whipping wind, "I have the name of the third goombah. It's Nicoletti. Paolo 'Small

Paul' Nicoletti. Can you run it and see what you find? Specifically, I need to know if he was on Oahu when Shannon was murdered."

"Sure, Kev. No problem." There's some discomfort in Flan's voice. "Listen, we didn't get to speak after the conference today. I wanted to apologize. I didn't mean to put you in that position. I shouldn't have done it in the first place, but once I did, I should've told you. I figured she'd tell the prosecutor who I was, but I never dreamed she'd tell him we slept together."

"I have one question for you, Flan."

Despite the wind, I can hear him swallow hard. "What's that, Kev?"

"Was she any good?"

Some uncontrolled laughter comes from his end, and I can tell that he is pretty drunk. "She was a wildcat, Kevin."

"You didn't bill me for that night, I hope?"

"I'll have to check my invoices. You should've seen the look on your face when the prosecutor said I slept with her, Kev."

"Trust me, I have a good idea of what I looked like, Flan. Listen, just forget about the whole thing. It never happened. We've got a lot of work ahead of us. The judge is one mean son of a bitch, and he doesn't like me one bit."

"I know. I heard most of it, Kev. That's why I left. I figured you'd be in a foul mood, and after what I had done, I decided to turn tail and run."

"Check on Nicoletti. Let me know as soon as you have something."

"You got it, Kev. Aloha."

I snap the phone shut and head back inside. I open the door to Nikki's room, where the lights are out, but candle flames are aglow. Nikki is lying on the bed naked, patting the space beside her with her hand, as though I were a puppy. I take the invitation and crawl under the covers beside her. Before I can remove my clothes, her lips are upon me.

"I'm sorry for before," she says. "I just don't want some haole girl to steal you away from me."

"No haole or Hawaiian is going to steal me away from you, Nikole."

"It's just that it seems I lose everyone," she whispers. "First my father to prison, then my mother to death. Now my brother to ice. Everyone slips away."

The candlelight illuminates the tears falling down her cheeks. In the glow, she looks like a nude hula dancer, like the ones that adorn the covers of all the local tourism magazines.

"I have no one now but you, Kevin."

"But you *do* have me, Nikki."

We make love in the glimmer of the candlelight, her tanned, toned body radiant in its gleam. As we drift off to sleep, entangled in an embrace, she whispers words more frightening to me than Palani, the Feds, and the Mafia combined.

"I so love you, Kevin."

CHAPTER 31

"Son, did I ever tell you about my last case as a capital defender in Houston?"

Jake and I are sitting together in the concrete coffin here at the jail, waiting on the corrections officers to produce Joey for our scheduled attorney-client conference. This will be the first time Jake and Joey meet. I asked Jake to join me so that we could use the good-cop/bad-cop routine since, despite my best efforts, I have been less than effective at eliciting from Joey any semblance of the truth. Milt and I played this routine all the time. But Milt and Jake are like night and day. Although I've diligently gone over with Jake his role, I remain skeptical that Jake Harper has what it takes to convincingly play a no-nonsense bad cop.

"Only that the end result was an acquittal," I say.

"My client was a thirty-four-year-old white male. He was filthy rich. So it was one of those rare occasions when I got paid by the client, a nice five-figure fee up front. His name was George Washburn, and he was charged with killing a twenty-two-year-old black male, a skinny kid by the name of Rudy Rivers."

"Was it a hate crime?"

"I guess you could call it that. Rudy Rivers was attempting to jimmy his way into Washburn's car, a brand-new, high-end Mercedes. Washburn had one of those alarms rigged up to his car, the kind that page you when your vehicle is being broken into."

I look at my watch. We've been waiting now twenty-six minutes.

"It was late at night," Jake continues. "Washburn was upstairs in the living room of his high-rise apartment building, six floors up. His pager went off. He looked out his living room window and saw this skinny black kid trying to break into his Mercedes. He went into his bedroom with a key in his hand. Then he unlocked and opened a desk drawer to find another key. Then he went into his closet. Then he unlocked and opened a long, steel case with the second key. He loaded the rifle. He attached the scope. He went back into the living room. He pointed it out the window. He set his sight."

"That's premeditation."

"By that time, Rudy Rivers had broken into the Mercedes and disconnected the stereo. Rudy Rivers was pulling the stereo out of the car when Washburn squeezed off two rounds. Nearly blew Rudy's head clear off."

Jake covers his eyes with his hands, and I steal another glance at my watch.

"As far as that jury was concerned," he continues, "Rudy Rivers was executed for trying to steal a nine-hundred-dollar car stereo. And that was fine by them. It took them not ninety minutes to return a verdict of not guilty."

I shake my head but say nothing.

"Rudy's family had just moved to Texas from Louisiana. The family was large; he was one of eight children, the only male. When the verdict was read, the entire family was sitting there in the courtroom. They had to watch that bastard Washburn hug me and listen to him thank me for all I'd done. They were screaming and crying, every last one of them. Rudy's mama grabbed me by my shirtsleeve on my way out the courtroom. With tears streaming down her face ruining her makeup, she asked me, 'Is this justice?'"

"What did you say?"

"I said, 'No, ma'am. This is Texas.'"

Jake's eyes are watering, the way my eyes sometimes water for Brandon Glenn. There is a rap at the door. *Some timing.* Jake's eyes look like a Maui waterfall. *Some bad cop.*

An oversize guard escorts our client into the room. Joey is so thin now, the guard could probably just have slid him under the door.

Jake puts on his best bad-cop face. Despite my objections, he practiced it in the mirror for forty-five minutes back at the office. I make the introductions and have Joey take a seat across from us.

I am used to clients lying to me. It's certainly nothing new. It is the criminal defendant's mantra: lie to the police, lie to the prosecutors, lie to your lawyer, lie to the jury if you take the stand. I have just recently come to the inevitable conclusion that Joey might just have told me the ultimate lie, that he did not murder Shannon Douglas.

I decide to start by throwing some softballs. This will hopefully lull Joey into a sense of security, such that he will feel at ease with telling some truths. This way, I'll better be able to gauge when he shifts gears and starts telling more lies.

"What's with the name Joey Bangs?" I ask.

Joey seems annoyed with the question. He looks around the room, twisting his head this way and that. Trust me, Joey, there's absolutely nothing to look at. I've stared at these four fucking walls waiting for you for more minutes than I care to count.

"It's just some stupid name my uncle gave me when I was in high school. I don't even know what it's supposed to mean."

"Who is your uncle?" I ask.

"My mother's brother. Married twenty-six years to my aunt Marie, but they don't get along very well. Look, did you come down here to talk to me about my family tree?"

Jake slams his fist down on the table. I eyeball him and mouth, *Not just yet.*

"Joey," I say, "did you know that Shannon was working for the FBI?"

Joey scrunches up his face as if I just placed roadkill on the table in front of him. "No, she wasn't. She was working for Carter, Backman and Knight. They're personal injury lawyers. She brought home her work all the time. Files with police reports from automobile accidents, discovery motions, pleadings, deposition transcripts. We even ran into one of her clients at the Willowbrook Mall."

"Carter, Backman and Knight had some legitimate cases to keep up appearances," I tell him. "Just like any firm, they took in new clients and handled matters in court. But, in reality, the firm existed so that federal agents could work undercover. To everyone around them, it seems they are a group of ambulance chasers, and their targets never suspect a thing."

Joey doubles over and begins to sob.

"Joey," I say, "we think the Fiordano family was one of their targets."

Joey sits up and looks at me through wet eyes.

"We think it's possible," I say, "that your father's syndicate knew this and that a member of the Fiordano family is responsible for Shannon's death."

"I'm not listening to this," Joey says, rising from his chair.

Jake slams his fist onto the table again. It sounds like a gunshot in the cramped concrete room. He stands, points his finger at Joey, and yells at the top of his lungs, "Do you know some lazy-eyed bitch-tits?"

I put my hand on Jake's shoulder and lower him into his chair. His face is red, and I can smell the booze on his breath. He's a really *bad* bad cop.

"Sit down, Joey," I order, and he does. "Do you know Salvatore Lopardi and Anthony Antonazzo?"

"Yeah. They're friends of my dad."

"What were they doing in Honolulu on the day Shannon was killed?"

Joey pauses, eyes up and to the left. "I don't know. If anything, they were here watching over me. I told you I let my dad know I was going to Waikiki. I think he was worried about me doing something stupid."

"Did you?" I ask.

"Did I what?"

"Do something stupid."

Joey shakes his head. "If you mean to ask me whether I killed Shannon, the answer is no, I did not."

"Joey, there's no easy way to put this. It's halftime and we're down by five touchdowns. We know you were at the beach where Shannon was killed."

Joey looks away from me, shaking his head. He doesn't get it.

I give Jake the signal, and he's up so fast his metal folding chair tips over, landing with an awful resonating bang.

"Police found your fucking sneakers spattered with Shannon's blood at the scene!" Jake yells. "You want to know what else they found? They found your fucking lip print on the inside Plexiglas of the lifeguard station a few yards from where Shannon's body was discovered!"

Joey is silent.

Jake remains on his feet, pacing the two and a half steps from wall to wall. Bad cop on the prowl. "I think we need to consider a plea," Jake says. "Maybe we can get you twenty-five years or so. You're a young guy. It's better than life."

Tears stream down Joey's face, but he says nothing.

"If we go to the prosecuting attorney," Jake continues, "we can show him evidence of your intoxication. He might knock it down to a second-degree murder charge, since voluntary intoxication would eliminate the specific intent needed to convict you of murder one. Maybe, if you're lucky, he'll let you plea to murder two, and you'll do fifteen years."

Joey looks at me, at me and not at Jake. "I was there."

I know you were, Joey. You thought you had me fooled.

"But I didn't kill her."

How can I believe you now?

"You have to believe me."

You know the saying. Fool me once, shame on you.

"I'll tell you everything that happened that night."

Fool me twice, and all that jazz . . .

CHAPTER 32

Joey was drunk, he tells us, as drunk as drunk could be. He exited a bar on Kuhio and stumbled through the streets of Waikiki in search of Shannon. The night sky was crystal clear, but he was in a fog. Too many tourists were walking ahead of him and behind, far too many to the left and to the right. So he escaped to the quiet, empty beach. He walked along the water for ten, maybe fifteen minutes. He grew dizzy, then dizzier. So he stopped and seated himself on the stairs of a deserted lifeguard station on an isolated stretch of sand.

Joey sat there for a bit, thinking thoughts drunk, desperate men sometimes think. He immersed himself in the silence and solitude, until the silence was broken and the solitude was no more. The voice sounded like hers, but it couldn't be. Could it? It could, yes, and it was, because the laugh, the laugh was unmistakable. It could belong to no one but her. It angered him that she could laugh at a time like this. It angered him more that she was not laughing alone.

Something prompted him up those steps. It could have been fear, but with all the liquor coursing through his veins, it likely wasn't that. It could have been curiosity. It could have even been something sinister, that much he admits. Whatever it was, it led him up those steps and through the unlocked door. It put him on his haunches and pressed his nose and lips to the glass. It was dark. But it was her. All five foot ten without heels and a body that could kill.

And there was him. Joey didn't know his name. He couldn't see his face. He didn't know his occupation, his religion, or the color of his skin. All Joey knew was that he hated him.

Joey watched as the pair plunked down together on the sand. He felt sick but managed not to puke. He kept silent and watched. He watched as they undressed each other. He watched as they *did things* to each other, things he cannot now say aloud.

It was all too much for him. He collapsed backward, knocking over a metal first-aid kit. He froze, certain they had heard the noise. A couple seconds that seemed like hours passed, then he heard her tell him, "Stop." He wanted to see what was happening, but he knew he could not pop his head back up, or he would surely be discovered.

And so he waited.

"My recollection becomes vague after that," Joey says. "I heard her sob, and I didn't know what to do. I was angry and sad and terrified. Then I heard two other voices, a man's and a woman's. They were speaking loudly; it sounded like they were drunk. I think they said they were on their honeymoon. Anyway, I smelled marijuana, and sure enough, a few moments later, they offered Shannon a hit off the joint they were smoking. After some coaxing, Shannon took a puff, and the couple asked her if she was okay. I heard one of them say she was bleeding."

I am listening to Joey's story, and even as I recall the newlyweds' statement to the police, I'm wondering how much to believe. Under any other circumstances, I'd say nearly none of it. He fooled me once; why risk being fooled again? But he speaks now with a certain sincerity. And if nothing else, I feel compelled to listen to the end.

"So when I was certain the couple had walked away, I opened the door to the lifeguard station and quietly walked down the steps. I said her name. She turned and saw me. She was startled at first, and then she seemed scared. I told her I didn't care what she did or what happened. I just wanted to hold her, help her, bring her back home."

"How did she react?" asks Jake.

"She yelled at me and called me a stalker. She demanded that I leave her there on the beach. The situation, her being drunk and crying, reminded me of the night back at her apartment in Manhattan, the night that led to my arrest. So I did what she said. I kept my mouth shut and I left."

"What happened to your sneakers?" I ask.

"My sneakers were wet from the surf and covered in sand. So I tossed them somewhere. As for the blood, Shannon *was* bleeding; some blood may have dripped on them when we spoke. I picked up a cheap pair of flip-flops at an all-night convenience store and wore them the rest of the night."

"Why didn't you tell me this earlier, Joey?" I ask.

"Because I knew you wouldn't believe me if I did."

You're probably right. "What does that tell you about what the jury will think, Joey?"

"That's why you have to find who killed her, Kevin. That's the only way you're going to get me home."

Easier said than done. "I'm trying my best, Joey."

"I promise I'll make it worth your while, Kevin. After all, I can assure you, I'll be a returning client."

"Oh, yeah, Joey? How's that?"

"Because as soon as I know who murdered Shannon and I get out of here, I'm going to go out and find him."

And then what, Joey?

"And then, I'm gonna kill the motherfucker."

PART III

SHAKA & AWE

CHAPTER 33

It is six o'clock on this, the eve of trial. The sun is setting above Waikiki Beach, turning the sky a brilliant red. The tourists are thinning out, returning to their rooms to shower for dinner and shows. In the parks, the barbecues are firing up, and the tiki torches are being lit. The restaurants and bars are bracing for the nighttime crowds. The street vendors are closing up shop. The street performers are painting themselves in silver and bronze. The streetwalkers still have five hours to go. It is six o'clock and the Hawaiian day is done. Waikiki is turning night.

I stand in the sand with Jake and Flan, on the spot where Shannon was killed. It is nearly six months to the day, and not a clue is left to be found. It simply seemed the right place for us to be.

I have since moved up North Shore to Waialua, a place more country than town. It is an hour from the hustle and bustle of Honolulu, a place more befitting the man I am trying to become. Not that I've had all that much success. I still curse at the top of my lungs at the dreadful traffic heading in and out of Honolulu. I eat my nails as if they were a delicious, nutritious New York delicacy. I still hate cigarette smoke, cell phones, and car alarms, and I'm unafraid to say so. But I like to think I've gained a modicum of tolerance and patience. Maybe even a little happiness.

Turi Ahina's case was dismissed for want of prosecution as planned. A steady flow of clients is now coming to my door, business cards in hand, singing Hoshi the same great song: Turi sent me. They all walk in with an unmarked envelope filled with $5,000 cash. And they all walk out with nothing but the lint lining their oversize pants pockets.

The Gianfortes have generously provided me with a second $50,000 retainer, exclusively for trial. Between that and the stream of clients sent by Turi, I could again be living the lifestyle I grew accustomed to in New York. But, for some reason, I have neither the need nor desire to.

I have avoided Palani Kanno and the Waikiki Winds hotel since the day I was attacked. Flan managed to interview J. J. Fitzpatrick, who claimed to have spent the night with his longtime girlfriend, Tracy Thorne. Flan's follow-up revealed that Tracy is a junkie with multiple boyfriends. Fortunately, she cannot recall which one she was with on the wild night in question.

Sometime after our meeting at the Whale Watcher Bar & Grill, Professor Jim Catus went to the Honolulu police and informed them of his scheduled tryst. He also informed them that he spent his first night on the island with one of Waikiki's working girls at the less-than-luxurious Leilani Inn. Flan attempted to locate that particular lady of the night, but was unable to penetrate this witness as he had one Carlie Douglas. Only a single bellhop admitted to seeing the professor on that ill-fated Sunday night, but that was apparently enough for Detective John Tatupu to clear Catus as a suspect.

I have not heard from the Feds since the night they warned me off Lopardi and Antonazzo. To my surprise and delight, neither have I heard from Lopardi and Antonazzo, despite our overt investigation into Paolo "Small Paul" Nicoletti, a well-known capo of the Fiordano crime family. That investigation has yielded little. The well of Milt's sources seems to have dried up. And there are no records of Nicoletti being on Oahu on or after the day Shannon died. The only evidence of his being here is the identification made by my girlfriend. Yes, I said it: girlfriend. The beautiful Hawaiian princess Nikole Kapua is now my one and only.

Nikki has been as constant a warmth in my life as the bright Hawaiian sun. She has shown me every pleasurable spot on Oahu from Hanauma Bay to Sharks Cove. Together, we've developed a threesome with the sea. As a New Yorker, my only experience with the water had been a ferry ride on New York Waterway, a six-minute excursion across the icy Hudson River. Now, I snorkel, scuba, sailboard, kayak, and surf. Well, I try to surf. But the last time I tried, the board knocked me unconscious and I had to be saved by a lifeguard, who more resembled David Hasselhoff than Pamela Anderson. Suffice it to say, I consider myself a surfer no more.

Unlike in New York, I now take regular days off. Sometimes even three or four at a time. Last month, Nikki and I flew to Maui, where we spent four days drinking mai tais and making love. I have since promised Nikki a trip to Kauai to visit her quaint, beloved hometown. I told her we'd go as soon as the trial ends, and I confess, I look forward to it, for more reasons than one.

Aside from the occasional streak of jealousy, Nikki is all a man could ever want. But for a brown-eyed brunette, she can sure turn green. Most recently, she admonished my next-door neighbor, a cute, redheaded University of Hawaii student, who thought she was doing me a favor by handing me some mail that had been left in her mailbox by mistake.

But I have attributed these streaks to the recent problems she's faced. Alika, all that's left of her *ohana*, hardly ever returns home. He remains strung out on ice, selling the drug and risking his life for the sole purpose of staying high. My custom is to pick her up after work and drive her to my place in Waialua, if only to take her away from it all.

But tonight, I will not see her at all. Tonight, Kevin Corvelli is all business. And his business is the trial of *State versus Joseph Gianforte Jr.*

Prosecuting attorney Dapper Don Watanabe made what he called a generous offer. Twenty-five years. As I am required by law to do, I relayed the offer to Joey, who cried

at the sound of it. There will be no negotiation. There will
be no plea bargain. There *will* be a trial. And there *will* be
a verdict.

Whether Joey killed Shannon or not, I don't truly know.
And I would not hazard a guess. Yet twelve jurors are
about to be asked to do just that. Regardless of whether
Joey is responsible for Shannon's death, my job is to zealously represent him and to create reasonable doubt. Regardless of what Joey did or did not do, my mission is
unequivocal: to strive for a verdict of not guilty.

We are barefoot, all three of us, our feet warmed by the
sand, sunglasses shading our eyes from the dropping sun.

"I want to thank both of you," I say, "for all the help
you've given me on this case. And for your friendship these
past six months. I'd be lost without either one of you."

Jake smirks. "All I get is money and thanks."

"What do you mean?" I ask.

"Well, I'm the only one didn't get laid through all of this."

"I think something can be arranged," says Flan. "Those
goodfellas Lazy Eye Sal and Tony Bitch-Tits are probably
getting lonely and bored of each other by now."

Although we haven't heard from Lopardi and Antonazzo, we have been keeping tabs on them. They returned
to Honolulu several times over the last six months, most
recently this past week. No doubt they are keeping tabs on
us as we keep tabs on them.

"Flan," I say, "you're not going to be permitted to watch
the trial, since I may have to call you as a witness during
our case-in-chief."

"That's okay," Flan says. "I'd prefer to keep my distance from Carlie Douglas as it is."

"Jake," I say, "I'll call you with updates during the breaks."

"There will be no need for that, son. I'll be sitting right there beside you."

"*Mahalo,* Jake. I truly appreciate that."

We have stood here before, many times, the three of us, scouring the beach, searching for clues, looking for answers. It is a narrow strip of beach. At high tide, the surf sometimes covers it all. It is the only portion of Waikiki Beach unlit by tiki torches at night. It is where Shannon was bludgeoned to death, and it is, practically speaking, the only spot on Waikiki Beach where the murder could have occurred and gone undiscovered until morning.

The lifeguard station stands empty. It has been photographed more times these past few months than most supermodels.

The last few tourists leave this strip of beach, and we are alone, but for the two white pigeons picking at the row of tall Polynesian shrubs blocking our view of the street, looking for any leftovers the tourists may have left behind.

I have a migraine. It's the same migraine that has visited me on the eve of every trial I've ever started. Tomorrow I choose those who will choose Joey's fate. The spotlight will hit me, a circle of illumination that will remain on me no matter what move I make, like a prisoner caught trying to escape over the wall. Every word I utter will be put in

print, analyzed under the media's microscope, and pre-
served for the jury's ultimate deliberations.

I marvel at Jake for merely making it to his age doing
the job that we do. Although Joey is not facing death, he
tells me emphatically he might as well be. He will not survive prison, he assures me. And this, if nothing else, I
wholeheartedly believe.

As the red-purple sky of dusk replaces the day's baby
blue, I step off the sand and onto the concrete. Thoughts of
Brandon Glenn fight their way back into my already over-
crowded mind. One last look at Waikiki Beach.

And then, like a thousand other commanders on a thousand other battlefields, I steel myself and wait for the dawn.

CHAPTER 34

I am trying not to yawn.

A hell of a way to start a trial, yeah, I know. But that's what I'm doing. I'm trying not to yawn. And trying not to yawn is making it worse. It's a psychological thing, I think. I never did look it up on the Internet, but right now that's not important. What is important is the opening statement I will make today. *If* I get to make it. If this son of a bitch ever stops talking.

Dapper Don Watanabe, the prosecuting attorney, has been at it for over an hour already. Decked out as he is in a brand-new navy blue suit by Hugo Boss, he struts the length of the railing back and forth like a runway model. The jury is not yet snapping pictures, but I fear they might. Even his entrance into the courtroom looked more like a movie star's stroll down the red carpet to the Kodak Theatre on Oscar night than a civil servant on his way to work to earn his hundred bucks a day. He's been standing before the jury for seventy-one full minutes. He spent the first six minutes clearing his throat before uttering a single syllable.

What really bothers me is that the jury seems to be hanging on his every word. Even though every word has been uttered at least a dozen times. It's as if he's laying out the evidence once for every juror. Let's just hope he doesn't do it again for each of the four alternates. In New York, any jury would become incensed with a long-winded prosecutor. But this jury seems to enjoy Dapper Don's repetitiveness, noshing on his words like a light afternoon snack.

I don't like our jury. But then again, I never do. Juries simply have too much power and absolutely no experience at wielding it. I wouldn't want twelve men and women with no medical training whatsoever to perform my triple-bypass surgery. And likewise, I wouldn't want twelve men and women with no legal training whatsoever to decide my legal culpability for a serious crime and determine whether I'll spend the rest of my life in an eight-by-ten cage. Of course, that's if I was innocent. If I was guilty, I'd put my fate in the hands of the twelve stupidest people I could find.

Our jury is an adequate cross-section of the Honolulu community. There are four Hawaiians, three Caucasians, three Japanese, and two Filipinos. They sit, as juries do, behind the rail closest to the prosecution table. The historical reason given for the parties' positioning is that the prosecution, not the defense, has the burden of proof. I tend to believe, however, that the real reason is that the jury would most fear the defendant, not the prosecuting attorney, jumping over the jury rail and strangling one of the jurors to death.

Joey doesn't appear capable of that. He's thin and withdrawn. His skin is pale, especially when contrasted with that of all of these Hawaiian residents. His suit is far too large for him now, and I asked his mother to buy him another, which she promised to have ready for him by tomorrow morning. He sits next to me, fidgeting as if covered in bugs, and I tell him to be careful with his body language.

"I'm nervous," he whispers.

"Me, too," I whisper back. "I think I left my iron on."

I look past Joey at Jake, who is visibly hungover and looks as though he never used an iron in his entire life.

"I realize," Dapper Don says, "I've taken much of your time this morning. But we must remember that we are all here today because a young woman is dead. And the evidence will conclusively show that the defendant, Mr. Joseph Gianforte Jr., is responsible for her death. It will show that he took that young woman's life in a cold and calculating fashion just a few miles from here on our own pristine Waikiki shore.

"The evidence will show that the defendant is the ex-boyfriend of the victim, Miss Shannon Douglas, and that she ended their relationship just days prior to her untimely death. That she left New York City for holiday here in Honolulu to meet her new lover the very day she was killed. That the defendant followed her from the East Coast of the mainland, thousands of miles to Oahu, to attempt to get her back. That he stalked her on the night of her death and found her, much to his dismay, on the white sand of Waikiki Beach, having taken another lover. That the defendant lay in wait, watching her and her paramour make love on the beach from his perch, concealed in a lifeguard station merely a few yards away. That when her lover left, the defendant descended from his perch and confronted the young woman, who wanted nothing more to do with him. That he with malice aforethought ultimately struck her with a rock-hard piece of reef, nearly the size of a softball, brutally ending her unfinished life."

Ordinarily, at this point, I would object on the grounds of torture by boredom and get a chuckle from the jury. But I know this jury will not appreciate my delightful sense of humor, and with Hideki Narita on the bench, I could very well spend the night in a cell next to Joey's.

"Let me remind you," Dapper Don continues, "you will hear testimony from the detective who investigated this homicide. He will describe for you in great and gruesome detail where, when, how, by whom, and in what condition Shannon's body was found. He will inform you as to what evidence was discovered, both physical and circumstantial, that links the defendant, indisputably, to this heinous crime.

"You will hear testimony from a forensic scientist, who will explain for you in great detail the science of latent-print identification and trace evidence, so that you may study the evidence in this case and make your own conclusions as to the guilt of this defendant.

"You will hear testimony from the medical examiner, who will tell you how Shannon was killed. He will tell you Shannon died from blunt-force trauma to her head and describe for you the likely height and strength of the person who did this to her.

"You will also hear testimony from Shannon's lover from that night, who heard a noise come from the very lifeguard station where the defendant lay in wait. And you will hear from Shannon's friend back East, who unfortunately informed the defendant of Shannon's tropical destination, unwittingly setting off the course of events which ultimately led to Shannon's death.

"Most importantly, you will see with your own eyes the bloodied sneakers left behind by the defendant near the scene of the crime. You will see photographs of the latent print he left behind at the lifeguard station where he hid and waited. And thanks to technology, you will see videos from hotel surveillance cameras showing not only when the defendant left and returned to his hotel, but that he left with the very pair of bright white sneakers found near the crime scene, and that he returned, of course, without them. And you will see the defendant, in the flesh, at a hotel near the scene of the murder less than an hour before Shannon and her lover walked to the spot of beach where she was killed. And, finally, you will learn that the defendant was convinced that Shannon Douglas had ruined his life, and so he took revenge by ending hers.

"Ladies and gentlemen of the jury, I am pleased to have had this opportunity to address each and every one of you in my capacity as a prosecutor and as an officer of this court. I only wish it were under much different circumstances. You have, each of you, an awesome responsibility, one which I know you will not take lightly. I am confident that after all the evidence is presented to you, you will return a verdict of guilty on the charge of first-degree murder against the defendant, Joseph Anthony Gianforte Jr. Thank you for your kind attention."

Dapper Don concludes with a slight bow, and at least half the jurors look as though they wish to applaud. He returns to his seat at the prosecution table, and all eyes turn to me.

"Mr. Corvelli," says Narita, "would you like to make your opening statement now, or reserve it for your case-in-chief?"

"I'll make my opening statement now, Your Honor."

"Very well. Proceed, Mr. Corvelli."

I stand and pick up my coffee, which is ice-cold from sitting on the table all day. I don't drink coffee. I don't like the taste and I don't need the caffeine. I'm jittery enough as it is.

As I walk past the counsel table, I trip over my own feet. The lid on the coffee is long gone, and the liquid spills all over Dapper Don and his sparkling new, blue Hugo Boss jacket.

"I'm terribly sorry!" I shout with all the sincerity I can muster.

Dapper Don rises from the table, dripping in cold coffee. If looks could kill, Joey would need to find himself a new attorney. Dapper Don removes his jacket and tosses it on a chair three seats away from where he sits. Some commotion disturbs the courtroom, mixed remarks of humor and insults about my clumsiness and carelessness. The judge raps his gavel, and I apologize to the room.

"Ladies and gentlemen of the jury," I begin, "my name is Kevin Corvelli, and I represent Mr. Joseph Gianforte. Let's hope I am better at lawyering than I am at walking with my coffee."

There's a chuckle from about half the jury. I get a smile from the rest.

"Of course, I would never do that on purpose. After all, I need my coffee to stay awake after Mr. Watanabe's lengthy and repetitive speech. I'm kidding, of course. I actually think Mr. Watanabe did a fine job, given what little he had to work with. He had to repeat everything a dozen times to make it seem like there is more there than there is.

"It's interesting though what Mr. Watanabe did with his suit jacket after it became drenched in coffee. He looked dapper in it just minutes ago. Now, he's tossed it aside three chairs away from him. It's as if he wants nothing more to do with it. Of course, I'll pay the dry-cleaning bill, and hopefully the stains will come out and it will be as good as new. If not, he'll most likely throw it away, and I'll have to buy him a new Hugo Boss suit."

"Objection," says Dapper Don, rising from his chair. "If counsel wishes to harp on the humiliation he caused me, he can do so outside the presence of the jury."

"I agree," says Judge Narita. "What's the relevance of this, Mr. Corvelli?"

"The relevance," I say to the jury, "is that sometimes people discard articles of clothing when the articles seem to be ruined. Even expensive articles like Nike footwear or Hugo Boss suit jackets. If Mr. Watanabe had a wealthy family and a few drinks in him, he may very well have tossed the jacket into the garbage as opposed to tossing it away from him onto that chair. Mr. Watanabe may very well have discarded the jacket like Joey Gianforte discarded the sneakers that became soaked with seawater and covered in sand.

"Of course, it is Mr. Watanabe's job to make sure all his pieces of evidence fit neatly into the puzzle he's trying to build. So he'll sculpt and twist those pieces every which way in order to fit his needs. But I ask that you, the jury, keep an open mind as is your duty to do so by law. Because, I submit to you, not everything is as it seems.

"Let's take the coffee for instance. Suppose no one in this room witnessed the incident. Suppose someone spilt coffee on Mr. Watanabe's suit jacket, but no one here knows who it was. The police would come in and examine the styrofoam cup, no doubt. Now, let's assume you twelve men and women are the police."

With a napkin, I pick the cup back off the defense table and walk back to the jury.

"I can assure you that there are no fingerprints on the cup because they've been wiped clean. I can assure you that my lip prints aren't on the cup because I don't drink coffee. There does, however, appear to be *someone's* lip print on the cup. After all, there's lipstick on it, as you can all see. It appears to be from the Sephora collection, Light Indian Pink. Not my shade. So the task of solving this crime goes to you twelve men and women. As crime solvers, what would you do? I'll tell you what you would do. You would seek the woman who wears Light Indian Pink. You would seek the woman who placed this lip print on the cup.

"Of course, as intelligent people you would know that lip-print identification is pseudoscientific nonsense. You might as well pick the names of ten suspects from a hat and have them draw straws. But you are desperate, and you have no other clues to go by. So you find the woman in Light Indian Pink."

I look around the courtroom as if seeking out the perpetrator. My eyes fall on Hoshi, seated behind Jake in the front row between members of the press. I point at her and she stands. Hoshi, the picture of innocence.

"You, miss," I say, "are you wearing Light Indian Pink?"

Hoshi nods her head three times as rehearsed.

"And did you take a sip of my coffee?"

She nods again, nods like a bobblehead doll to help our cause.

I turn back to the jury. "If you men and women were the police, that young woman would be your one and only suspect. And Mr. Watanabe, or someone like him, would stand before another jury and make the case that the young woman in Light Indian Pink, indisputably, committed the crime of defiling Mr. Watanabe's suit jacket. But as

we all know, she's not the culprit. And to convict her based
on this lukewarm evidence would be to convict her despite reasonable doubt, which juries are expressly forbidden by law to do.

"The same goes for my client, Joey Gianforte. The police do not know who killed Shannon Douglas, yet they
were desperate to solve this crime. They chose Joey Gianforte, not out of malice, but out of convenience. The physical evidence that Mr. Watanabe seems so excited about is
not evidence that Joey killed Shannon Douglas; it is evidence that he was in the wrong town at the wrong time.
And being in the wrong town at the wrong time does not
a murderer make.

"Despite the length of time Mr. Watanabe took to talk to
you, he neglected to tell you an awful lot. He neglected
to tell you that the lover Shannon Douglas was supposed
to meet the next day was her law school professor, Jim
Catus. He neglected to tell you that this professor arrived a
day early to surprise Shannon. He neglected to tell you
that this professor kept his visit to Honolulu a secret from
police for several weeks following Shannon's death. He
neglected to tell you that this professor admits to observ-
ing Shannon take another lover the night before their
scheduled tryst. He neglected to tell you that this professor hopes to use as his alibi a two-bit prostitute from
Waikiki.

"Mr. Watanabe also neglected to inform you that the
local man Palani Kanno, the lover Shannon took that night,
left his post at the Waikiki Winds hotel for fifteen minutes

after starting work, leaving this man, who admittedly struck Shannon and caused her to bleed, more than enough time to drive his moped back to the spot where he left her and to finish the job.

"Mr. Watanabe also neglected to tell you that Shannon tested positive for marijuana upon autopsy, and that the local man, Palani Kanno, admitted buying marijuana from a fellow doorman, named J. J. Fitzpatrick, at the Waikiki Winds. He neglected to tell you that J. J. Fitzpatrick then abandoned his post for the remainder of the night, heading for heaven knows where. Perhaps to Waikiki Beach to find the half-naked, drunk girl who enjoys sex with strangers, and to share with her some of the vile weed he sold to Kanno.

"Mr. Watanabe neglected to tell you about many people who had both motive and opportunity to kill Shannon Douglas. He neglected to tell you about them because he knows that one of them very well could be Shannon's killer. He neglected to tell you about them because if he did, he could pack his briefcase and turn in his badge. His career as a prosecuting attorney would be over, because he would have done exactly what it is the defendant's job to do. He would've shown you enough reasonable doubt to choke a horse.

"Ladies and gentlemen, the murder of Shannon Douglas is a terrible tragedy. A tragedy which has been compounded by the arrest and prosecution of an innocent man. It is my sincere hope that once you acquit Joey Gianforte of this terrible crime, the police will reopen their investigation, as they should have done months ago. That they will find Shannon's killer and finally bring to him the justice he deserves.

"As a criminal defense attorney, I don't often have the pleasure of standing beside an innocent man. But, ladies and gentleman of the jury, I do today."

I think.

CHAPTER 35

I was bitten by a spider. But I didn't develop any supernatural powers whatsoever. I can't sling webs or climb walls. I have neither superstrength nor superspeed. Not a lick of spidey sense. Just a big, red fucking welt the size of a golf ball that itches like hell.

Life up North Shore isn't all it's cracked up to be. Waialua is considered country, and despite all my efforts, I am still a city boy at heart. So when I first moved to Waialua and came across ants, spiders, and centipedes, I panicked, packed my bags, and spent the next four nights in an upscale Waikiki hotel.

After Flan explained to me the relative harmlessness of the creatures found in my new home and helped me take measures to rid myself of them, I reluctantly moved back in. But that first night, I came face-to-face with a gecko. And he wasn't selling car insurance.

The next day, I found myself at a North Shore animal

shelter in search of a kitten. I told the woman at the shelter
I wanted a companion, not some muscle for my war on
geckos. She led me to a nine-year-old, gray long-haired
Maine coon. I told her I was adamant about getting a kitten.
I didn't want a *used* cat, someone else's sloppy seconds. But
she told me she was unable to find this cat a home, and
that he was on his last day. If I didn't take him, they would
have to put him to sleep. Not the kind of sleep you wake
up from feeling refreshed. A permanent sleep. The big sleep.

So I took him, and I named him Grey Skies, *Skies* for
short.

I know what people say about guys with cats, so I decided to toughen him up. I bought him a black collar with
metal spikes. The collar only made him look as if he be-
longed to one of the Village People, so I took it off. Skies
couldn't care less either way.

Skies is the most laid-back creature I have ever seen. He
doesn't chase anything. Not insects, not lizards, not even
his tail. I half-expect to come home one day to find him
and the gecko sharing a malt.

Nikki loves him, which is a good thing because he
sleeps with us in my bed. I made up the second bedroom
just for him, complete with a $200 cat bed. But he thinks
it's beneath him, and he won't sleep in any bed other than
mine.

Skies is my new alarm clock, too. He woke me this
morning and I got an early jump on the day. I drove my
Jeep from Waialua to Honolulu and got to court before 8:00
a.m. Sitting on each table in the otherwise empty Lawyers'

Room was a copy of the morning's *Honolulu Advertiser.* The headline read GIANFORTE MURDER TRIAL UNDER WAY. Without reading the article I took each copy of the paper and tossed them into the trash. I no longer get any satisfaction from seeing my name in print.

This morning we will have the opportunity to voir dire the prosecution's expert witness, who intends to testify about lip-print identification and the latent print left by Joey at the lifeguard station at the crime scene. My personal stakes in this case have risen, and keeping the forensic scientist from testifying about the lip print left at the lifeguard station is all the more important.

The case is called and I immediately renew my objection regarding the trial court's failure to conduct a full hearing before admitting lip-print-identification testimony on the grounds that it is novel scientific evidence. In renewing my objection, I also renew the judge's ire. Narita warns me to stay focused on the matter at hand and threatens me again with contempt of court.

I take my seat at the counsel table, and Dapper Don Watanabe calls his witness to the stand. Alison Kelly is a fiery Irish redhead with emerald green eyes that look as if they can cut glass.

"Redheads are my favorite," Jake whispers in my ear.

The jury is not in the courtroom for this, the voir dire of the witness whom the prosecution wishes to qualify as an expert. If she qualifies, she will be permitted to testify during the prosecution's case-in-chief as to the lip print found in the lifeguard station at the beach. The print is evidence of Joey being a few feet from where the body was discovered, quite possibly the single, most damning piece of evidence against him.

Joey is not in the courtroom either. He is suffering from stomach problems, no doubt a result of the stress caused by this trial. He asked that we not delay the day's proceedings, but that the voir dire of Alison Kelly be conducted without his being present.

Dapper Don is at the podium, adorned today in Brooks Brothers. He quickly and effortlessly takes Alison Kelly through her education, publications, and past employment. Then he moves on to the meat of the matter.

"Ms. Kelly, would you please tell us the name of your present employer, and your position with that employer?"

"I am employed as a forensic scientist with the Honolulu Police Department."

"Do you specialize in any particular area of forensic science?"

"I do. My specialty is latent-print examination."

"Please, Ms. Kelly, briefly describe for us what latent-print examination entails."

"Police investigators gather latent prints, such as fingerprints or other impression evidence from a crime scene or other piece of physical evidence, and then gather a sample from a suspect. I am given both of these. I perform a side-by-side comparison, searching for as many points of similarity as possible between the two. If there are enough points of similarity found, then we have a positive identification that the suspect is the individual who left the prints at the crime scene or on the physical evidence."

"She's really beautiful, isn't she?" Jake whispers in my ear. "How old do you figure she is? Late forties?"

"Aside from fingerprints," Dapper Don says, "what other types of impression evidence do you examine as a positive means for identification?"

"Well, there are lip prints."

"Stop right there," he says. But she had already stopped. This back-and-forth has no doubt been rehearsed ad nauseam. "Is there a scientific name for the study of lip prints?"

"Yes, there is. It is called cheiloscopy."

"Is cheiloscopy a generally accepted form of identification in the scientific community?"

"Yes, it is."

Jake is back at my ear. "She kind of looks like that doctor on *Star Trek,* don't you think?"

"Bones?" I ask him.

"No," he whispers back, a little too loudly. "The female doctor on *Next Generation.*"

"Have there been articles written about the subject?" asks Dapper Don.

"There have been several articles." Alison Kelly lists the names of the articles and where they can be found. I came up with a similar list last night on the Internet, and I check them off as she calls them out.

"To your knowledge, has there been any dissent within the scientific community with respect to the methodology of studying lip prints, or whether lip prints could be used for purposes of positive identification?"

"No," she answers, "there has not."

I attempt to rattle her cage by briskly moving for my briefcase, as if I have volumes of dissent waiting for me inside. I, in fact, have nothing, not a single sheet of useful rebuttal. But my action has the intended effect on her.

"There could be some dissent on the subject," she back-pedals, "but I am not aware of any."

Dapper Don gives her a look that says, *That wasn't in the script.* Then he tries to reel her back in. "What is the basis for identification of impression evidence?"

"That everything is unique if looked at in sufficient detail, and if two things are sufficiently similar, they must have come from the same source."

"And does that apply to lip prints?"

"Absolutely," she says. "In fact, lip-print comparison is very similar to fingerprint comparison."

"Yet lip-print comparison is seldom used. Why is that, Ms. Kelly?"

"Because unlike fingerprints, it is very unusual to find lip prints at a crime scene, or on a piece of physical evidence such as a weapon."

Jake pushes a yellow legal pad toward me. It reads, *Do you think she'd go out with me?*

I feel like I'm in the sixth grade. I write, *I'll ask her during cross-examination.*

"How long have you been employed in the area of forensic science?" asks Dapper Don.

"Eighteen years," she says.

"How many latent-print examinations have you completed in your career?"

"Roughly, one hundred thousand."

"Have you ever testified as an expert witness before?"

"Yes, I have. On over fifty occasions."

Alison Kelly testifies about the classification of lip
prints, their division into five main types: diamond grooves,
long vertical grooves, short vertical grooves, rectangular
grooves, and branching grooves. It's all uninteresting, yet
Jake hangs on her every word like some eighth grader
with a crush on his pretty, young pre-algebra teacher. To
simplify the pattern, Kelly explains, she divides the lips
into four quadrants, then studies each quadrant individu-
ally to look for similarities between the control print and
the print found at the crime scene.

My ears perk up like a cat's when she is asked about our
specific case. She testifies that she found thirteen similarities between Joey's sample print and the print found on the
Plexiglas at the lifeguard station. Talk about your unlucky
number thirteen. Thirteen similarities were more than
enough for Alison Kelly to positively identify Joseph Gianforte Jr. as the individual who left the lip print at the lifeguard station on Waikiki Beach.

Dapper Don thanks her and tenders the witness. I stand
and carry my notes to the podium. "Good morning, Ms.
Kelly," I say.

She nods politely and offers a smile. She was properly

prepared and will use as few words as possible during my cross-examination.

"You stated during direct examination that you have testified as an expert witness on over fifty occasions, is that correct?"

"Yes."

"On how many of those fifty occasions did you testify concerning lip-print identification?"

"None."

"Well, in your eighteen years as a forensic scientist, how many opportunities have you had to examine lip prints for use in identification of an individual?"

"For an actual case?"

"Yes, Ms. Kelly, for an actual case."

She shifts uncomfortably in her chair. "Twice."

"Two times in *eighteen years*?"

"Yes."

"And what types of cases were those?"

"One in which a woman was struck by a hit-and-run driver. Her lip print was discovered on the hood of the suspect's vehicle."

"And the second?"

"A burglar, who was apparently thirsty, took a sip of water from a glass in the home he was burglarizing."

"Were you called to testify in either of those cases?"

"No, I was not."

"Why weren't you called to testify?" I ask.

"Objection," says Dapper Don. "Ms. Kelly cannot

speculate as to why she wasn't called to testify in a particular case."

"I'll rephrase, Your Honor," I say. "Do you know why you weren't called to testify in either of those two cases?"

"Yes, I do."

"Please, tell us why you weren't called to testify in those two cases, Ms. Kelly."

"Because neither of the cases went to trial. Both of the defendants pled guilty."

"So in both of those cases, lip-print identification was merely used as a scare tactic to assure guilty pleas, and not as substantive evidence of guilt, isn't that right, Ms. Kelly?"

"Objection!"

"Sustained."

"Would you agree, Ms. Kelly, that lip-print identification is novel scientific evidence?"

"It is seldom used, so I suppose you can say so."

"Are you aware of any published studies in peer-reviewed journals that provide empirical proof of the study of lip-print comparisons showing their individuality, which you contend has been generally accepted within the scientific community?"

"No, none that I am aware of."

"Any published studies that describe the methodology to be used in lip-print comparisons?"

"No, none that I am aware of."

"Any published studies that describe the characteristics of lip prints which are to be used in comparing known standards and crime-scene prints?"

"No, none that I am aware of."

"I am not aware of any either, Ms. Kelly," I say. "Because there are none."

"Objection!"

"Sustained. Mr. Corvelli, you will refrain from testifying."

"I apologize, Your Honor. I have no further use of this witness."

I return to the defense table, confident that I accomplished what I set out to accomplish. If Narita follows the law, then Alison Kelly will not be permitted to testify about lip-print identification. At the least, we will be granted a full hearing on the admissibility of lip-print identification.

But the look on Narita's face tells me he has no intention of following the law. The judge straightens his spectacles and sits up as high as his miniature frame will allow him. "This Court finds that Alison Kelly qualifies as an expert in the field of forensic science, specifically with respect to latent-print examination. Ms. Kelly's testimony regarding lip-print identification is admissible. This decision is based on her testimony that lip-print identification is generally accepted within the scientific community. That the technique has been around for over half a century, that articles have been written on the subject, and that she is unaware of any dissent within the scientific community on the methodology or whether lip prints could form the basis for positive identification.

"The Court acknowledges Mr. Corvelli's objection, and that lip-print identification involves a unique comparison that has not been used very often in the history of the court system. Nevertheless, this Court, in its discretion, finds the evidence to be admissible, and it will be up to the jury to determine the amount of weight to assign this evidence.

"Tomorrow morning, at nine o'clock, Mr. Watanabe, you will call your first witness to the stand."

"I look forward to it, Your Honor."

That makes one of us. Narita's decision is a major blow to the defense, one from which we may not recover. I gravely fear that by pressing his lips up against the Plexiglas of that abandoned lifeguard station, Joey inadvertently gave his freedom the proverbial kiss of death.

CHAPTER 36

I don't like shopping. I buy whatever I can on the Internet to avoid going to the mall. I don't like crowds. I don't like salespeople looming over my shoulder, asking me if they can help. I'm a big boy now, and I can find my own size, thank you very much. I refuse to try anything on at the store, and I refuse to come back for an exchange. I pick items out and purchase them as quickly as possible with little thought to price. I bring the items home and put them away, taking them out only when I'm ready to wear them. If something doesn't fit, I return it to my closet and let it remain there for six months. Then I throw it out.

Nikki calls me eccentric, but it's really just that in the fifteen years I've lived on my own, I haven't learned to take care of myself very well. I don't like cleaning, so I have a cleaning woman in my home once a week. I don't like washing dishes, so I only use paper plates and plastic utensils. I don't like pumping gas, so I travel twenty miles out of the way to go to the only full-service gas station I've found on the island. But that a girl like Nikki stays with me tells me at least *some* good must come along with all the bad.

Tonight Nikki and I are at the Ala Moana Center, Hawaii's world-famous open-air shopping mall. I reluctantly agreed to the distraction after convincing myself I could do absolutely nothing further to prepare myself for tomorrow's witness.

I am standing next to a rack of bikini tops at Maui WaterWear as Nikki models swimsuits, which she wants to bring with her on our upcoming trip to Kauai. I am growing increasingly uncomfortable, and probably getting somewhat red in the face. Not because of Nikki; I've seen all there is to see of her. But three other hot women are trying on two-piece bathing suits themselves, and it is a little more than a man on trial can stand.

A leggy strawberry blonde in an orange two-piece string bikini prances around the store like a gazelle in heat. My eyes become transfixed and I am helpless to look away. Nikki steps out of the dressing room in a blue-gray two-piece and catches me midglare.

"Do you like what you see?" she scoffs.

Think, Corvelli, think. "Not at all. I was just thinking someone should get that girl something to eat." *Smoooooooth.*

"Don't bullshit me, Kevin! If you want a haole, then go get yourself a haole!"

Nikki is making a scene in the small store, and I feel a foot tall. The leggy strawberry-blond gazelle stops in her tracks. The salesclerks stop ringing at the register. The doors to the dressing rooms open and heads pop out. All eyes are on us.

My cell phone starts ringing, and for the first time I can remember, I'm glad to hear it sing. I dig into my pants pocket as Nikki huffs and puffs and returns to the dressing room. I pull the phone from my pocket and read the caller ID. The call is from a number I don't recognize, and my first instinct is to hit IGNORE. But the call is from the 201 area code, the area code I know represents an area of northern New Jersey.

I open the phone and put it to my ear. "Speak."

"Is this Mr. Corvelli?" a woman's voice asks.

"Yes, this is he."

"You don't know me, but I may be able to help you."

"I'm already very happy with my wireless phone service. Thank you anyway."

"No," she says, before I can snap the phone closed. "I may be able to help you win Joey's case."

"Who is this?"

There is silence for nearly a minute on her end of the phone. I don't want to push for the name and have her hang up scared.

"I understand you're looking for Paolo," she finally says.

Nikki has finished her quick change and is back at my side. I don't like for her to listen in on my conversations, but at this point I can say or do little. Together, we step out of the store and back into the mall.

"Paolo Nicoletti?" I ask.

"Yes. Him."

"As a matter of fact, my investigator has been trying to trace Mr. Nicoletti's whereabouts. We would like to ask him a few questions."

"Well, I'm sure Paolo won't be very forthcoming with answers, but maybe if you find him, you'll learn what you need to know."

"Is Paolo here on the island of Oahu?" I ask.

"He is. He's holed up at a hotel."

"We've already checked with every hotel on Oahu, and he's not registered as a guest at any of them."

"He's using a fake name. He's registered under the name Victor Trozzo."

"Do you know where he's staying?"

There is another long pause. "The Pacific Edgewater in Waikiki."

A million questions flood my mind, but I don't know how long I can keep this woman on the phone.

"Why are you helping me?" I ask.

"Because I know that Joey didn't kill that girl."

"How do you know that?"

"Paolo knew that Shannon Douglas was working for the Feds."

My mind is racing. I can't even prove Shannon was working for the Feds, let alone that anyone from the Fiordano family knew about her employment. I need to know who this woman is without asking her directly.

"Why do you want to help Joey?"

"Because, I love him."

"You love him?"

"Of course, I love him," she says, her voice cracking in the beginnings of a cry. "My name is Marie. I'm Joey's aunt."

"So you know this Paolo Nicoletti well?"

"Yeah. You could say that."

"How well?" Though I think I already know the answer.

"*Too* well. I'm married to the son of a bitch twenty-six years."

The line goes dead, and I snap the phone closed. I take a seat on one of the mall benches, and Nikki sits silent at my side.

I speed-dial Flan and he picks up on the first ring.

"We've got Nicoletti," I say. "He's using the alias Victor Trozzo, and he's staying at the Pacific Edgewater. Remember, we just need evidence that he was here on Oahu when Shannon was killed."

"I'm on it."

"There's more, Flan. He knew Shannon was working for the Feds."

"Son of a bitch! Nicoletti is our killer! How did you get all this?"

"His wife."

"His wife sold him out? Shit, she sounds just like my ex-wife."

"Maybe," I say. "But she has more of a motive than just fucking her husband over."

"Oh, yeah? What's that?"

"She's also Joey's aunt," I say. "Flan, be careful. This guy is a lot more dangerous than Carlie Douglas."

"Hey, Kev, you didn't see Carlie when she pulled out the handcuffs. You weren't there in that hotel room when she whipped me with my own belt."

"Well, at least I can be thankful for that."

I snap the phone closed and look at Nikki. I'm hoping she'll stand up and say, "Meet me at Macy's in a half hour," or some shit like that. But she just sits there, silent, making me feel bad.

I chew through the nail of my right index finger and speed-dial Jake. He answers on the fifth ring.

"Jake, I've got some interesting news."

"I missed the Astros going to the World Series when I first came out here," he slurs. "Can you *believe* that?"

Jake's drunk.

"Jake, listen to me."

"Forty-five years I waited for the Astros to go to the big dance, and I missed it."

"Jake, we found Nicoletti."

"Do you listen to Johnny Cash?"

"Jake, did you hear what I just told you?"

Now Jake is mumbling the lyrics to "Cocaine Blues."

"Jake!"

"I like that Alison Kelly, son. You were too hard on her today."

"Well, you'll get to see her again when she testifies at trial, Jake."

"Kevin, do you know that you're like a son to me?"

"I know that, Jake. It's late. Get some sleep. I'll see you in the morning at the courthouse."

"Did I ever tell you that I have—"

I snap the phone closed before he can utter another word.

Nikki tells me she'd like to go home, and I'm quick to oblige. We step out of the mall and into the night, where my orange Jeep glows under the artificial light in the parking lot.

The ride to Kailua seems longer than usual, probably because Nikki won't speak. I'm not sure whether she is angrier about the leggy strawberry blonde or the phone calls, so I don't know which to apologize for.

"I'm sorry about tonight." That should cover it all.

She nods but says nothing.

"The case will be over soon."

If nothing else, one thing about Nikki is clear. She does not like sharing me. Not with mermaid bartenders who like silk ties. Not with leggy strawberry blondes who prance around like gazelles. Not even with young men from New Jersey facing life imprisonment for crimes they insist they did not commit.

"Winning this trial means a lot to you," she says.

"Yes, it does. If my client is really innocent, which I somehow believe he is, it will eat away at me forever if he has to rot in prison. I may never know the truth, but not knowing will be just as bad. If there's even a chance he's innocent, he has to be set free. The problem is that a good many juries have difficulty grasping that concept, the concept of reasonable doubt."

"If you can show that this other guy you were talking about on the phone may have done it, will your client be set free?"

"That's the gist of it," I say, pulling into Nikki's gravel driveway.

"Would they put this other guy in jail and give him a trial?"

"Probably not without a full confession. There's little chance at this point of anyone else being tried for this murder."

"So, even if your client goes free, the police won't look for the real killer?"

"No," I say, shaking my head. "The police will continue to insist that they had the real killer, and they'll close the case. The prosecutors will blame the not-guilty verdict on bad investigative technique by the police. The police will blame the verdict on bad lawyering by the prosecuting attorneys. The public will blame the verdict on an incompetent jury."

"They won't give you any of the credit?"

I laugh. "Hell no."

"Kevin, you work so hard, so many hours. You put yourself in danger. The media portrays you as a shark. Your clients are usually bad people, who are completely ungrateful for all you do for them. Why do you do this? Why do you continue to practice criminal defense?"

"Nikki, some people are just made for this shit."

CHAPTER 37

"The prosecution calls Detective John Tatupu to the stand."

Tatupu is the criminal defense attorney's worst nightmare: a good cop. Born to full-blooded Hawaiian parents on Molokai and raised in the poorer sections of Oahu, he overcame a speech impediment to become a highly decorated officer with the Honolulu Police Department. Tall, well built, with boyish good looks and distinguished gray hair, he has the female jurors' attention before uttering a word. Well dressed and as articulate as any police officer I've ever met, he will make a formidable witness.

Word is that Tatupu is a genuinely good man, who has stood up in the face of corruption, risking his career and his own safety to preserve the integrity of the department. He is friendly and polite, and worse yet, he exudes sincerity. All of this makes my job more difficult. My job is to discredit him on cross-examination, to criticize his techniques and undermine his experience, to put into question his virtue and decency. I have gone toe-to-toe with a lot of cops. The bad ones make it easy, even fun. Nothing is sweeter than embarrassing a bad cop on the stand. But grilling a good cop is like giving a small child the middle finger. It makes you feel like shit, and everyone in the room hates you for it.

Dapper Don Watanabe walks Tatupu through the preliminaries while Jake takes a nap at the counsel table. I assure Joey that it's all part of the plan, but that I can't discuss the plan with him until the trial's over. Luckily for us, Jake doesn't snore.

The body, Tatupu says, was discovered at dawn by a group of early-morning surfers at the far end of Waikiki Beach, near Diamond Head. One of the surfers called Emergency Services from his cell phone. Tatupu, who was at the Honolulu Police Department's Waikiki service station, was the first officer on the scene, less than three minutes from the time the call came in.

Tatupu checked the victim for a pulse, although there clearly was no need. The color and feel of her skin told Tatupu that the girl was already long dead. Paramedics arrived and made the formal pronouncement at 6:27 a.m.

A crowd quickly gathered, and Tatupu immediately directed his team to secure the crime scene by roping off a small portion of the beach. The crowd proved difficult to disperse, but his team controlled the crowd and prevented any unnecessary moving of things and walking about.

Photographs were taken of the victim and the surrounding area. Gasps resonate from the jury box as a picture of Shannon's bloodied corpse is passed around like some Fabergé egg at a second-grade show-and-tell.

Footprints were evidently washed away by the tide. The only fresh prints in the sand were those of the surfers that discovered Shannon's body.

The murder weapon was a bloodstained piece of reef. Discovered by Tatupu a few feet from the body, it contained no usable prints.

The lifeguard station, also swept for fingerprints, yielded only those of the two lifeguards who had complete access to it. However, during a follow-up investigation, police technicians discovered a single, full lip print on the inside Plexiglas of the station.

A pair of sneakers, believed to belong to the defendant, was discovered hidden behind some plant life near the scene of the crime. Lab results conclusively showed that the shoes contained traces of the victim's blood. Furthermore, video from the Hawaiian Sands hotel clearly showed that the defendant left the hotel in bright white Nike sneakers and returned in a pair of black flip-flops.

Tatupu was put in charge of the investigation. He quickly learned that the victim had spent the evening between two bars, Margaritaville and the Bleu Sharq. He interviewed the bartenders at both spots and learned that the victim was last seen leaving the Bleu Sharq at approximately 2:45 a.m. with a local man named Palani Kanno.

Tatupu questioned Palani, who admitted to having sex with the victim and getting into an argument, resulting in a physical altercation. Palani stated that he left her for the

Waikiki Winds hotel, where he worked as a doorman. And that when he left her, she was very much alive.

Palani was cleared as a suspect after his story of going to the Waikiki Winds to buy marijuana and then taking over a shift was confirmed by witnesses and video from the hotel's surveillance cameras. And after witnesses, a pair of honeymooners, came forward and attested to seeing the victim alive, though bruised and bleeding, at a time after Palani had already begun to work his shift.

Once Palani was cleared as a suspect, Tatupu continued his investigation by contacting friends and family members of the victim through local law enforcement back East. A young woman by the name of Cindy DuFrain admitted to police that she informed the victim's ex-boyfriend Joseph Gianforte Jr. of the victim's destination a short time after dropping Shannon off at the airport.

Tatupu soon learned that the defendant took a flight from Newark shortly thereafter and arrived in Honolulu just hours after Shannon.

Surveillance cameras at the Hawaiian Sands hotel captured the defendant leaving his hotel in the early evening and returning shortly before sunrise. Another camera at the Kapiolani Surf Hotel put the defendant in close proximity to the crime scene less than one hour before Palani left the victim on the beach.

Tatupu and his department followed all other leads, including a professor from the victim's law school named Jim Catus. The professor volunteered to police that he was in Honolulu to meet with the victim, and that he arrived a day earlier than she expected. The professor also admitted to seeing the victim with another man, and later soliciting a prostitute at the Leilani Inn.

Yes, Tatupu and his department followed all leads, but in the end, all roads led to the defendant.

Dapper Don's direct examination of Detective Tatupu lasts for more than three hours. During those three hours, as Jake napped and Joey sat in fear, I made a decision. I would not risk losing credibility with the jury by pursuing half-cocked theories about the professor, or Palani hopping on his moped to finish off his victim. I would not pursue the motiveless J. J. Fitzpatrick or the Fed-protected Tony Bitch-Tits and Lazy Eye Sal. I would, instead, do what I did in the trial of *People versus Brandon Glenn*. I would follow my gut instinct and pursue only the one suspect that I knew had both motive and opportunity. The one suspect who could conjure in the minds of this jury a certain reasonable doubt. I would pursue only Paolo "Small Paul" Nicoletti, alias Victor Trozzo.

The courtroom is restless as Dapper Don takes his seat. Narita calls for order in the courtroom. He bangs his gavel, awakening Jake with a start.

"Mr. Corvelli," says Narita from the bench, "it is nearly time to break for lunch. Would you like to begin your cross-examination of Detective Tatupu after the recess, or would you prefer to start and stop?"

"Your Honor," I say, "my cross-examination of the detective will be very brief. If it pleases the Court, I'd like to conduct my cross-examination now."

A collective groan comes from the courtroom, and Narita bangs his gavel again. I don't eat lunch when I'm on trial. My stomach is too tied in knots. But I'm sure the jury is bored and hungry, so I do my best to sweeten the deal, even though I know I am out of line.

"Judge, perhaps if I finish before lunch, the jury can have the rest of the day off?"

Grudgingly, Narita and Watanabe agree. I walk to the podium and check my watch. Twelve oh two.

"Good afternoon, Detective."

"Good afternoon, Counselor."

"I'm curious. Approximately how many homicides occur each year on the island of Oahu?"

"I would say approximately twenty, give or take."

"Only twenty?" I comment, neither asking for nor getting a response. Ordinarily, I would hammer this point home. Homicide detectives get relatively little action here on the islands, making them inevitably less experienced than most urban homicide detectives. Ordinarily, I would remark about the hundreds of homicides in New York City each year. But the jury loves this guy. I can see it in their eyes. Attacking him would only alienate them from me, and it would do my client no good. I'll let the jury make the inference on their own.

"Detective," I say, "I would like to discuss the sneakers. Those that allegedly belong to Joseph Gianforte and purportedly contain trace evidence of the victim's blood. Can you tell me precisely how and when the victim's blood came to be on those sneakers?"

"I assume when he struck her."

"You *assume*. Do you, in fact, have any physical evidence that shows that Joseph Gianforte struck the victim at all?"

"You mean aside from the dead body?"

"Detective, the body of the victim is evidence only that *someone* struck her. It is not at all evidence that Joseph Gianforte struck her. So I ask you again, did you, during the course of the extensive investigation you described during direct, discover *any* physical evidence whatsoever that indicates that Joseph Gianforte struck the victim?"

"Nothing other than the circumstantial evidence I mentioned earlier."

"Ahhh, the circumstantial evidence. Well, let's consider that. Is it possible that the victim's blood could have ended up on those sneakers by some way other than Joseph Gianforte's striking the victim?"

"Anything is possible."

It is the testifying officer's fallback position. It infers that what I am asking skirts on the edge of the realm of possibilities. In other words, yes, what you are asking is possible, just as it is possible that aliens in UFOs really abduct people for their experiments and then return them to the earth. Just as it is possible that hired mediums such as television's John Edward really communicate with the dead. Just as it is possible that the Bush administration really believed there to be weapons of mass destruction in Iraq.

"You testified," I say, "during direct examination that Palani Kanno gave you a statement. Is that correct?"

"It is."

"And in that statement, Palani Kanno admitted to engaging in an argument with the victim on the beach. Is that correct?"

"Yes. It is."

"And he also admitted to engaging in a physical altercation with the victim on the beach, did he not?"

"He did."

"And he admitted to striking the victim, didn't he?"

"He said that it was in self-defense, yes."

"Did he tell you whether his striking the victim caused her to bleed?"

"He said it did not."

"You also testified during direct that you were contacted by witnesses, honeymooners I believe you said, in connection with this case. Is that correct, Detective?"

"That is correct."

"And those honeymooners told you that they observed the victim alive on the beach after Palani Kanno left her there to go to the Waikiki Winds hotel, correct?"

"Correct."

"Would you please remind the jury what else the honeymooners told you?"

Tatupu knows what I am searching for and doesn't want to give it to me. But he has to, or else it will appear as if he is trying to conceal it. His concealing it would work better for me because it would allow me to drag it out of him in front of the jury. But he's too smart for that.

"The honeymooners told me that they observed Miss

Douglas weeping, and that she appeared slightly injured. She was bleeding from a cut on her face."

"She was bleeding. So is it possible, Detective, that Joseph Gianforte came across the victim subsequent to Palani Kanno's striking her, but before she was struck with the death blow, and that was how and when those sneakers came to have on them traces of the victim's blood?"

"As I said before, anything is possible."

"Is it possible then, Detective, that Joseph Gianforte discarded the sneakers simply because they were soaking wet from the surf and covered with sand?"

"Objection," says Dapper Don. "Calls for speculation."

"Withdrawn, Your Honor," I say. "The detective would only have told me that anything is possible anyhow."

"Objection!" cries Dapper Don again.

"Sustained," says Narita. "Further commentary will not be tolerated, Mr. Corvelli."

I ignore the judge and return my attention to the witness. "Detective, would you remind the jury where the sneakers were found in relation to the victim's body?"

"In some greenery, maybe ten yards from the deceased."

"During direct examination, you inferred that the fact that Joseph Gianforte's sneakers were found with traces of the victim's blood on them near the scene of the crime increased the likelihood that he was the perpetrator, did you not?"

"I did."

"And, Detective, you stated that perpetrators routinely

hide items that might link them to their crimes, is that correct?"

"Yes, that is correct."

"And you stated, Detective, that it is the traces of blood found on the sneakers that link these sneakers to this crime, correct?"

"Yes."

"Considering the proximity of the spot where these sneakers were found to the victim's dead body, would you say that these sneakers were well hidden?"

"Not particularly, no."

"Would you please remind the jury how far the ocean is from where the victim's body was discovered?"

"Just a few feet."

"Then let me ask you this, Detective. Assuming Joseph Gianforte owned these sneakers and assuming he committed the crime in question, why would he have tossed the sneakers with the blood still on them only ten yards away from the victim's body, instead of simply washing them off a few feet away in the surf?"

Tatupu eyes Watanabe, but Dapper Don can offer no help. We wait while the detective thinks.

"It was very dark," Tatupu says. "He probably didn't see the blood."

"I see," I say. "But, Detective, you made it clear to this jury that Joseph Gianforte discarded these sneakers and hid them in the plants because they linked him to the crime by virtue of the fact that they were spattered with the victim's blood. So, Detective, if he didn't see the blood on them, why would he have discarded them at all?"

I do not ask the judge to compel the witness to respond. I let the question hang in the air. The longer the silence the better.

I have just two more questions for Detective Tatupu. Two questions I have committed myself to asking, the consequences for doing so be damned.

"Detective," I say, "are you familiar with the name Victor Trozzo?"

Tatupu looks around, thinking over the question, swirling the name around in his head like a connoisseur tasting a fine wine. He doesn't know where I am heading, and this troubles him. But there is only one answer he can give.

"No, I am not."

"Detective, are you familiar with the name Paolo Nicoletti?"

This time his answer comes quicker. "No, I am not."

"Maybe you should be, Detective. Your Honor, I have no further questions at this time, but I reserve the right to recall this witness during the defendant's case-in-chief."

I turn and face my counsel table. Jake is awake and nodding his approval with his head. Joey stares at me, his eyes wide, frozen in a look that conveys an unequivocal fear. I have seen the look of fear in those eyes before, fear from the grim specter of life imprisonment. But that look of fear pales in comparison to the look of fear he wears now, at the mere mention of his uncle's name.

CHAPTER 38

The repercussions of my actions at trial are fast and furious. I am hating myself. I should have known better. Lex Luthor went after Lois Lane. The Joker went after Vicki Vale. The Green Goblin went after Mary Jane Watson. And Paolo "Small Paul" Nicoletti took no time at all in going after Nikki Kapua.

I spin my Jeep onto the gravel driveway, jump out, and run for the red front door. It is locked tight. I pound on it. I pound on it almost as hard as my heart pounds in my chest.

"Nikki, it's me!" I shout as loud as I can.

I hear the locks turn, then the door opens slowly. The whites of her eyes are caught in red spiderwebs; tears like waterfalls stream down her cheeks.

I enter the cottage and close the door behind me. I try to kiss the tears away, but there are far too many for that.

Nikki is shaking. I try to steady her and lead her to her

room. The light is off and the shades are drawn. I can barely see her as she sits on the bed.

"Tell me everything," I say.

She tries to catch her breath and takes my hand in hers, forcing the words from her throat.

"I was walking home from Longs Drug Store; there was something I needed to pick up. There were footsteps coming from behind me. They were moving fast, much faster than mine. I got scared and picked up my pace. But so did the man behind me. He grabbed me. I tried to scream, but he covered my mouth and dragged me behind some bushes."

Rage and fear and every terrible emotion imaginable are building up inside me. I feel around for love and sympathy, but they've been smothered by my hate.

"It was dark. I tried to bite his fingers, but I couldn't even open my mouth. And then, he started talking in my ear."

"What did he say, Nikki?"

"He said, 'Your boyfriend and his friends have been poking their noses into things they have no business poking their noses into.' He said, 'It stops tonight, or I'll have your pretty little head.' He said, 'Tell your boyfriend not to mention my name anymore, not to even *think* it, or I'll slit your throat from ear to ear, you little hula whore.'"

The image of Shannon Douglas involuntarily fills my mind. Then the image of her grows darker. The bloodied face transforms. The image of Shannon is replaced by an image of Nikki, bloodied and frozen in the same gruesome pose.

"Did you see his face, Nikki?"

"No. No, I didn't. It was dark, and he held me facing the opposite way."

"How about his voice? Did you recognize his voice?"

"Yes, I definitely did."

"Whose voice was it, Nikki?"

"Kevin, it was the man from the aquarium."

Earlier, after I received the urgent call from Nikki, I telephoned Flan and told him to put a tail on Nicoletti. He was unsuccessful at tracking him down the previous night, and no one at the Pacific Edgewater was of any particular help. It's as if everyone knows just by looking at him just how dangerous Nicoletti really is.

The moniker Small Paul is like labeling Archie Bunker "Mr. Tolerance," or Edith "Mrs. Intellect," or Meathead "Conservative Mike," or . . . You get the point: I like *All in the Family,* and Paolo Nicoletti is one big son of a bitch.

As Nikki rests on the bed, my cell phone chirps, and I pull it from my pocket. The caller ID reads FLAN.

"Speak."

"Kev, Trozzo has checked out of the Pacific Edgewater."

I knew that the mention of his names at trial would prompt Nicoletti to make a move. I just didn't anticipate his making a move against Nikki. After I finished my cross-examination of Detective Tatupu, I had Jake stonewall the Gianfortes, so that I could leave the courthouse without speaking to them about why I mentioned Nico-

letti's name at trial. Still, I had little doubt that someone
would mention it to Nicoletti himself.

For a few days I won't have to mention Nicoletti at trial,
while Dapper Don Watanabe parades his witnesses during
the remainder of the prosecution's case-in-chief. Then it
will be my turn. It will be my turn to offer proof of Joey's
innocence by offering proof of Paolo Nicoletti's guilt.

"Keep looking, Flan," I say, before snapping the cell
phone shut.

Nikki refuses to call the police. And she is adamant that I
not do so on her behalf. She fears it will bring attention to
her brother and his illicit business, and she will not risk his
arrest and conviction. She will not make any move that
may land Alika in a mainland prison, where she will never
lay eyes upon him again. After a half hour of argument, I
lay down my arms and drop the subject.

"We're not safe here," I say.

"Yes," she says. "We are. Come with me."

She stands and takes my hand. We exit her room and
walk across the small foyer that leads to Alika's bedroom
door. She opens the door and steps into the room, leaving
me in the frame. The room is illuminated only by moonlight, but I can see that the room is in shambles. Clothes
and ashtrays and empty beer cans are strewn about like at
a frat house during Oktoberfest.

On her knees, from underneath the unmade bed, Nikki
withdraws an old Adidas shoe box. She slowly lifts the lid

and reaches in. She pulls out a matte black .40-caliber Smith & Wesson pistol.

"Is it loaded?" I ask.

She nods.

"Is it registered?" I ask, considering the Hawaii Penal Code.

She gives me a look. Ask a stupid question . . .

She hands me the pistol, and together we return to her room. We sit in the darkness with few words between us. Few words and a loaded gun. After forty-five minutes, she lies down and quickly falls asleep.

I place the gun on the nightstand and lie down next to my girl.

But I don't sleep a wink all fucking night.

The sun rises, as it tends to do, and we replace the pistol under Alika's bed. I insist that Nikki come with me to Honolulu, so we leave together in my Jeep. I drop her off at Ala Moana Center and instruct her to mill around the crowds. I give her some money and beg that she stay there until the time comes for her to take the bus to work.

I arrive at the courthouse just in time to watch Alison Kelly take the stand. There are no surprises during direct examination, as Dapper Don takes her through the history and methodology of lip-print identification. The fiery redhead testifies as expected as to the similarities discovered between the lip print found in the lifeguard station and the sample taken from the defendant.

Exhausted from lack of sleep and smothered in fear, I
listen to her testimony in a daze. Fortunately, the questions
I will need to ask her on cross-examination are printed
neatly in order and clasped together in a bright green binder.
For now, we can only put into question Alison Kelly's methodology and the practice's acceptance within the scientific
community. During our case-in-chief, we will put our expert on the stand. But it would be foolish to rest Joey's fate
on the jury's believing that he wasn't on Waikiki Beach
that night. He most certainly was, and there is no way
around that. The only viable argument is that he was there,
but left her alive and in one piece. That someone else then
came along and struck her dead.

"Mr. Corvelli," says Narita from the bench. "Your witness."

I slowly pick myself up from the chair.

"Son," says Jake, stepping over to my side. "Let me handle the cross-examination."

For the first time since I met him, Jake is bright-eyed
and bushy-tailed. He looks downright handsome in a freshly
ironed beige linen suit.

"Are you sure?"

"Oh, I'm sure, son," he says, taking the green binder
from my hand.

"Go get her, tiger," I say, grateful, as exhausted as I am,
to be sitting back down in my seat. Jake is as skillful and
confident at the podium as the great Milt Cashman himself. He deftly crosses Alison Kelly on every point Watanabe covered, moving seamlessly from my binder to his

own notes like an artist switching colors at his canvas. I'll be damned if Jake Harper isn't the most talented cross-examiner I ever laid eyes on.

And I'll be damned if Jake doesn't use his last question on cross to ask Alison Kelly for a date.

CHAPTER 39

"And she said yes!"

"That's so sweet," Nikki says to me, rubbing suntan lotion on my back.

The first week of trial is finally over, and the weekend is here. After Jake set his date with Alison Kelly for next Saturday night, Dapper Don Watanabe called the county's chief medical examiner to the stand. Dr. Derek Noonan testified as to the cause and time of Shannon's death, and the likely height and strength of the criminal perpetrator. Jake did another outstanding cross-examination, kicking hell out of Noonan's conclusions like a professional wrestler on 'roids. Unfortunately, by having the medical examiner testify on Friday, Dapper Don ensured that the jurors will spend their weekend with the image of Shannon's bludgeoned head etched into each of their minds.

Flan is still scouring Oahu for Nicoletti. The airlines have no record of his leaving the island, but he could be using yet another name. Investigators, now on my payroll in New Jersey, are gathering as much information as is available about Nicoletti for use in our case-in-chief. It is certainly a working weekend. But not for me.

Nikki and I are basking in the warm Hawaiian sun on Kailua Beach. We rented a tandem kayak to paddle out to Flat Island, but that was when we were feeling more ambitious. We lie instead on our towels, our eyes closed and arms intertwined, listening to the waves pound the windward shore.

Unlike on the sands of Waikiki, no crowds are here. Just a few avid parasailors and sailboarders taking advantage of the wind. The courthouse is but a forty-minute drive from here, but right now, it seems a hundred thousand miles away.

"The trial should be over by the end of next week," I say. "So if you can take the time off from work, we can fly into Lihue the following Monday."

"I'm so excited," she says. "I miss the feel of old Hawaii, the beauty of Kauai."

"We can stay as long as you'd like."

Jake promised me he'd make my court appearances while I was gone. Now that I've seen him in action, I have every intention of taking him up on his kind offer.

"I know some remote places on Kauai," Nikki teases, "where we can swim naked and make love under spectacular natural waterfalls."

"Sounds even better than the helicopter tours."

With the grace of a salamander, Nikki slithers on top of me.

"Have you been watching the news lately?" she asks.

"No. Not since the trial started."

"Well, you look incredibly sexy in the courtroom sketches. Alika didn't really get a good look at you the day you ran into him at the house. Now he finally knows what you look like."

"How's your brother been lately?"

She sighs. "I still hardly ever see him. He's high all the time. He's still selling ice and smoking half his supply. I'm so very scared for him, Kevin."

"Do you think he would consider getting help? I could probably get him into a good program."

She gives me another look. Ask a stupid question . . .

"So," Nikki says, "now that you've been here several months, can I assume you are here in Hawaii to stay?"

"That's a very safe assumption" is all I say.

A very safe assumption indeed. Since I intend to propose marriage to Nikki on our very first night on Kauai.

CHAPTER 40

Justice evolves only after injustice is defeated. I don't know what that means. I read it fifteen years ago on a Public Enemy album cover and added it to every academic paper I had to write. Once I was sworn in as an attorney, I used it in every motion, every pleading, every piece of correspondence to the court. I shoveled it onto juries, and they ate it up like the Rooty Tooty Fresh 'N Fruity breakfast meal at IHOP. Soon other attorneys were singing the words during their own closing statements. It took a ninety-one-year-old retired cabdriver on a jury in Queens to finally ask me what the hell it meant. I admitted I had no idea, and that he'd have to ask Flavor Flav.

Jurors are a lot like dogs. They don't necessarily understand what you're saying; they only respond to the tone and pitch differences in your voice. In other words, it's not what you say, it's how you say it. A simple question like "So are you telling this jury you had *blueberry* pancakes for breakfast?" if asked correctly, can get the jurors' attention and help to extinguish a witness's credibility. Especially if that witness isn't too bright. Suffice it to say, I didn't so much enjoy my last meeting with Palani Kanno, but I'm going to have a lot of fun now.

It is Monday morning and Dapper Don Watanabe has just completed his direct examination of the pugilistic doorman from the Waikiki Winds hotel. Dapper Don put Palani on the stand not only to clear him as a suspect, but to confirm that someone was in the lifeguard station to make the noise that interrupted Palani's romantic interlude.

"Your witness, Mr. Corvelli," says Narita from the bench.

"Thank you, Your Honor."

I take my place at the podium and offer Palani a broad smile. We're not on *his* island. We're not in front of *his* hotel. This time, we're on *my* turf. And, yes, Palani, you stupid son of a bitch, this time, it's personal.

"Good morning, Mr. Kanno."

He nods but says nothing. Watanabe has instructed him to use as few words as possible.

"We have met before, have we not?"

He nods again.

"You'll have to speak up for the court reporter."

"Yeah, we met."

"I may look different from the last time we left each other."

"Yeah, you're no longer one sharkbait. You got tan."

"And my face looks different, too, from the last time you saw it."

"Yeah, you heal up real good."

Palani is smug, and I don't like smug. By kicking the hell out of this guy on the stand, I'll accomplish two goals. The first is that I'll show the jury that Shannon Douglas was quick to intimately associate herself with a local low-life and, thus, could easily have got herself killed by just about anyone. The second, of course, is personal satisfaction.

"You like hitting people, don't you, Mr. Kanno?"

"Objection," says Dapper Don. "Argumentative."

"Your Honor," I say, "Mr. Kanno testified that he struck Miss Douglas on the beach, and I know for a fact he struck me several times in the face. It's a legitimate question."

"The objection is sustained," says Narita.

That's okay. I just told the jury what I wanted them to hear.

"Mr. Kanno, you testified that you were at Waikiki Beach with the victim on the night she was murdered, did you not?"

"Yeah, I already said that."

"Yet you didn't kill her, is that correct?"

"That's right."

"And you didn't witness the murder either, did you?"

"Nah."

"So it must be possible for someone to have been at the scene of a crime and not have committed or witnessed the crime himself. Am I right?"

He thinks about the question, wondering if I'm trying to trick him. Finally, he nods and says, "Yeah."

"Good. Now will you please explain that to Mr. Wata-nabe and the Honolulu Police Department, because it seems they can't grasp that very *reasonable* possibility?"

"Objection!" cries Dapper Don.

Narita sustains the objection and admonishes me.

"Mr. Kanno," I say, "you testified that you met Miss Shannon Douglas at a bar in Waikiki called the Bleu Sharq, is that correct?"

"Yeah."

"And you danced with her, correct?"

"I said all this already."

"Bear with me, Mr. Kanno. I realize you have doors to open, and I'll try to have you off the stand as quickly as possible. Please, don't hit me."

"Objection!"

"Withdrawn," I say.

As I'm looking back at the dirty look on Dapper Don's face, I see Flan entering the courtroom. I specifically in-structed him to avoid doing so, as I may need to call him to testify during our case-in-chief. But here he is, barreling up the middle aisle, waving a manila envelope in his hand.

"Your Honor," I say, "may I have two minutes to con-sult with my colleague?"

"You have ninety seconds, Mr. Corvelli."

I step to the rail and Flan whispers in my ear. He tells me what is in the envelope and where he got it from. I look back toward Palani and decide I'm through with playing games. It's time to make some real progress toward saving Joey's ass. Not to mention my career.

"Mr. Kanno," I say, "at any time while at the Bleu Sharq, did you lose sight of Shannon Douglas?"

"Yeah, when I went to the bathroom."

"Would you please tell the jury what you were doing in the bathroom, Mr. Kanno?"

Palani can lie in answering this question, and I will have to accept his answer. But he doesn't know that, so he decides to tell the truth.

"I was smoking one joint."

"How long were you in the bathroom smoking marijuana?"

"Maybe ten minutes."

"When you exited the bathroom, did you find Shannon Douglas right away?"

"Nah, I didn't."

"How long did it take you to find her?"

"Maybe fifteen more minutes."

"Mr. Kanno, did you ever come to learn where Shannon Douglas was during that time?"

"Nah."

"Do you know if Shannon Douglas spoke to anyone, or if anyone spoke to her, while you were in the bathroom and/or while you were looking for her after that?"

"Nah, I dunno."

I open the manila folder and leaf through the items. Everything is in there, just as Flan said. I step over to the counsel table, take a sip of water, and wink at Jake, even though he doesn't know what the hell is going on. I go into my briefcase and flip through the file, pulling from it the single item that I need.

"Your Honor," I say, "I would like this item marked for identification as Defendant's Exhibit Nine."

Jake has copies of the item, and he hands one to Watanabe and one to the court officer with the pretty purple flower in her hair.

"May I approach the witness?" I ask.

"You may," says Narita.

"Mr. Kanno," I say, coming as close to him as I have in nearly six months. "Do you recognize the man in this photograph?"

From above the top of the photograph that I hold in front of my face, I see Palani's eyes flare in angry recognition. He nods slowly at first, then more quickly. Like a mad-as-hell, take-no-prisoners, pissed-off bobblehead doll.

"Yeah," he says, "I do."

"Do you know his name?"

"Nah."

"Then, would you please enlighten the jury as to where you saw the man depicted in this photograph?"

"The Bleu Sharq."

"When did you see him at the Bleu Sharq?"

"On the night that girl was killed. Just before I found her, he knocked into me, on purpose like."

"Did you speak to him?"

"Nah, but that big haole said something to me. That's why I remember him."

"What did he say to you, Mr. Kanno?"

"He said, 'Watch yourself, you fucking coconut nig-gah, or I'll bash in your fucking skull.'"

I step back to the counsel table and take another drink of water. Jake can't hide his smile. Joey looks bewildered. But that bewilderment is about to turn into something else altogether.

"Let the record reflect," I say, "that the man depicted in the photograph marked as Defendant's Exhibit Nine is identified by the Federal Bureau of Investigation as Paolo 'Small Paul' Nicoletti, a capo of the Fiordano crime family in northern New Jersey."

An uproar explodes in the courtroom, but I hear one distinct voice, yelling at me from the top of his lungs, calling me a two-faced son of a bitch. I turn and see Joseph Gianforte Sr. being pulled from the courtroom by three armed officers.

The judge raps his gavel and threatens to clear the courtroom.

Palani's run-in with someone at the Bleu Sharq while searching for Shannon seemed rather extraneous while we sat on the beach, smoking *pakalolo* from a pipe. But Flan's coming to the rail minutes ago triggered in me an instant total recall. Flan went to my office earlier today, funny man that he is, with an envelope filled with Vicodin and a note reading, *Just in case today's witness gets out of hand.* While he was sitting there, speaking to Hoshi, a FedEx package arrived. He saw that it was delivered from Mahwah, New Jersey, and asked Hoshi to open it right away. The package was from Marie Nicoletti, Joey's aunt, and it contained a cash receipt from the Bleu Sharq for two Peroni bottled beers, dated the night Shannon was killed. With the receipt was a handwritten note that read, *I found this in the bastard's pants pocket.*

With Palani's testimony on cross-examination, I have established that Paolo Nicoletti was at the Bleu Sharq on the night Shannon was killed. Nicoletti now has a target on his back. But I know that I now do as well. It is now a matter of who is mentally tougher, of who can outlast the other, of who can squeeze the trigger first.

CHAPTER 41

Nikki is staying with Julia, one of her sexy bartender friends. Alika, too, has been warned to steer clear of the cottage in Kailua until after the trial. Flan and Jake spent last night at the Kapiolani Surf Hotel, while I opted for the Grand Polynesian, which reminds me just how Bond-like I, Kevin Corvelli, really am. Suffice it to say, I am dressed in the same suit I wore yesterday, and my cell phone battery is ready to die. It is definitely an inconvenience to be hunted by the mob.

Today's testimony should be anticlimactic. Cindy Du-Frain has been called by Dapper Don Watanabe to testify against her former friend. Cindy is petite and pretty, with a few scattered freckles and mousy brown hair. She appears more than a little melancholy over the death of her best friend. Or perhaps she's glum over today's duty, which would make things all the better for us.

Dapper Don is decked out in Ralph Lauren for what

should be the conclusion of the prosecution's case. He greets Cindy DuFrain but does not get the warm smile he received from all his previous witnesses. Even Palani had offered Dapper Don a jovial "Howzit."

"Miss DuFrain," Dapper Don says, "I know that being here must be very difficult for you. I'd like to thank you for traveling all this way from New York to testify at this very important trial. I only wish you could see our lovely island under different circumstances."

Cindy DuFrain's testimony can only hurt us, so I hope the jury isn't listening. To let the jury know that it's all right not to pay attention to this testimony, I feign boredom and pretend not to be listening myself.

"Would you please tell the jury how you knew Miss Shannon Douglas?" asks Dapper Don.

"She was my friend. I knew her since high school in Tennessee. Most recently, we went to law school together in New York."

Cindy DuFrain speaks casually, in a conversational tone. Attractive and articulate, she makes an effective witness.

"Do you also know the defendant, Mr. Joseph Gianforte Jr.?"

"I do," she says sadly without looking at him.

"Would you please identify him?"

I tell Joey to stand and he does.

She looks in his direction and offers him a sorrowful smile. "That's him."

Dapper Don asks Cindy for details about her relationship with Shannon. He is no doubt concluding his case with

Cindy to give the jury an image of Shannon Douglas less two-dimensional than the photographs he passed around. Cindy paints Shannon as a vibrant, intelligent, fun-loving girl with aspirations of going into federal law enforcement.

"Miss DuFrain," Dapper Don says, "prior to Shannon's leaving New York for holiday here on Oahu, did she tell you where she was going?"

"Yes, she did. In fact, I drove her to the airport. She said she needed to get away. That she planned to spend a couple of weeks soaking up sun in Waikiki."

"Miss DuFrain, did you relay this information to anyone else?"

"Yes, I told Joey."

"Miss DuFrain, what did you tell the defendant?"

Cindy shifts uncomfortably in her chair. "Well, Shannon had recently broken up with Joey, and he was understandably upset. He came to the apartment and asked me where Shannon was because he couldn't get in touch with her. I told him to calm down, to try to get over her. I told him Shannon wouldn't be around for the next couple of weeks. He persisted in asking me where she was, and I finally told him she left a short time ago for Honolulu."

"What do you know of the relationship between Shannon and the defendant prior to their breakup, Miss DuFrain?"

"They were very close. They were inseparable."

Dapper Don walks her through what she knows of the events leading up to Joey's misdemeanor conviction in New York. I object at every turn, but Judge Narita consistently shoots me down. Dapper Don introduces an e-mail communication from Joey to Cindy, which describes for the jury precisely what Joey told me. Only it doesn't sound nearly as truthful. The dam containing Joey's motive has been collapsed; the terrible truth is flooding in. And I am helpless to stop it.

The sheer intensity of the relationship between Shannon and Joey is damaging to us, and I attempt to distract the jurors by rummaging through my files.

"Miss DuFrain," Dapper Don continues, "would you describe the breakup between Shannon and the defendant as being very sudden?"

"Yes, it was very sudden."

"Do you know, Miss DuFrain, just what caused the breakup?"

"Shannon and Joey had broken up once before. And during that breakup, Shannon started seeing someone else. A professor at our law school."

"What was his name?"

"Professor Jim Catus."

"Go on, Miss DuFrain."

"When Shannon and Joey got back together, she tried to break it off with Professor Catus, but she was having a difficult time."

Joey's knuckles are turning white as he grasps hold of the defense table with both hands. His face is a shocking crimson, and I pour him a tall glass of water, hoping he'll cool down. It does us absolutely no good for the jury to see him angry.

"So," Cindy continues, "Shannon broke up with Joey because she felt guilty. Guilty for cheating on him and guilty for putting her career above him."

I try to hide Joey's face by bringing some papers up to mine. I've inadvertently grabbed the brochures from Diamond Head Diamonds, the store I stopped in to pick out an engagement ring for Nikki. The rings are costly, to say the least.

"It was one thing when Shannon and Joey were just dating . . ." Cindy says.

I replace the brochures in my briefcase and pull out a close-up photo of the victim's left hand. And that is when I see it.

". . . but once Joey proposed, Shannon couldn't live with herself."

In the photograph, on Shannon's left hand, a strip of stark white skin on her fourth finger contrasts deeply with her leftover summer tan.

"They were engaged?" Watanabe asks Cindy on the stand.

"You were engaged?" I ask Joey in his ear.

"Yes," Cindy says.

"Yes," Joey whispers to me.

I turn Joey around at the counsel table and speak to him as low as I can. "Did you give her a ring?"

"Yeah," he whispers, "a two-carat diamond."

"Did she give it back to you when you broke up?"

He shakes his head.

"You son of a bitch, Joey, *why didn't you tell me this?*"

"I didn't think it was rel—"

"Just shut the fuck up," I say much too loud.

"Mr. Corvelli!" shouts Narita from the bench. "If I ever hear you use that kind of language in my courtroom again, you will spend the night in lockup!"

"I'm sorry, Your Honor."

Dapper Don gives me an unsympathetic look and says, "I tender the witness."

I stand and first walk over to Jake. "Call Flan and have him meet us at our office in an hour."

Jake gets up to exit the courtroom, and I step over to the podium, a glass half-full of water in hand.

"Aloha, Cindy," I say. "May I call you Cindy?"

"Aloha. Of course, you may call me Cindy."

I look back at Dapper Don, stifling my urge to stick out my tongue. With seven words, I have already gained an air of familiarity with the prosecution's final witness. Something Watanabe wasn't able to accomplish at all.

"Cindy, you testified during direct examination that Joey and Shannon were engaged, is that correct?"

"Yes, it is."

"Do you know if Joey gave Shannon an engagement ring?"

"Yes, he did."

"Have you seen the ring, Cindy?"

"As a matter of fact, I helped Joey pick it out."

"Would you please describe the ring for the jury?"

"It was a two-carat, princess-cut diamond with a platinum band."

"Cindy, do you know how much the ring was worth?"

She looks at Joey as if to ask if it is all right for her to reveal the cost. I assure her that it's okay.

"It was in excess of twelve thousand dollars," she says.

"Did Shannon wear the ring often after Joey gave it to her?"

"Yes, Shannon never took it off."

"Did Shannon return the ring to Joey after they broke up?"

"No, she did not."

"Cindy, you testified that you drove Shannon to the airport when she was leaving for Honolulu, did you not?"

"Yes, I did."

"Think carefully, Cindy. Was Shannon wearing the diamond engagement ring when you dropped her off at the airport?"

"Yes," she says quickly, "she was."

"Are you absolutely certain?"

"Yes, I am. I remember because I made a comment about it. I asked Shannon if she wanted me to hold the ring for her while she was gone. She said, 'No, it'll help to keep the guys away.'"

From my peripheral vision, I see Watanabe frantically searching through his file. But Dapper Don already knows what I know: no two-carat-diamond engagement ring was found on the victim's person or in her hotel room, and it certainly was not in the possession of the defendant at the time of his arrest.

A $12,000 diamond engagement ring is missing. Clearly, whoever killed Shannon also took the ring. The ring we all know that Joey does not have.

Ladies and gentlemen of the jury, I give you reasonable doubt.

CHAPTER 42

Court recesses for the day, and Jake and I are out the door as quickly as our legs can carry us. When we get to our office, Flan is already in the conference room waiting for us. I have Hoshi bring us a map of the island of Oahu, and I spread it across the conference-room table.

"We find the ring and we find our killer," I say.

"If it is Nicoletti," Flan says, "wouldn't he have brought the ring back to Jersey?"

"I don't think so," I say. "I don't think he would have risked taking it on the plane. He couldn't have known for sure that the police weren't onto him. And I doubt he opened a safety-deposit box here on the island, though we'll check for one, too, if it comes to that. My guess is that he would've gotten rid of the ring as quickly as possible here on Oahu, probably by pawning it using another false name. Hopefully, whoever he pawned it to will remember him, even though more than six months have passed. Even if we can't identify Nicoletti, finding the ring should be enough to get Joey off the hook."

"If Nicoletti killed Shannon to keep her quiet like we think he did," Flan says, "he may have just tossed the ring in the trash."

"A criminal like Nicoletti wouldn't toss away twelve grand," I say. "Besides, if he was thinking that way, he would never have bothered taking it off her dead hand in the first place."

I ask Hoshi to bring me three copies of the yellow pages.

"Gentlemen," I say, "we are looking for a two-carat, princess-cut diamond engagement ring with a platinum band. We need to check every pawnshop and jewelry store on Oahu that trades in pre-owned diamonds. It would probably have been brought to them within the first two days of the murder before police would have been able to put out word."

I use my Sharpie to divide the island into three sections.

"Jake, you take Honolulu and the rest of the leeward side. Flan, you take windward Oahu. I'll take central Oahu and all of North Shore."

Flan and Jake start rifling through the pages of their phone books, jotting down names and addresses. I take mine and head for the door.

"The clock is ticking, gentlemen," I say. "Thank you and good luck."

———

Oahu has fifty-six pawnbrokers and over three hundred jewelers. The pawnbrokers have been given first priority. After hitting a handful of brokers in Wahiawa, I pull my cell phone from my pocket to see if Jake or Flan have made any more progress than I. Of course, since I didn't sleep at home and charge it last night, the bastard battery is dead.

My home in Waialua is only a fifteen-minute ride from here, so I jump in my Jeep and drive. I hate cell phones, but I hate even more not being able to contact Nikki to make sure she's just fine. I pull in front of my home, jump out of the Jeep, and grab my mail. As I walk across the street, I see, sitting stone still, a handsome gray cat that looks a lot like Skies. So many strays are in this neighborhood, I wonder how they all eat and survive.

I step inside and lock the door behind me. I walk into the kitchen and plug my cell phone into its charger, then return to the living room to check for messages on my landline. The light is not blinking.

That's when I see him. He steps out of my bedroom and in front of the front door. He stands there between me and my only means of escape.

"Sit down," Nicoletti says in a throaty voice befitting his size.

I take a seat in the chair next to the phone, sweat suddenly dripping from my forehead, stinging my eyes. My breathing quickens; nausea creeps into my gut.

Nicoletti seats himself on the couch across from me.

"What the fuck do you think you're doing in that courtroom?"

"I—"

"Shut the fuck up!" he shouts. "I already know what you been doing, and I'm putting a fucking end to it here and now."

Nicoletti pulls a cigarette from his pocket and I wonder if he's armed. He certainly wouldn't need to be. The size of the hands lighting his cigarette could wrap around my neck at least twice. This is probably not the best time to tell him how much I loathe cigarette smoke.

"I like Joey Bangs," he says. "You know who gave him that name?"

I nod but say nothing, afraid to open my mouth.

"Yeah, Joey said he told you. But did he tell you why I gave it to him?"

I shake my head, not saying a word.

"I gave him that name in high school because he was banging every chick in his class."

He allows himself a long, hearty laugh.

"As much as I like Joey Bangs, I'm not going down for this murder, Counselor. And I know that's where all this is heading if I allow you to continue doing whatever it is you are doing."

The landline rings and I move for the phone. But Nicoletti gets up and throws me back down into the chair.

"Sit still, you motherfucker!" he shouts, pulling a handgun from the small of his back. "One more move and your little girlfriend's gonna be serving mai tais out of your fucking skull!"

The answering machine picks up the call, and I hear

my voice from a much happier time: "You've reached Attorney Kevin Corvelli. Please leave a message after the tone."

The tone sounds.

"Kev, it's Flan. I tried your cell but it must be dead. I found the ring. It was at a pawnshop in Kailua. The bastards wouldn't give me the name at first. But I gave them a few hundred bucks and they folded like a cheap suit. I'm billing you for that, by the way. Well, listen, I wanted to tell you in person, but fuck it. It wasn't Nicoletti at all. The name of the fucker who sold the ring to the pawnbroker is Alika Kapua."

CHAPTER 43

I am already in my Jeep, well on my way to Kailua, when I realize I've forgotten my cell phone. Convinced by Flan's phone message that I would now be pursuing a new lead, Nicoletti let me go free with the caveat that I not go to the police and describe our impromptu meeting in my home. I readily agreed on the condition that he go outside and locate Skies, whom he accidently let out my front door. My foot feels stuck to the accelerator as I race toward the Kapua cottage in search of further evidence that Nikki's brother, Alika, murdered Shannon Douglas in a robbery gone awry.

Scared away by the very real threat of Paolo Nicoletti, the cottage will be empty, although I have no idea for just how long. Clearly, selling ice alone did not generate the income necessary to feed Alika's own habit. I seriously doubt that the Douglas robbery was his first. His new-found hobby is no doubt why he acquired the gun. I have read in the *Honolulu Advertiser* about a rash of robberies in Mililani in recent months. They remain as yet unsolved, yet are attributed to the ever-growing ice epidemic plaguing the Hawaiian Islands. I would bet my bottom gecko that Alika Kapua is responsible for his fair share of these crimes.

No one can accuse me of being the most ethical attorney in this world. But no chance in hell am I warning Nikki of the storm about to rain down upon her brother. For a long time, I was impervious to the victims of the crimes of the people I was hired to defend. But something over the past six months took hold of me. Something in the photos of Shannon Douglas, both alive and dead, made me angry about her murder. Something in Joey's voice made me feel sorry for his loss. Justice is rarely, if ever, the goal of the criminal defense attorney. But for the first time in my career, I can truthfully say that it is mine.

I am hopeful that my actions will not destroy any chance I have of creating a future with Nikki. I am hopeful that when she sees the evidence, she will weep but understand. I am hopeful that when I bring the evidence to Tatupu and Watanabe, Alika will be arrested and Joey will be freed. I am hopeful of a hell of a lot. But the reality of it is that it would be foolish of me to risk Joey's freedom and my career on the strength of a single pawn slip.

I park my Jeep four blocks away on the darkest street I can find. I hike on foot toward the cottage, maneuvering behind bushes and parked cars whenever possible. When I get to the cottage, I curse myself for demanding that Nikki lock all doors and windows before leaving to stay with her friend. I intend to anonymously call police to the scene if I discover anything useful, and I would prefer there be no evidence of an amateurish break-in. But, looking around, I realize I really have no other choice.

I creep around to the back of the cottage, my hands shaking with every step. The night is cool as far as Hawaiian nights go, yet I find myself drenched in sweat. I remove my suit jacket and wrap it tightly around my right fist, as I've seen done so many times on the silver screen. With the jacket tightly secured, I throw a right jab into the window leading into the living room and nearly break my fist. The glass, however, is none the worse for wear.

With my right hand throbbing in pain, I search the small yard for something more solid to break the glass. I slip back into my jacket, then with my left hand pick up a rock. It is large and ivory, and it reminds me of the piece of reef that was used to kill Shannon. I cock my left arm back and whip it at the window, shuddering at the sound of breaking glass.

I reach my hand through, careful not to cut myself while attempting to unlatch the lock. I do so, ripping only my suit and not the skin on my arm. I open the window, take a deep breath and climb in. I stand completely still as my eyes adjust to the darkness. I try to conjure some rational thought, but I left all logic somewhere outside. I am running on lunacy.

I look down at my hands and realize I'm leaving prints around the area of forced entry. I've been admonishing clients for years about how stupid they must be to leave such evidence behind. I realize for the first time that I haven't at all thought this through. I have only a vague idea of what I'm looking for, but I am confident that I will know it when I see it. I could very well find the companion receipt to the pawn slip, his bloody clothes, or even the fruits of other robberies. Whatever I find, I'll leave it where it is, find a phone, and call the cops.

In the darkness, I feel around the cottage the way I did that first night with Nikki. I navigate the small area blindly, searching for the door to Alika's room. Once I find it, I open it, take another deep breath, and step inside.

The mess of dirty clothes, ashtrays, and empty beer cans is illuminated by the half-moon outside. My first instinct is to drop to my knees and reach underneath the bed, to feel around for the old Adidas shoe box and pull it free. The box is light and I open the lid to see for myself what I already know to be true. The weapon is gone.

Still on my knees, staring helplessly into the empty box, I suddenly hear the sound of footfalls outside followed by the jingle-jangle of keys. Nikki, I know, is working the evening shift at the Bleu Sharq, which means that Alika Kapua must be coming home.

I replace the lid on the shoe box and stuff it back under the bed. I stand up and bolt out the door into the small foyer leading to Nikki's room. I dive into her room just as I hear the front door creak open.

I slowly close the door to Nikki's room, careful not to make a sound. I pant frantically in the darkness as I hear

the television in the living room turn on. I glance around
the room, looking toward the windows for escape. The
half-moon illuminates this room even brighter than Alika's,
giving it and me an eerie glow.

Nikki's bedroom is back in the disarray it had been in
the first time I was here. Clothes and beauty items are
strewn haphazardly across her furniture. Ledgers and loose
papers are piled high upon her desk. Even the mementos
and photographs with cropped-out heads are back.

I pick up one of the photographs to examine it, a tiny
sense of betrayal tugging at my heart. Nikki's smiling face
rests on the shoulder of a tall, bare-chested man. The headless man boasts a tattoo on his chest, one I immediately
recognize. A weeping tiki god. I rifle through the pile of
pictures, all of them of Nikki, all of them with the same
bare-chested, headless man.

Palani Kanno.

I feel dizzy, faint enough to drop. I forget about the
television sounding from the living room. I forget about
Alika, undoubtedly carrying his gun. I forget about the
danger lurking just outside the door.

I pick through the items on her desk and find a half-
filled journal. I open it and scan the dates. I see my name
peppered throughout the pages, but the focus of my search
is not my name. I am looking for the name of Palani Kanno.

I flip backward through the pages until I spot it. I search
for the beginning of the passage so that I may read it in
context, but time is short, and instead I start somewhere in
the middle.

. . . *and this guy she screamed at and called a "stalker" left her there alone on the beach, just as Palani had done before him.*

Palani. I was shaking just thinking about him, thinking about him having sex with this HAOLE in the sand! I felt short of breath, dizzy. It felt like animals were eating my insides! My life, my love, my WORLD was torn to shreds!

I felt nauseous, close to vomiting. I couldn't help but curse her aloud. She heard me. She looked toward the shrubs where I was hiding and took a couple of steps toward me.

Without even thinking about it, I found myself feeling around in the dark for something, some rock or reef, a weapon of some sort. How could she do this to me? How could she cause me all this PAIN after listening to me beg her to stay away from Palani at the bar? How could she come to my island and take from me the only LOVE that I had left in my life?!

"Is someone there?" she asked. "Help me," I cried, hoping to bring her closer to where I hid. She moved toward me slowly, cautiously . . .

Seeing her eyes through the bushes caused something in me to just SNAP! I picked up the piece of reef, raised it above my head, and leapt at her from behind the shrubs. The reef struck her right in the skull and we both landed facedown in the sand.

The piece of reef was red with blood. My hands were shaking, but I managed to turn her limp body over in the sand. Looking at her bloodied face, I didn't know what to do . . .

But I knew what I had done.

I don't hear the door open when it does. I hear only the voice from behind me as the light flickers on.

"I'm pregnant, Kevin."

I turn, see her eyes locked on the journal still glued to my trembling hands.

"I wanted to wait, to tell you on Kauai. We are going to have a *keiki*."

I stare at Nikki, an incredulous look plastered on my face. My world is turning inside out. The past six months suddenly seem like a dream.

"I would like to give our child a Hawaiian name," she says, "if that's okay with you."

"Nikki, what have you done?"

"You mean *that*?" She points at the journal, her other hand hidden behind her back. "I told you that I like to write."

"*You* killed Shannon Douglas."

"Don't do this, Kevin," she says, shaking her head. "Just let it go."

"*Let it go?*"

"The trial is almost over. Then we'll leave this place, forever if you want."

"Do you *hear* yourself, Nikki?"

"We can move away from here and raise a family. Kevin, we have a child on the way."

I slowly shake my head, but say nothing. For just the slightest instant, I am tempted to run from Oahu, to run from the law. To change our names and find a home somewhere across the sea. But then I think of Shannon. And then, I think of Joey. I think of Jake and of Flan and the man I'm striving to become. And the choice becomes no choice at all.

"Never," I say.

The word rings like a bell, and with it, she brandishes a butcher's knife. She charges at me like a bull at a matador, and like a matador, I deftly dodge out of the way. As I move, she swings the knife, tripping, then falling clumsily across the bed.

I bolt for the door just as she screams, *"Alika!"*

That is when I see him, high and wild-eyed, loading a clip into his gun.

I run for the red front door and make it out of the cottage, hitting the street at full speed. I look back and see Alika in the moonlight, chasing me with pistol in hand.

"Shoot him!" Nikki cries, but Alika doesn't yet have a clean shot.

I swerve in and out between parked cars, ducking my head as much as I can. The scene is surreal and I fear I'll faint, my legs already threatening to give out on me. I dart across the street, heading toward a house, leaving myself wide-open for the shots.

I hear them first. Two rounds like cannons. A split second of silence, then two more. My knees buckle, and to the ground I fall, my chin striking the pavement, my teeth damn near biting through my tongue.

Facedown on the pavement, the taste of blood in my mouth, I wait for the pain I know will inevitably come. I slowly feel around my chest for the exit wounds. I'm frozen on the blacktop, my knees bloodied, and my right wrist fractured from the fall. The bullets must still be inside me. I cannot move; yet here I am, sitting prey.

That's when I realize that the second two shots came from the opposite direction.

I look backward to find Nikki, kneeling over her brother under the light of a streetlamp, weeping at his bloodied body.

I look forward to find a familiar figure, standing stone still, eyeing me over the barrel of a smoking gun.

Then, like a mirage, the lone figure vanishes behind some houses, and I pull myself up from the ground. I remove my jacket to see that the bullets never struck me, and I breathe out for perhaps the very first time tonight.

I take the painful ten steps toward Nikki, all the while eyeing the weapon Alika dropped to the ground. With my sore right leg, I kick it across the street, where it ricochets harmlessly off the curb.

Nikki is hysterical, shaking and screaming at her brother to wake up. I look at his face and know immediately he will not. His eyes are open wide, seeing nothing. His mouth is full of blood. And where his heart once beat are two gaping holes.

"Give me your cell phone," I say in her ear.

She rocks back and forth, speaking gibberish to herself.

"Give it to me!" I yell.

She pulls the cell phone from her belt and drops it to the ground.

I pick it up and dial 911.

"There's a man dead," I say into the phone. I give the emergency operator my name and the address where we can be found. She tries to keep me talking, tries to get as much information from me as she can. She asks me many questions, some of which I answer, others I decline.

Sirens sound in minutes, and before I snap the phone shut, I answer one final query.

"No," I say into the cell, "I did not see the shooter."

CHAPTER 44

Some criminals have compelling reasons to confess their crimes. Other criminals simply *have* to confess their crimes, whether it is to the police, to their lawyer, to their shrink, to their spouse, or even to themselves in the form of a diary. Confessions somehow make sins easier on the soul. And easier on the American system of justice. In this case, Nikki made things easier on me by confessing to the murder of Shannon Douglas in a hysterical rant to police at the scene of her brother's death. And, of course, Nikki's detailed handwritten journal confirmed her sordid story.

My Hawaiian hula girl is now in jail awaiting sentencing after pleading guilty to second-degree murder. With the overcrowding in Hawaii's prisons, she will likely be shipped to a prison on the mainland, where she will be locked away for at least the next couple of decades of her life.

Nikki was not the first girl that lied to me about being

pregnant with my child, but she was the first to do so in an effort to keep me from turning her in for criminal homicide. For an instant, I believed her. Then I remembered how Palani had told me that his former girlfriend, whom I now know to be Nikki, also told him he had knocked her up. Fool me once, shame on you. Fool me twice, shame on me. Or some shit like that.

It would be easy to simply say that Nikki was a rejected girl, acting in a jealous rage. But it was much more than that. Her *ohana* was torn apart by an evil haole, who involved her father in the drug trade that got him sent away to prison. That same haole was responsible for addicting her mother to ice, which led to her psychosis and ultimate suicide. Nikki was also losing Alika, the only *ohana* she had left, to the dangerous underworld of ice, when Palani rejected her and moved quickly on to another haole, a beautiful, young law student named Shannon Douglas.

Haoles stole the Hawaiians' land, Nikki once told me, then they stole her family. She was not about to let one steal her first and only love. Nikki warned Shannon of this while Palani was in the bathroom smoking a joint at the Bleu Sharq. Nikki took Shannon outside for several minutes, threatening her. But Shannon refused to listen, and for that she was killed.

The murder of Shannon Douglas was, indeed, a crime of passion, and a sloppy one at that. Still, had Alika not regularly ransacked Nikki's room and stolen the diamond ring, he would still be alive today. Nikole Kapua would have got away with murder. And I would be married to a killer.

Because Nikki *did* love me. Of that much I am certain.

Dapper Don Watanabe stood tall in a Louis Vuitton suit in open court and apologized to Joey after moving to dismiss all charges. Afterward, he sincerely thanked me for my service to the community in helping to catch a killer. He called me an honorable adversary. I can't say I agree with that, but I can say that Donovan Watanabe is the classiest and most admirable prosecutor I have ever come up against.

Joey's ultimate account, as unbelievable as it sounded at the time, was mostly truthful. However, his keeping from me crucial information nearly cost him his future. From his being at the scene of the crime to the two-carat diamond ring he gave to his girl, Joey just didn't see these tidbits as vital. Joey said he has seen enough of the courtroom to last him a lifetime. And I think the world is much better off that Joey has decided for certain that he won't be returning to law school.

Joey thanked me in an eight-page, heartfelt letter. He informed me that although Hawaii is a beautiful place, he is unlikely to ever set foot on the islands again. Not even on his honeymoon, whenever the hell that might be. Though he tells me he's presently seeing Cindy DuFrain.

Joey's parents, Senior and Gina, thanked me personally at my office. I didn't have to shake their hands, but each insisted on a hug. Senior reasoned that since his son really wasn't guilty, he shouldn't have to pay for the defense. Gina told him to shut the fuck up and to give me another hug.

Paolo Nicoletti initially came to the island, like Lopardi and Antonazzo, to keep an eye on Joey. He flew back here for the trial to offer moral support in his own shadowy way. He rather liked Shannon for his nephew, and he followed her that night to see if he could talk to her and perhaps help her and Joey patch things up. Meanwhile, Lopardi and Antonazzo were supposed to have their eyes on Joey, not on strippers and bottles of Scotch. Once Nicoletti saw Shannon dancing with Palani, he became disgusted, bumped into him, and left.

I can live with never seeing Paolo "Small Paul" Nicoletti again. Though, if I did, I'd like to ask him if his confrontation with Nikki during the trial ever truly happened. I suspect that Nikki, who encountered Nicoletti at the aquarium, used what she heard me say over the phone at the Ala Moana Center to make the whole thing up. I suppose I'll just never know.

The Feds that pulled me over and jacked me up against their car weren't Feds at all. They were hired guns, ex-cops on the Fiordano payroll whose mission was to help me stay focused on finding the real killer and avoid bringing attention to the Fiordano criminal enterprise.

Shannon Douglas was, indeed, working for the FBI, but not in the capacity we had thought. She actually worked as an intern in the counterterrorism division, serving as an ambassador to the Department of Homeland Security, aiding in the exchange of sensitive information.

Professor Jim Catus was asked for his resignation by the law school after the administration became aware of his flying off to meet a student for a sexual tryst and instead spending a night with a $600 prostitute. The administration may never have got wind of it had I not anonymously sent the dean of the law school a transcript of the entire trial with the relevant sections about Catus highlighted in yellow.

Coincidentally, the Waikiki Winds hotel also received highlighted portions of the trial transcript relevant to Palani Kanno. The trial transcript prompted management to conduct an unannounced drug screening, and Palani and J. J. Fitzpatrick were subsequently relieved of their duties. I now have little doubt that Palani's attack on me was also motivated by jealousy over my dating Nikki. But, little did he know when he was pummeling me, I'm one vengeful son of a bitch.

Neither Flan nor I ever heard again from Carlie Douglas, but Joey received a letter from her apologizing for all the terrible things she'd said about him in the press. Joey responded with a defamation lawsuit. Evidently, he doesn't let things go that easily himself.

The media portrayed me as a hero, and the articles and television spots have served as a catalyst for my now booming practice. I thanked every reporter politely and gave them each a full interview, with the exception of

Gretchen Hurst. I politely told her to go fuck herself. Instead she flew back to the mainland to further exploit for ratings the family of a new missing girl.

Milt Cashman showed up with his new bride on Oahu last week. His fifth wife, a twenty-four-year-old fashion model, attempted to pass me one of her private cell phone numbers during dinner at Duke's, when Milt got up from the table to use the restroom. I, of course, declined it. When Milt asked me what I thought of his new bride, I told him that I thought she was beautiful.

With my practice booming, I had the pleasure of offering Flan a full-time position as an investigator with my firm. He readily accepted and promised to request permission before bedding down any witnesses in the future.

Unable to handle my new, overflowing caseload alone, I asked Jake Harper to be my partner. He accepted my offer and thus the law firm of Harper & Corvelli was born.

Jake also made a resolution not to drink . . .

. . . with anyone who isn't serious about drinking.

That's working out just fine, since his new girlfriend, Alison Kelly, takes her drinking seriously. Together, they can be found at Margaritaville, dancing the night away, on any evening when Jake doesn't have court the next morning.

I am alone, but I find it easier to live with myself these days. I often read Joey's letter, thanking me more for catching Shannon's killer than for helping set him free. I learned that I delight in making a difference in people's lives. So I took the money I set aside for Nikki's engagement ring and the trip to Kauai and made donations to some worthy charities in the name of Brandon Glenn. Brandon cannot live on, but I can make certain that his name forever does.

If geckos are truly harbingers of good luck as people say, then I must be the luckiest son of a bitch on the face of the earth. My apartment is lousy with them. Skies and I watch them slither around as if they own the place. So, together, we have decided to move to a small resort community called Ko Olina on the leeward side of Oahu.

Now with Skies in my lap, I read Joey's letter again. He writes, *I suppose the old saying holds true. One man's paradise is another man's prison. You know how I feel about Hawaii, and I know how you feel about New York, so I fear we may never see each other again.*

Petting Skies with one hand, I fold the letter and tuck it neatly in my drawer, wondering whether geography means as much to me now as it did before.

My cell phone vibrates in my pocket and I reach for it, flip open the clamshell, and put it to my ear without checking the caller ID. "Spea—" I take a deep breath. "Aloha," I say.

It's Hoshi. She wants to know if I'll be in the office at all today.

"Maybe later," I tell her. "Maybe not."

I set the phone down on my desk and shield my eyes against the sun seeping through the blinds. As much as I try to avoid it, my mind often wanders back to the night I was nearly killed.

Alika Kapua was killed lawfully in defense of my life.

Still, the shooter that gunned him down has never come forward. I have no illusions. But for that gunman, I would not be alive today. I would not be hiking up Diamond Head crater and watching the sun rise and set. I would not be walking in the park watching the birds, or driving leisurely in my Jeep admiring the coast. I would not be relaxing on the beach or taking long jogs in the sand. But for that gunman, I would not be swimming alongside giant sea turtles in the azure Pacific, drinking in the sun and jumping over waves, dreaming of tomorrow's infinite possibilities.

Okay, so I don't really do any of those things. But I sure as shit am happy to be alive.

EPILOGUE

I am lying facedown on Kailua Beach on the windward side of Oahu when I hear a familiar voice from no more than three or four yards away.

"Aloha, Mistah C!"

"Aloha, Turi," I say, picking myself off the sand.

Turi sits on the beach next to me. As he looks out at the sea and Flat Island, he displays a chubby smile upon his chubby face. It's the first time I've seen him in months.

"I never got to tell you, Turi."

"What's that, Mistah C?"

"*Mahalo.*"

"Oh, that," he says. "That was nothing. I never liked that moke anyway."

"Well, Turi, I owe you my life. If there's anything I can ever—"

"I know, I know, Mistah C. We got each other's backs. That's what friends are for, brah."

I nod, not much unlike a grateful bobblehead doll. Thanks to some professional surfing on the Internet, I now have a bobblehead doll of a Hawaiian hula girl sitting upon my desk. Only instead of her head, she bobs her hips. Very sexy.

"I saw you in the neighborhood that night," Turi says, "and I figure I better keep my eye on you. Can't have nothing bad happen to my lawyer, eh?"

"Good thing for me it was your neighborhood, Turi."

"What did I tell you when we first met, Mistah C? It's my *island,* brah. Now that over there"—he points to Flat Island—"I tell you what, that's yours."

"*Mahalo* again, Turi," I say, happy yet somehow unable to mirror his smile.

"Don't look so sad, brah. C'mon, smile, Mistah C. The sun is shining. The birds are singing. The waves are hitting da shore. The *'aina,* the land, it's ours."

I nod my head but say nothing.

"C'mon, smile, Mistah C. It's one fucking beautiful day, yeah?"